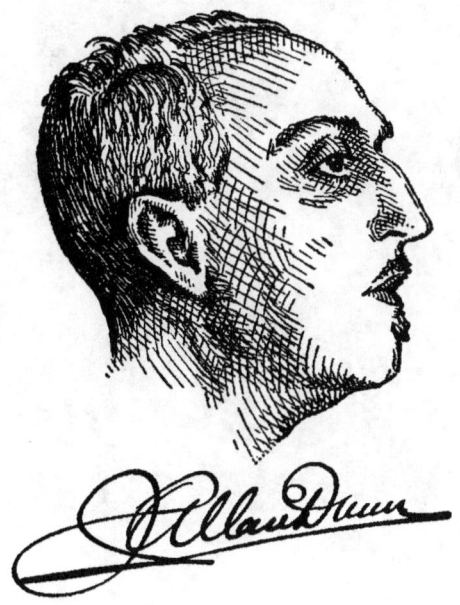

# In the
# GRIP of
# The GRIFFIN

## THE COMPLETE BATTLES OF
## GORDON MANNING
## & THE GRIFFIN
## VOLUME 3
## J. ALLAN DUNN

ALTUS PRESS • 2014

© 2014 Steeger Properties, LLC, under license to Altus Press • First Edition—2014

EDITED AND DESIGNED BY
Matthew Moring

INTERIOR ILLUSTRATIONS BY
Joseph A. Farren

PUBLISHING HISTORY

"Sign Sinister" originally appeared in the February 4, 1933 issue of *Detective Fiction Weekly* magazine. Copyright 1933 by Popular Publications, Inc. Copyright renewed 1960 and assigned to Steeger Properties, LLC. All Rights Reserved.

"The Scarlet Seal" originally appeared in the April 15, 1933 issue of *Detective Fiction Weekly* magazine. Copyright 1933 by Popular Publications, Inc. Copyright renewed 1960 and assigned to Steeger Properties, LLC. All Rights Reserved.

"Death Has Its Fling" originally appeared in the December 16, 1933 issue of *Detective Fiction Weekly* magazine. Copyright 1933 by Popular Publications, Inc. Copyright renewed 1961 and assigned to Steeger Properties, LLC. All Rights Reserved.

"The Griffin Returns" originally appeared in the September 22, 1934 issue of *Detective Fiction Weekly* magazine. Copyright 1934 by Popular Publications, Inc. Copyright renewed 1961 and assigned to Steeger Properties, LLC. All Rights Reserved.

"The Griffin Runs Amuck" originally appeared in the November 3, 1934 issue of *Detective Fiction Weekly* magazine. Copyright 1934 by Popular Publications, Inc. Copyright renewed 1961 and assigned to Steeger Properties, LLC All Rights Reserved.

"The Six Scarlet Seals" originally appeared in the December 1, 1934 issue of *Detective Fiction Weekly* magazine. Copyright 1934 by Popular Publications, Inc. Copyright renewed 1962 and assigned to Steeger Properties, LLC. All Rights Reserved.

"The Griffin's Gambit" originally appeared in the March 2, 1935 issue of *Detective Fiction Weekly* magazine. Copyright 1935 by Popular Publications, Inc. Copyright renewed 1962 and assigned to Steeger Properties, LLC. All Rights Reserved.

"The Griffin's Living Death" originally appeared in the March 16, 1935 issue of *Detective Fiction Weekly* magazine. Copyright 1935 by Popular Publications, Inc. Copyright renewed 1962 and assigned to Steeger Properties, LLC. All Rights Reserved.

"In the Grip of the Griffin" originally appeared in the May 18, 1935 issue of *Detective Fiction Weekly* magazine. Copyright 1935 by Popular Publications, Inc. Copyright renewed 1962 and assigned to Steeger Properties, LLC. All Rights Reserved.

"The Seventh Griffin" originally appeared in the October 5, 1935 issue of *Detective Fiction Weekly* magazine. Copyright 1935 by Popular Publications, Inc. Copyright renewed 1962 and assigned to Steeger Properties, LLC. All Rights Reserved.

THANKS TO
Joel Frieman, Monte Herridge, Everard P. Digges LaTouche, Ray Riethmeier and Jonathan Sweet

# TABLE OF CONTENTS

*Airplanes Soared Overhead, Police Patrolled
the Penthouse and Gordon Manning Sat with
the World's Greatest Scientist to Protect Him
from the Griffin's Fiendish Death Plot*

I T  WA S  a fit night for plotting a murder, or for committing one. The old trees and the overgrown and untended shrubbery about the ancient house were lashed by the storm until the tortured boughs rasped against each other and the autumnal leaves blew free in gusty drifts.

Thunder pounded like distant, heavy cannonading. Lightning flared in ghastly lavender illumination that briefly showed the tossing tree tops, the high chimneys of the old building and the tilting headstones of the long forgotten dead in the private graveyard; and the hundreds of wild acres that surrounded it; untended, practically unsaleable (although the property was within fifty miles of New York City) because of a clouded title.

The lightning turned a desolate mere into a sheet of purple flame; it showed the family vault of stone, iron-grated and iron-doored, itself lurching forward into the uncertain clay. It was a sinister landscape even when the sun shone. To-night it seemed the setting for a Witches' Sabbath.

A bolt of levin blazed. There was a crash and the limb of a great elm javelined to the ground, almost grazing the roof of a big black sedan that, expertly driven by a chauffeur with the face of an undertaker, had turned in from the road to the muddy lane and now dimmed its lights.

Three men got out. One, who stayed between the others, was clearly a prisoner and a none too willing one. He was defiant as he was hustled along between the sagging tombstones towards the vault. One man showed the hooded ray of an electric torch and they stumbled among the tall weeds, burred and brambly, over the low mounds and sunken, shallow pits where the water collected above the dead.

"You trying to throw a scare into me?" demanded the captive.

"You ain't seen the half of it yet," said one of the others. "If you do get scared, buddy, you needn't be ashamed of it. There's plenty reason."

He touched a spot beneath one of the skulls, carved in semi-relief on the scaling stone façade of the mortuary, and instantly the iron gratings swung out and the iron door slid aside to show the ghastly interior. The two guards thrust him in to the dimly lighted place that smelled of sickly decay, the stench of a charnel house.

The door clanged to, the gratings closed and the lights on the car came on full as it plowed up the lane to the back of the house where it slid, in a controlled skid, into the wide doorway of a great barn. The chauffeur did not come out again. The employees of the Griffin never entered the house that was recently bought by Mr. Silbi, tenanted by a gaunt, gruff couple whose surly silence had been barely broken enough to announce that they were caretakers.

The house was a blind, a cover for life and activities that went on underground—in extensions of the cellars, in cement walled crypts where men labored as slaves—men known only by numbers, men once honored for their proficiencies in the arts and sciences and higher mechanics; now servitors of the Griffin, cowed by his knowledge of their guilty secrets. Men who had been disqualified for malpractice or for chicanery.

There were no orgies here, but there were often grim rituals of experimental surgery, tests of death-dealing machines and potions, the assembly of delicate contrivances to further the mad and evil wishes of Mr. Silbi who was known to a shuddering nation as the Griffin.

An inhuman monster, an insane genius whose bent was all

*"You ain't seen the half of it," said
one of the Griffin's killers.*

destruction, whose warped ego, inflamed with grandiose dementia, resented all that was constructive and who deemed
himself destined to eliminate those against whom he felt envy.
Stark mad, but infinitely cunning, cold blooded as a lizard
spawned in Gehenna, arrayed against the sons of men even as
Iblis, the fallen angel, hurled down from heaven because he
refused to salute Adam, God's last creation.

Iblis, spelled backwards, became Silbi.

Once this mortal Iblis had been cast down, manacled, flung
into durance. Gordon Manning, ex-Army Intelligence man,
explorer, adventurer, scientist, consulting attorney and, first and
foremost, investigator, had accomplished this at the request of
the governor and the police commissioner; and the Law, in its
blindness, had not destroyed the fiend who had murdered hideously a score of the most valuable citizens, but had sent him
to Dannemora, to the institution for the criminally insane.

His cunning had freed him. Like the fabled beast, whose

name he used as a symbol, he was free to rend, to claw, leaping and swooping like the creature of mythology, half lion, half eagle. He had slain and would slay again, until Manning once more bested him, or killed him—unless he killed Manning first.

Perhaps he hated Manning as much as his hellish soul and spleen could hate while his lunatic conceit rated the investigator as the only opponent worthy of him.

To-night he waited in an inner chamber, subterranean, bomb-proof, until the man he had sent for should be brought before him. One he expected to make use of by bending him to his diabolic purpose.

THE ROOM was circular. Its wall of reinforced cement was hung with sable tapestries emblazoned with the signs of the zodiac, for the Griffin believed in the influences of the stars upon human destiny and never set the date for a murder without consulting them. Hidden neon tubes gave a soft glow. The ceiling had been made of dark purple glass in which there glowed the constellations, illumined at will by the Griffin.

The door was of steel, also tapestried, so that it blended with the walls. The floor was covered with thick rugs. The Griffin sat at a carven desk, whose legs were supporting griffins, in a throne-like chair. His face was hidden beneath a mask of some close-clinging tissue like goldbeater's skin, yellow, making him hideous and terrifying, as his high-bridged beak of a nose thrust out, with his protruding cheek bones, his stern chin, his black eyes glittering through slits.

Now he was at his devilish ease. From some source strange strains of music played, barbarically. There was the odor of burning amber, the fumes controlled by the ventilation ducts that kept the filtered air of the chamber at an even temperature.

Before him was a crystal bowl, slowly revolving, lighted from its base. Whorls of colored flame perpetually changed their pattern within the sphere. There was a disk of bronze hung between two crystal rods. Papers lay beneath the weight of a griffin of gold-bronze, superbly modeled, with ruby eyes.

These things, all his elaborate laboratories, his luxuriant living quarters, his unique establishment; Manning had once discovered and destroyed. But the Griffin's enormous financial resources had not been eliminated. The Griffin was rehabilitated. He had his new aerie, secret, invincible, his corps of groveling slaves. He was Himself again—Iblis, Son of the Morning, the Destroyer of Destinies!

The flat top of his desk was black onyx. On it lay astrological charts. He had worked out a horoscope and the result pleased him as he checked over his reckonings, muttering through the leprous-like mask the names of heathen gods and goddesses connected with the planets that ruled the houses of the Zodiac.

Marduk. Ishtar, Ninib. Nebo. Nergal, Sin and Shamash! Names as old as ancient Babylon, used to conjure with by the priests of the world's earliest cults.

"This time it cannot fail," he chuckled. "All the signs point to danger for this upstart, his house is invaded by malign controls. And now, for Manning."

He touched a point in the heavy carving of the desk and the bronze disk began to hum, to vibrate, while its shining surface clouded. Its pace increased until triple rods of crystal, set in a lute-like frame, the model of an Egyptian sistrum, gave off a clear, chiming note. The Griffin touched another button and the hum of the disk was steadily maintained as he spoke into it, knowing his message would be transmitted to Gordon Manning's private telephone at Pelham Manor, sure he would find the investigator at home, sure he would be waiting there, keyed up to hear the Griffin's next murderous, boastful announcement.

Last time Manning had foiled the Griffin. This time there would be no failure.

"Manning? Good! Doubtless you have been expecting me to communicate with you. You were not so amusing in our last encounter, Manning. Much too serious.

Manning, in his own library, listening with grim face to the message, fancied that the Griffin, menace though he was, cunning and powerful, was more erratic than he used to be before he had gone to Dannemora. When the fiendish desire to kill flooded his inflamed brain it seemed for the while to render it super lucid. The phantasmagoria it conceived took definite shape with the means to carry out his wicked will. But it must some day burn up in a spontaneous combustion generated by its overcharge of mad, fevered energy.

Manning made no answer. He waited to hear the name of the man selected as the Griffin's next victim, the day that the Griffin fixed for what he called his elimination.

"The name, Manning," the Griffin's deep voice continued, "is Harvey Allison, the upstart who thinks he can control cosmic forces. It seems that he is now endeavoring to perfect certain experiments on behalf of the government, to whom he has offered his preposterous plan of controlling the force of split atoms in a power that can annihilate, in one charge, the mightiest of armies, of fleets of the sea, the air, or submarine and subterranean activities.

"The supreme hypocrite claims that demonstrations of this power will force peace upon the other nations and that the world's safety will be accomplished by the United States.

"He does not add what lies behind this screen of altruism. The whole world, paying tribute to those who can thus threaten them! If he accomplishes this thing it makes Allison supreme, even though he pretends he gives it to the United States. He will still carry the secret in his brain. Bah!

"He assumes divine prerogatives, he seeks to harness the heavenly energies. We shall see, Manning, we shall see on the eleventh of this month.

"What makes this particular problem interesting is that certain ultra-socialistic organizations have taken him seriously. They want his secret. So, because of certain attempts, he has been given a police guard. One trusted officer is with him night and day. And now you also will defend him. The attempts have been crude. As I have told you before, Manning, study a man's habits and it is easy to dispose of him. The date will be the eleventh of this month.

"This time, Gordon Manning, you lose."

The voice ceased. Manning still heard the exotic music as he sat with the telephone arm gripped in his hand until his knuckles showed white against the tan.

And the Griffin touched the connection and the hum of the disk died now. Again he spoke into it.

"Bring in the man who came to-night."

THE TAPESTRY was pulled aside and a gap showed where the door had opened noiselessly. Through this entry came a strange being. It looked like a hobgoblin of the fairy tale legends. Its head was infantile in size, but wrinkled like that of an old man, set upon an enormous pair of shoulders. The chest showed tremendous development and power and the body was only a torso. It ended abruptly below the hips. The creature's long arms acted as legs and it came striding in, knuckles to the ground, like some grotesque ape, clad in a shaggy sweater that looked as if it might be natural fur.

This was Al, the Griffin's devoted familiar, a joke of Nature in a cruel mood, born legless, mute and almost dumb; bought by the Griffin from a traveling circus. Malice could sparkle in Al's eyes and the strength of his crippled trunk was phenomenal. Now he fawned as he came up to where the Griffin sat, nuzzling like a faithful dog.

Al wore a long, straight-bladed knife in a leather scabbard that was slung about his thick neck, belted about his chest. Its handle was brass, and it was balanced by lead for a throwing-knife. In the circus Al had specialized in a knife-throwing act and his aim was precise and, on occasion, deadly.

Back of him, thrust into the room by two guards who did not enter the chamber, but stood back of the doorway, the prisoner pitched into the chamber and caught his poise adroitly with more than a suggestion of athletic or acrobatic training.

He was dressed in clothes that proclaimed the penitentiary

outfit for outgoing convicts. Save for a certain fixed sullenness about his face, there were no other signs. Evidently he had been employed out of doors, for his features lacked the usual waxen pallor of a prison inmate and his hair had been allowed to grow for the time immediately before his release.

He was well built, lean, and not ill looking, save for his sullen expression; defiant rather than hangdog. A man of decided intelligence who might have gone as far along the upward path as he seemed to have descended on a lower. He glowered at the Griffin.

"What's the idea of the Chamber of Horrors and this freak out of a sideshow?" he demanded. "I've seen bones before—and legless wonders."

He was belligerent, but as he glanced about the chamber and again at the masked figure of the Griffin, he appeared less confident, impressed against his will by the atmosphere of the place.

"What's the idea of the snatch?" he went on. "I think I'm met by pals outside the College and then I get a rod shoved into my ribs and I get a ride to this dump. What's the big idea?"

"Nothing but what may turn out to your advantage," said the Griffin in his deep voice. "Sit down, Burns. That was, I believe, your latest alias. Make yourself comfortable. You might glance over this dossier."

Half against his will, the man took the paper offered, sat in the comfortable appearing chair that was indicated.

"I could stand a drink, and something to smoke," he grunted.

"Presently," said the Griffin. "Read that first."

The man looked indifferently at the document, then intently, last of all with a growing fear. Here were set down the intimate details of his life for the last twenty years; things that he believed the police did not know, intimate matters he had been sure no man surmised.

"How the devil did you get this dope?" he muttered.

"My friend, I am the devil," said the Griffin complacently.

"It pays to serve the devil, though you may not have found it so hitherto. You may have heard of me, even in Ossining. I am the Griffin."

Burns, alias many other names, late 17745 of Sing Sing, with other numbers to his name that penitentiaries had given him, twitched a little. His nerves were shaken. He had heard of the Griffin. In the underground gossip of Ossining the Griffin had loomed large as a master-criminal, a monster of deviltry and cunning. His escape from Dannemora had set him on a pinnacle for those still behind gray walls of stone and bars of steel.

The Griffin beckoned and the two men back of the still open door advanced. They also wore masks, of gray linen, tinted to suggest skulls. It was melodramatic, but in this place they did not seem out of keeping.

"You have his finger-prints?" asked the Griffin. He received the record, studied them, compared them with others and chuckled. He waved the two men back. The door slid to, the tapestry fell.

The man grew suddenly belligerent, with a burst of anger.

"You trying to frame me?" he cried.

The Griffin grinned and his mask wrinkled.

"You are already framed," he answered.

Burns started from his chair. Al's knife rose halfway from its sheath as he gazed for permission from his master to complete the cast. But there came a yelp of anguish from Burns. His eyes bulged from his head, his face twisted in anguish, his hands were clamped about the arms of the chair as an electric current held him there, galvanized, helpless, suffering. The current died and the man sank panting into the deceptive cushions.

"Just a foretaste, my friend, of what may be your ultimate end," said the Griffin. "If the authorities knew all that paper held it would not be long before you would be in the autopsy room back of the Execution Chamber, after you had squatted in the hot seat. I have the power to send you there, or to keep you free of it, to condemn you for your past sins or reward you for services rendered—to me. Look at this disk of bronze—*look at it!*"—he commanded compellingly—"and tell me if you know this name."

Burns scowled villainously. He was missing something. Back in the dark, unused recesses of his mind he wondered vaguely if he had been mistaken for his brother—if he were being punished because his brother was on the police force.

Letters appeared in flickering incandescence on the disk. They spelled a name that had not been included in the man's record. Now he realized the Griffin knew all. His eyes gleamed with a long smoldering hate, fanned to fire by the wind of fury.

"I know it," he snarled. "The canting hypocrite!"

Again the Griffin chuckled malignantly.

"Good," he said. "If I give you a chance to serve me, and to even a score with this man, will you obey with eagerness?"

"Give me the chance!"

"The chance is yours if you prove clever enough to pass the test," the Griffin told him. "Revenge is sweet. Is it not, 17745?"

The man snarled again.

"He sent me there, he branded me with that number," he cried. "He made a caged beast out of me and called it duty. I'll measure up. If I could put him where he placed me I'd give the rest of my life to do it."

"Your wish may be accomplished," said the Griffin and there was a mocking ring to his tones that the other missed. "Your instructions will commence to-morrow. Meantime you will be well served though your quarters may prove confining and, perhaps, a trifle reminiscent of your recent habitation. But at least the food will be better. There will be liquor and something else I fancy you crave more. Though that is a habit you must keep in hand for the present."

"You're going to give me some snow?" asked the other, half incredulously.

"A certain prescription. Be careful of it. It will not be diluted like the drug the trusties slipped you in Ossining. That is all."

Again the tapestry moved, the door slid aside. At a gesture from the Griffin, Al stalked grotesquely forward to lead the way for the bewildered Burns. Light glowed blue in a curving corridor. The steel door closed again. Alone, the Griffin reached for the silver mouthpiece of a Turkish hubble-bubble. He lit the fragrant weed in the bowl, tinctured with hashish. The air bubbled in the rose-scented water and wreaths of smoke made wispy patterns.

MANNING ADMIRED Harvey Allison first, then liked the man for his sheer humanity. He was both an advanced intellectual and a gentleman of the utmost courtesy.

He was a rare combination. If his head was occasionally in the clouds his feet were firmly planted on the earth. He was primarily a gentleman and a scholar, far from the ordinary conception of what such an ultramodern scientist might be. He was perhaps the foremost man of the age, since he did not stay at theories, but proved and made them practical and of value to his fellowman and Allison was altogether a charming person to meet.

He had the skull of the born scholar with eyes far apart and seeking, a tolerant mouth; the nose of the adventurer—whether of uncharted seas or unknown cosmic realms.

He was the opposite of the Griffin. Here, Manning reflected, was the true genius, a power for good, while the Griffin was like an evil jinni bent only upon malice.

Allison, if his claims were well founded, and Manning did not doubt them, was possessed of a force that was stupendous, that could not be comprehended. Men thought of it in terms of war, of destruction and it was true that, so used, it would prove irresistible. But Allison looked beyond that. If he could secure world peace, that was but a step in the progress he imagined. That atomic power of his could provide light, heat, energy that would release all men from the slavery of producing necessities and set them truly free for higher efforts. With it he could defeat climate, eliminate present fuels, outleap electricity, harness cosmic forces to the chariot of ascending evolution.

That, he owned, was still his dream, but it was more than a vision. He had isolated the idea and made it concrete. In his brain there glowed a divine inspiration.

Something of this, beyond public knowledge, Manning knew through his associations with the secret archives of the Government. Now that he had met the man he believed in him. Allison had the brow of a prophet, the inner glow of one set apart, appointed.

His workshop was a penthouse, set high on a Manhattan skyscraper, secured to him by special privilege of the magnate who had built the towering edifice as self-tribute to a successful career. These were the days when successful financiers raised buildings, as the Pharaohs erected stele needles and pyramids.

"I've heard of you, Manning," said Allison cordially. "It seems that I am marked down by this maniac who styles himself the Griffin. A fanatic, of course. Star-gazer and so on. Well, I have been threatened before. I could paper my main room with warnings and death warrants from every variety of communist, syndicalist and the generally deluded who think that world progress must be based upon destruction.

"Perhaps you know Dougherty?" he went on. "He has been appointed my special bodyguard to protect me from annoyance and my penthouse from sabotage. I am happy to say that he has become my close friend and also my assistant."

Manning shook hands with Detective Sergeant Dougherty who laughed at the idea that he was able to assist Allison. But it was clear that the upstanding Irishman was an admiring adherent of the noted scientist and that, aside from science, the two liked each other.

The police commissioner had told Manning about Dougherty.

"He's due for an inspectorship," said the commissioner. "He deserves it. There's not a braver, straighter man on the force than Tom Dougherty. I wish I had a dozen like him. He leans over backwards when it comes to honesty and he's got intelligence. Allison rates him highly and I miss him badly. He's been an efficient bodyguard but, if the Griffin's in on this, we'll see he's reënforced. What do you propose?"

Manning was not backward in his proposals.

"Here," he said, "is a man born once in a century, once in ten centuries. His brain holds value greater than that of all the treasuries of the world. His success means not merely the supremacy of the United States but, far more than that, the establishment of world friendship. He is the outstanding product of modern intelligence. He told me, half jestingly, that he preferred his penthouse laboratory because, if the atoms should run amuck and there should be a catastrophe it would cause least damage on the top of a high building.

"It makes it easier for us to protect. It is most vulnerable from the sky. As for that...."

"I'll see to that," said the commissioner, "that the sky is clear not only during the twenty-four hours of the eleventh, but from sunset of the tenth until sunrise of the twelfth. Washington will help us in this. They know the value of Allison. We'll not let a mosquito get within an air mile of the Whistler Building. And we'll not let a stranger, we'll not let *anyone* get on that roof or into that penthouse. Inside, it's up to you, Manning. You and Dougherty, though of course I'll give you all the men you want. You'll be in a state of siege. I defy the Griffin to get through."

"I defy him," said Manning, "but I don't underestimate his resources. He is not an ordinary man. He is a fiend. His genius is as facile for evil as Allison's is for good. I only trust I can get a glimpse of him."

"I'm with you in that," said the commissioner. "Manning, if you get a chance to kill that devil, don't hesitate."

"I have no intention of seeing him go to trial a second time," said Manning grimly. He did not count his chickens before they were hatched, much less the brain children of a griffin.

But his hunch told him that the Griffin had counted all defenses, calculated them as a master chess-player reckons the possible moves of a skilled opponent.

The sky might be guarded, all approach to the penthouse protected; but the Griffin had a plan. His mine was planted, the fuse would soon be lit.

IT WAS midnight. The beginning of the zero hours—twenty-four hours of constant vigil to guard the life of Allison and the secret he alone held. That secret was nearing completion.

Allison, Manning and Dougherty stood in the laboratory of the penthouse. It was skylighted with glass, proof against ordinary missiles, layers held together by shock absorbing glucose. The sky was clear. The stars shone in a cloudless sky and seemed to gaze benignly on the mortal who sought to solve the riddle of the infinite; to learn the law that kept them in their orbits, that marshaled the constellations and fixed the planets and controlled the blazing suns.

Allison was serene. Constantly he encountered minor setbacks, but he was convinced he was on the right track. His last experiment was a profound success that had startled Manning and Dougherty and left them solemn after the demonstration they had witnessed.

The laboratory was a place of shining glass and metal, of rods and spirals and strange-shaped containers—condensers and transformers, inducers and reducers, generators and converters, elaborate contrivances of which they could only guess the use.

They had seen a million volts released without thunder, sending a purple glare high into the heavens, then subdued, eliminated. The primal force that held the atoms indivisible had been split. Allison was a god.

Manning had been with him as guest and guardian for forty-eight hours, relieving Dougherty for short watches.

Now the three were together for twenty-four hours. No one else was in the penthouse. The servants had been given a holiday. All through the building detectives and private operatives saw

that nobody penetrated to the roof. The whole building was
being thoroughly searched, every hour. Its own watchmen were
supplemented by picked men from Centre Street.

The penthouse was shut off, in a state of siege. It was, of
course, amply provisioned. Dougherty had volunteered as cook
and butler.

"I'm no Oscar of the Waldorf," he said, "but I can handle
plain food. I've made you a menu."

It was simple, but satisfactory. Eggs, bacon, coffee and melon
for breakfast. A simple luncheon. Canned turtle soup, steak,
asparagus and baked potatoes for dinner, with a dessert.
Manning had ordered and taken in all the food. He had provided water, even a supply of ice. He was leaving nothing to
chance. He included tobacco, cigars, cigarettes and certain
liquors from his own supply. They would fare well enough, but
they would use nothing that was on hand, not even the running
water. The servants were not let off because they were in any
way mistrusted, but because Manning was resolved to eliminate
all chance of outside interference. The Griffin's money might
bribe one of them to do some apparently insignificant thing
which might prove the loophole he needed.

How the Griffin would strike was beyond Manning's ken,
beyond the ideas of Dougherty. That the stroke would be subtle
and sudden was certain.

Allison surrendered himself to their dual keeping with a
laugh.

"I am yours for the next twenty-four hours," he said. "To
guard and keep. For that period I shall do no more work. I have
earned a rest and I intend to relax and enjoy it. Do not take
your own responsibilities too heavily," he added. "The Fates look
down, my lot is determined. Whatever happens, I have made
some advancement in the right direction. Even to have pointed
out the way is satisfaction."

Dougherty said something almost incoherent. His voice was
strained and harsh. Manning felt the terrible tension, but he

was primed with the thrill that always prefaced an encounter with the Griffin. He felt that Dougherty was going stale from his steady stress of guardianship to which the climax now seemed imminent. The sergeant had changed within the last twenty-four hours and Manning wondered if he would crack, but his jaw was steady and there was a glint in his eyes that proclaimed resolution. Allison rallied him.

"You're not yourself, Dougherty," he said. "Let's go into the living room and get some refreshment. Afterwards, if you smoke, I'll play to you both. I know Dougherty doesn't play the piano, but how about you, Manning? My instrument is the violin."

"I never got farther than chopsticks," Manning confessed, "but I'm a music lover."

"I find it lets me down," said Allison. "Clears up the cobwebs and all the trash left over from concentration on a problem."

Manning glanced upwards through the vaulted skylight. He could see dark shapes soaring, manbirds on motionless wings, their cruising lights gleaming on patrol. There were police planes and army pilots. All landing fields had been notified not to fly over that part of Manhattan without reporting it in advance. No unknown airplane could penetrate that flying cordon.

Surely the place was impregnable. The elevator doors to the penthouse were locked, the door at the head of the stairway was closed. The building swarmed with armed and alert officers, the approaches to it were heavily guarded. The penthouse was shut off, it was rendered invulnerable.

YET MANNING, keyed-up to the expectancy of disaster, felt his spirit vibrating with premonitory alarm. He had no fear. He did not know what fear was. But he had seen many strange things in his Oriental travels, in African kraals; things inexplicable to ordinary knowledge, in old temples, spirit-houses, where phantoms had seemed to gather and take shape, chilling the hearts of warriors.

The Griffin's apparent concession in naming the twenty-four

hours in which his victim should die was in reality a crafty maneuver. It increased strain to the snapping point, while vigilance was so widely extended that, with Manning and Dougherty, it was stretched to extreme limits.

Now Manning felt certain phenomena that did not materialize out of his own consciousness. They were as automatic as the lifting hackles, the quivering nose and trembling body of a hunting dog that scents a dangerous quarry. There was evil in the penthouse, crouching, cowering, amorphous at present, invisible. At any moment it might assume some form, make itself manifest.

There was the same sort of atmospheric pressure that makes a dog howl hideously while old women predict the passing of a soul. Manning felt as if something clammy crawled down his spine, as if ghost hackles were rising on his neck, his skin goosefleshing.

Dougherty was rated the bravest man on the force. He, too, seemed haunted. Allison was the least concerned. He led the way into the living room and produced his cased violin from a carved chest.

Manning took it from him, went with it through the tall glass doors to the parapet, closing the doors behind him. He exercised the greatest precaution in opening the case, examining the violin, the bow, the cube of rosin. He had not forgotten the Griffin's hint, which, of course, might turn out to be only a false lead, that some habit of Allison might be used as the means of destroying him.

There was nothing wrong. Out here on the roof terrace the air was cool and sweet. The lights of the theater district glowed below. All about, the towering buildings were dotted with squares and oblongs of illumination. The lighted spires gleamed like beacons. The low murmur of the city came up to Manning and now he felt nothing of that impression, that emanation of evil he had experienced within.

Allison smiled as he took over the violin.

"I played that last night for a little while," he said, "after my formulas had proven themselves. Now I shall give you a concert."

Dougherty and Manning smoked and sipped highballs. Allison declined a drink. From now on they partook of nothing that Manning had not personally inspected and provided.

Allison's music was excellent and varied. He played the chansons of French voyageurs, barcarolles of Venetian gondoliers, sweet lieders of Germany, a stately Largo; passing from berceuse to minuet, from lilting gypsy airs to stirring marches, as the mood led him. Different music, this, from the barbaric strains Manning sometimes heard as the Griffin ceased talking through the telephone.

The room was delightfully furnished, artistically lighted. Through the tall windows they looked west, towards the Hudson. A few pinnacles cut the skyline where the stars glittered and the planes kept their vigil. Allison played with consummate skill for over an hour. Then he set down the violin and poured himself a drink.

"A nightcap," he said. "I haven't been sleeping too well lately, but I feel I shall to-night. Here's to your healths, my friends and guardian angels, and, incidentally, here is also to my own health. I'll turn in. See you both in the morning, although I suppose you'll be peeping in on me, to see I haven't been spirited away or otherwise eliminated."

"He's got nerve," said Dougherty as Allison disappeared into his bedroom. "I'm damned if he hasn't got more than I'd have, in his shoes. How about turning in, Manning? If you like we'll split watch until breakfast time. Two four-hour tricks."

Manning shook his head.

"I couldn't sleep," he said. "Go ahead and get a few hours if you feel like it. Things seem serene enough, but I haven't had the long session you have for the past few weeks. I'm out of sleep until the time's up."

"I feel the same way about it," said Dougherty. "I think I'll shift into pajamas and a dressing-gown, just the same."

He went to the bathroom of a guest chamber and presently came out looking far more fit and vigorous than he had done since dinner of the previous night. He took a prowl about the terrace, returned and began to look through a pile of geographical magazines. Manning found a book that interested him, but he could not lose himself in it. He still sensed that form of evil lurking, lurking for the appointed hour.

FOUR TIMES in all they looked in on Allison, who slept like a tired child. Four times Manning inspected the guinea pigs in open cages he had placed here and there on the floors to detect any creeping, deadly vapor that might turn the penthouse into a lethal chamber for all of them. He had investigated all ventilation and heating ducts, but he was being thorough.

The night passed. The sky over the Hudson River turned gray, warming as the sun rose in the east. Vague mists dissolved about the tall buildings. Manning went outside. The planes caught the sun and were no longer shadows, but brilliant, tangible machines intent upon their task. They were being relieved by fresh planes and pilots every four hours.

There could be no danger from the sky. Manning could find no trace of it on the roof. He made a short patrol, assuring himself that the doors and gates were still locked—from within—plain-clothes men at their posts.

Dougherty was preparing breakfast. He had changed back into regular clothing. The smell of coffee came from the compact kitchen. Allison appeared, shaven, smiling, refreshed.

"Eight o'clock and all's well," he announced. "I'm hungry. How about chow, Dougherty?" he inquired as he looked into the kitchen.

Eight o'clock! A third of the allotted time had passed. Sometimes the Griffin waited until the last minute to strike.

Dougherty appeared. The table was already set in the dining room, where the sun was pouring in. A pair of canaries were singing lustily. Manning had inspected the guinea pigs once more. Allison opened a window. There were flowers outside and flower boxes gay with blooms inside the room. It was a gay appearing place that morning, but Manning was tense as a coiled spring. His hunch had heightened. The Evil Presence was still manifest despite the smiling morning, the sunny room.

Dougherty carried a dish with musk melons upon it.

"Your favorite fruit," he said to Allison. "They're nice and cold. We'd better eat them first and I'll cook the omelette and bacon later so they won't be spoiled. Where are you sitting, Mr. Allison?"

Manning had bought the melons, consulting Allison as to his taste. Dougherty sat with them, dividing a melon equally with a silver knife, scooping the seeds out deftly and placing them in a bowl. He placed one half on Allison's plate, the other on his own.

"How about you, Manning?" he asked. "Choose your own?"

There were two more melons. Manning did not immediately reach for one. He was a little surprised that Dougherty had helped himself to the other half of the first melon, but figured that he might have done that with some remote idea of reassurance, or of determination to taste the same food as Allison. It seemed unnecessary.

There was another matter, also a slight one, but arresting to Manning's keen perceptions. Dougherty's hand had been perfectly steady while he divided the melon with the silver knife, but he had used his left hand. It was an unusual thing for a normal person to do. He had not noticed before, and he was sure he would have, that Dougherty had shown himself ambidextrous or left-handed.

Manning caught himself remembering the original meaning of the word sinister—"opposed to dexter—pertaining to the left." Sinister-handed! It was an ill-omened phrase. Dougherty had seemed nervous, which was natural enough—Manning's nerves were also taut. Now, for the first time, he caught sight of the sergeant's eyes in the sunlight. The pupils were....

Dougherty spooned up some of the rich orange pulp, swallowed it. Manning reached for a second melon and a knife.

"Pretty nearly perfect," said Dougherty. "Try it, Mr. Allison."

Allison did so, smacked his lips.

"Delicious," he said; "sweet as hon—"

He never completed that word or any other one. He began spasmodically gasping for breath. His mouth opened wide and his face seemed suddenly drained of blood. Then he slid from his chair in a heap, the spoon falling from his hand.

"It's a stroke," said Dougherty. "I'll get a doctor."

He started to his feet. Manning also.

"Never mind a doctor," he said. "I'm afraid he's gone. But not you. You're staying here."

Dougherty stared at him. His eyes glittered with excitement.

"Okay," he said. "You notify 'em if you want to."

"Put up your hands!" ordered Manning.

"Are you crazy?" Dougherty partially obeyed.

"Higher," snapped Manning. "I may be. I'll know better when his half of the melon has been analysed. I may apologize to you then, but I doubt it. I'll let you put down your hands on one condition, that you finish that half, or start to finish it. One spoonful of that pulp, 'sweet as honey,' will be enough."

The face of Dougherty was suddenly transformed. His lips curled back and showed his teeth in a snarl. He thrust his right hand high, but his left—the sinister hand that had halved the fruit, darted for his right side.

His second gun—the first one known to Manning and revealed several times as a service weapon in a holster as regularly worn—came from the inner pocket of his coat. It spat fire twice before he fell with Manning's bullet in his chest. The shock of the slug and its placement had knocked him down. Manning was bored through his shoulder, high up, his collarbone was broken.

The sergeant, still snarling, dying even then from the wound, fired again, left-handed, but the shot went wild as Manning's relentless aim crashed lead into the man's skull. It was a duel to the death, though he would have preferred to take his man alive.

But the Evil lurking there had materialized too swiftly. The Griffin had struck. Two men lay dead. One of them Allison.

There was pounding at the stairway door and Manning opened it. Officers came in, stood amazed and aghast.

"Who killed him?" demanded an inspector.

"He killed Allison, I killed him," said Manning quietly. The game was over. The Griffin had lost a pawn, but he had called checkmate. "Get the commissioner right away," Manning ordered. "And the Medical Examiner."

"Dougherty killed Allison? That's impossible," said the in-spector as another officer went to the telephone, a third knelt beside and between the dead men.

"I'm not contradicting you," Manning answered. "Get a set of Sergeant Dougherty's finger-prints sent up from the official file. Get a print man here, too. Ask the Identification Bureau if they've got any other prints similar to Sergeant Dougherty's. They should be not far from identical."

"I DON'T know what has happened to Sergeant Dough-erty," Manning said to the police commissioner. "I hope he'll show up, but I doubt it. The Griffin got him, inside of the last forty-eight hours, during the time I relieved him. He was going to see his girl, poor devil. As for this chap, you can see he's the double of the sergeant. He fooled you, and it was easy for him to fool Allison and myself. Look at those sets of finger-prints. Nobody but twins could have them so alike. Did you know the sergeant had a twin brother, Commissioner?"

"God help me, I did," said the commissioner. He had come up from the ranks and his knowledge was wide in police affairs. Now his seamed face was troubled. "But I had forgotten it. We all agreed to forget it, years ago. Dougherty's twin was a bad lot. Tom got him out of trouble time and time again when they were both lads, but he couldn't stop him. It was Tom who recognized him eight years ago in New York and turned him in. He was wanted for homicide. He got ten years. It was hard on Tom, but he did his duty. And his brother cursed him for a canting hypocrite. We never spoke about it, we forgot it for the sake of Tom's feelings—and his promotion. I should have thought of it. I blame myself for this, Manning."

"It was not your fault," Manning tried to reassure him. The commissioner pulled himself together.

"I don't see now how it was done," he said. "They both ate the fruit."

"It's not entirely a new method," said Manning. "Not often used outside of the Orient. It's a Malay trick. The killer mixes poison with honey and smears it on the underside of a knife. Then he shares a meal with his victim, divides a melon with the poisoned blade and is careful to eat only the upper and harmless portion. The method is common in Treggannu and they use either cyanide or physostigmine, which is taken from the Calabar or Ordeal bean. He was nervous and he used his left hand to cut the melon, as he did to shoot with afterwards. I think you'll find Tom Dougherty's twin was left-handed. Of course he disguised it at first. Then I saw his eyes. He had taken dope to nerve himself. It was too late then, but I knew what had happened when Allison started to pronounce the word 'honey.'

"The Griffin knew, of course. He knew of the killer's hatred against his brother, and he undoubtedly had something hanging over him that forced him to revenge himself on his brother and also kill Allison. He was probably given the choice of being given over to the police or doing this job for a big reward he would never have collected. The Griffin would figure the odds of his capture, though it was a smart move of his to offer to get a doctor."

The Medical Examiner reserved announcement on the poison used until the melon was analyzed.

"No doubt as to what killed the other one," he said. "Either bullet would have done it." He opened the clothing over the murderer's chest and showed the wound. It was not bleeding much, but there was a brighter crimson mark on the opposite breast, too regular for a birthmark.

It had been recently tattooed there. The upper half of a griffin in scarlet ink, indelible and sinister.

*Manning Gets an Invitation to a Murder, to
Watch an "Ingenious Method"—an Invitation
Sealed with the Terrible Scarlet Griffin*

THE LITTLE graveyard was a place forgotten. A private cemetery, no longer visited. Its tombstones sagged and some were fallen. The stone had flaked and the inscriptions were illegible, if anyone had cared to read them. Sumach and thornapples and blackberry brambles discouraged investigation. Old yews and native cypress shadowed the dismal spot. There was a vault of stone that was still intact, though it had tilted as the soil had shifted with the centuries on the slope which the vault crowned. The vault had a gate of wrought iron secured by a rusty chain and padlock, and a door that seemed to await the Resurrection morning.

Behind the slope, across neglected pastures, stood a house of brick and stone that had been nobly designed but had suffered the wear of the elements for fifty years without human occupation or reinforcement. Once there had been a garden and still a few roses bloomed, stunted, and hedges once trimmed grew wild.

The land was part of a great grant by King George to one of his overseas subjects. Most of it had been sold. This had been a portion bequeathed to a minor heir. At the back of the house were great, gaunt lilacs guarding an alley where once George Washington had walked in his unsuccessful wooing of Marion Philipse, visiting there.

There was a cloud about the title. The old, proud family had gone into oblivion. But someone had recently risked buying the forty ragged acres. The house was almost a ruin, with its rotting sills and leaking roof, its sagging shutters and mouldering paint, within and without.

To-night, dim through the driving, persistent rain, a light gleamed downstairs. Some thought the newcomers were merely caretakers for the purchasers. They made no attempt to farm, little to offset the impending ruin of house and land. They were a tall, taciturn Yankee and his equally lean and silent wife; they attended strictly to their own affairs, paid their bills in cash.

The place had long been dismal, desolate and deserted. The light in the window did little now to dispel its dreariness. Rain dripped from the dark trees, beat upon the sunken mounds in the pale gleam of a sun that fought and failed against the gloomy, swiftly gathering night.

The new owner was recorded as a Mr. Silbi. A foreign sounding name, surely not New England, like that of Cyrus Allen, now living in the house. None locally had ever seen Mr. Silbi.

Surrounding this forty acres was more deserted land, also with clouded title. Two big tracts of it, wooded and hilly. On one of them was a weedy mere that had once been a lake. No one ever fished there. Once a girl had drowned herself in it. These wild acres had been considered by real estate developers with an eye to summer bungalows and country homes, but the uncertain titles checked them and the land lay slowly reverting to wilderness.

They said the ghost of the suicide haunted the mere, that weird blue and green lights flickered above the graves—corpse-candles lighting the phantoms back to their beds of clay. Some swore that a party, taking the back road by mistake, had seen the vault open, with an unearthly glare revealing broken coffins and scattered bones, and a fearful goblin, capering, hairy and legless, its head neckless and tiny; walking on its hands, in the midst of the charnel place.

AN OWL hooted its melancholy note. A nightjar swooped with a screeching whistle. A few bullfrogs croaked in sheer

*"Damn you for a
fiend!" he cried. "I'll
get rid of you too...!"*

defiance of the rain. Thunder muttered and lightning flickered
incessantly as the smouldering sunset died.

The state road was two miles away. The dirt lanes were little
better than quagmires, rutted by those who stole the timber
from the old Luddington Grant. Few passed after nightfall.

A mighty, closed car came surging through the slush, driven
by an expert who used the power of twelve tremendous cylin-
ders with consummate judgment, whose steel wrists and fingers
controlled their force with ease as the big black sedan threatened
to skid and swerve.

Behind drawn blinds a man sat who was dressed—as his
chauffeur was—in black. Sable, from wide-rimmed slouch hat,
turned down, to his shoes. He was wrapped in a black cloak
like a condor with folded wings. His vulturine features, half
hidden between upturned velvet collar and the brim of his
sombrero, were offset by a close trimmed Spanish beard, twin-
forked and upcurled mustachios. His eyes were yellow of iris,
his high-bridged nose was thin and bony, like a bird's beak.

This was the mysterious Mr. Silbi and he sat couched in the
deep cushions with an expression infinitely feral, evil and
content.

The sedan slowed, turned to a miry rise, plowed up a lane, its headlights spraying through the darkness and the filtering rain, now beginning to slacken.

The driver showed no hesitation. This was not his first visit. Mr. Silbi did not tolerate mistakes. He was well served, as was Iblis, Prince of Darkness, cast out by God because he refused to abase himself before the latest creation—Adam.

Iblis, the Moslem Satan, becomes Silbi when spelled backwards. No one in Grangers' Mills had noticed it. Nor, as yet, elsewhere.

They surged about the house across the muck of an old byre and the car disappeared in the dark maw of a staggering barn, still held together by its frame of timbers hewn two hundred years before from forest giants. The driver stayed there. Silbi emerged, his black cloak flapping in the wind and rain, only his beaklike nose showing. He ascended a rear stoop and rapped on a door that was instantly opened and closed behind him.

The lean, bony woman who was the consort of Cyrus Allen held an oil handlamp as they passed on to a front room with a blotched Empire mirror over a black marble hearthplace, old, blistered and blackened portraits on the walls, furnished with chairs whose brocade was mildewed and frayed, chairs by Heppelwhite, a loveseat, a spinet, an inlaid sideboard by Sheraton upon which stood a tarnished empty candelabrum.

"Put down the lamp, woman," said Silbi imperatively. "Bring another, with your husband. Have him fetch kindling and logs and light a fire. It should have been laid. It is colder than the soul of Lucifer. Begone!"

## II

THERE WAS a dramatic and tragic air about him, an aura of force, the hint of a dynamic will never at rest within; that made his somewhat stilted phrases not unfitting as he stood wrapped in his cloak with his yellow, evil eyes gleaming in the lamplight while his distorted shadow fell upon the paneled wall like the shadow of a swooping bird of prey, hunting carrion.

There was a touch of madness in his lambent orbs that stared the woman down as she looked at him with a certain latent rebellion that dissolved like ice at the gate of hell.

He chuckled hideously as she turned away, in a low but frightful cackle of malice and satisfaction. Then he turned impatiently to the empty hearth, chafing his hands. For all the vigor that seemed to seethe within him, his face was pinched and carved with suffering, and the hands he chafed were cold. There was a ring upon one long, clawlike finger, a ring of gold with a deeply incised design of a demi-griffin, its eagle wings outspread, with tufted beak and pointed ears, its lion's tail showing above the sheer line of the coup.

There came a shriek from the woman in the dark hall and Silbi laughed noiselessly with intense enjoyment, his red tongue tip showing between his teeth. He knew the cause.

The next instant a strange shape came into the room, a creature with a microcephalous head, no bigger than an infant's, set neckless upon the shoulders of a blacksmith. The body ended at the hips, it swung between two enormous arms that raised the trunk clear from the floor with hands set knuckles down. Silbi's grotesque fancy had dressed this unfinished being in a sort of turtle-necked sweater with long hairs woven into it like those of an Angora goat. There could not be much intelligence in that contracted cranium, but the eyes showed delight and obedience.

The freak was mute, but it babbled inarticulately as it came noiselessly to the side of its Master, the man known to a horror-stricken world as the Griffin, the monster once caged but kept alive by the law of the land for the criminally insane. Now he was free again, launched again upon his fanatical crusade against those whom he envied, or fancied had done him wrong; always the choicest citizens.

The Griffin patted the monstrosity as if it had been a dog.

He called it by its monosyllabic name and the creature lip read the title and fawned with hands that could crush a potato to pulp, stroking those of Silbi, the Griffin.

Al—that was its name, the Griffin's title for the misbegotten object he had bought from a traveling show. Al—one of the gruesome group of demons in Persian mythology that sit in sandy places meditating impure designs.

This Al was peaceful enough now, but it was not hard to imagine it surcharged with malevolence, handicapped but horrible. It could travel from beams or trees with the effortless ease of a chimpanzee, it could have wrestled on even terms with an orangutan with those long, sinewy arms where the sheathed muscles scarcely showed more than the constricting muscles of a boa. It could walk and even run on its arms as well as an ordinary man could travel on his legs.

The Griffin motioned it to a corner where it stood squat in the shadow with eyes still twinkling from the fright it had given the woman.

There was light outside the room again. Cyrus Allen and his wife both carried lamps. Allen had kindling wood and paper. He fixed them in the grate and went away to bring back a double armful of logs. The flames gathered strength and soon the fire was roaring up the chimney, sending dancing shadows about the room with shafts of light as the wood snapped and distributed its heat. The Griffin warmed his hands, then stood with his back to the blaze, arms folded.

"WELL, ALLEN," he said, "have you completed the device? Are you ready to demonstrate it to me, as I asked? You got all the apparatus you asked for, I believe?"

"I got the tools and the machinery," said Allen slowly. "They came at night, like you said they would, like the other things came. Mine is set up in the vault. They took the stuff in through the passage back of the paneling in the dining room. The other stuff's been set up in the cellars. I ain't inspected none of it. It ain't in my line. The men are living here, keeping upstairs, using the back way. My wife's fed 'em, but she's through. It's too much work for her. I don't aim to stand having that freak swinging around, spying, noiseless. It scares my wife, coming on it unexpected, like I did once, in the vault. It ain't human. Also the work's getting too hard for her."

"Hard labor, eh?" asked the Griffin. His tone was almost jovial, but his eyes were the eyes of Satan, the eyes of an old he-goat in the dark. "You'd like to avoid hard labor—for her, or yourself, I suppose," he added.

"I'm not afraid of work," said the man, "but I ain't got that contraption ready for you. I don't aim to *have* it ready, not unless I know what you're going to use it for. It don't figure legitimate to me. I could fix it, easy, but I won't," he went on, with growing firmness. "We're quitting, the two of us, right now. Give us what's coming to us and we'll leave to-morrow morning. This place ain't right. We just waited for you to come...."

Cyrus Allen had worked himself into indignation, but now he faltered under the baleful look of the Griffin's sardonic expression.

"You want what's coming to you?" asked the Griffin. "I wonder? Let me see, Allen, when you and your wife came to see me in town, at my studio, you said she was an excellent housekeeper and that you were an expert electrician. If I remember right, you told me of certain inventions you had made and that should have brought you money, if the capitalists had not robbed you. There was another one you were eager to complete. You said you preferred a quiet place, for yourself and your wife. A quiet place like this—"

"It's *too* quiet," broke in Allen passionately. "It ain't right or natural, the way things are run. You didn't say my wife should work her fingers to the bone for a lot of cranks, half of 'em foreigners—"

"Well, well," the Griffin said soothingly. "You may quit if you want to, only, I want you to remember that I showed you the crystal globe, the Orb of Truth, with its swirling fires. You remember that, Allen?"

"I remember looking into it. It gave me a headache."

"It gave me the creeps," his wife spoke up, and then the Griffin's diabolical laughter checked them to silence. He laughed like a demon who watches some tortured soul racing down a corridor in Hades that will end in a blazing pitfall; his eyes were like the eyes of a snake watching the fluttering of a fascinated and already helpless bird.

"The Orb of Truth brought out your hidden thoughts, your memories and your fears," the Griffin said at last. "You told me *everything*. You signed a paper, which was duly witnessed. Let me read it to you."

They listened with whitening faces, with terror growing in their eyes. The woman shook like an autumn leaf in a cold wind. The man broke the spell with a screaming oath.

"Damn you for a fiend!" he cried. "I'll get rid of that and you, too!"

The Griffin did not move, but Al came in three great hitches, and reaching upwards, gripped the man's arms at the elbows so fiercely that he howled with anguish, unable to shake off the legless creature whose fingers clamped down on his nerves and paralyzed his efforts.

"Fool!" said the Griffin. "This is a copy. And if anything should happen, at any time, that would disappoint me in you, any act of disobedience, the signed and witnessed confession would be released, automatically. That you were hypnotized into telling the truth does not alter the facts that can and will be eagerly substantiated. In the State where you committed the crime, kidnaping now brings life imprisonment. If you were able to clear yourself of the question as to whether you killed the child, you could not avoid that. Hard labor for both of you, for life!"

He gestured to Al, who released Allen. The New Englander stood stricken with despair that was reflected on his wife's wan face.

"I'll fix that contraption for you to-night," he said humbly.

"I thought you would," said the Griffin. "See that it is successful."

## III

GORDON MANNING was the last client that afternoon at the down town gymnasium where business men tried to keep themselves physically fit and offset the depression by virility. There was no partner available for handball but the professional. That suited Manning well enough and he threw himself into the game with an ardor and finesse that left his opponent panting, chagrined, and frankly admiring.

Manning went into the shower and let the needle sprays run icy cold. He had played hard not merely to win, but to help him forget the problem of the Griffin, to prevent it becoming an obsession that would rob him of his best judgment by incessantly suggesting he was no match for the monster, that the handicaps were too severe. The handball game had temporarily sidetracked even the workings of his subconscious mind as he set every energy to the task in hand.

But the poisonous leaven was there. The task had to be taken up again, helpless as it seemed. He was the only man who had ever defeated the Griffin, who had ultimately sent him to the asylum for the criminally insane at Dannemora. Now it was all to do over again. The Griffin had scored. The people looked to Manning to rid them of the menace.

He was well equipped for it, late officer in the Army Intelligence, scientist, world traveler, soldier and adventurer. He had been called in when the police had failed, given special commissions by the New York Police Commissioner and the Governor of the State; commissions still in effect. The Griffin, with his organization, his own intuition spurred by insanity that amounted to evil genius, had written satirically congratulating himself upon obtaining a worthy opponent. He had mailed the letter with its heavy gray paper, its purple ink and scarlet seal, upon the same day Manning had secretly accepted the commission. Not even the press had known—under restriction of publication—of his under cover appointment; but the Griffin had discovered it.

The Griffin professed to call it a game. He condescended to name his victim, to state a twenty-four-hour limit to the time of mysterious murder.

But he had inevitably planned his moves, made all his preparations, studying the problem intricately during the weeks between killings, when he was silent. A silence that was like the steady drip of water upon Manning, waiting, waiting, for the inevitable boasting announcement of a crime so devilishly planned that no protection availed against the madman's craft.

That first capture had been largely owing to Manning's blocking of one of his diabolical murders. Failure had so inflamed the Griffin that rage had made him almost futile, careless of consequences in his wild desire to restore his fallen ego. Manning believed that the bringing about of another failure was the best chance once more to secure this fiend in human shape.

The man was a devil loosed on earth. He had killed a score of valuable men who could hardly be replaced. He meant to keep on killing. He juggled with astrology and divination, doubtless believing himself an appointed destroyer.

Once, since the Griffin's escape, Manning had foiled him, saved his intended victim, not so much by discovery of the devilish device employed as by strict vigilance and alertness at a crucial moment.

Then Manning had seen him, had gripped the cloak he wore, only to lose him in a surging crowd where the Griffin's minions took advantage of the confusion.

Soon the Griffin would strike again, when he was ready, the victim selected, studied, all moves considered.

Manning, brown, lean, dressed, nodded to the old trainer who ran the gymnasium, and stepped outside, swinging his favorite weapon, a cane made from a steel tapering rod on which were shrunk scores of rings of leather. It was as efficient as a sword in his skillful hands. He asked nothing better than a chance at the Griffin, cane against gun or other weapon. His morale was not shaken, but he had a hunch, certain vibrations that tuned-in to evil emanations, that told him it was not long before he would be hearing from the arch-enemy, the man who hated all other men.

Ever since the last attack, the police force, public and private, had been trying to get clews concerning the Griffin's whereabouts or those of his agents. His former elaborate organization had been shattered, but he still had great resources and he was rebuilding his force. All clews had failed. There had been no real clews. The score stood two to one, since his escape, in the Griffin's favor. And now....

MANNING'S POWERFUL roadster had been standing at the curb. He stood with his hand on the doorturn, looking at the button to his siren at the hub of his steering wheel. On the black circle a scarlet oval showed red as blood, sinister as blood. An *affiche* of thick paper embossed with the signet of the Griffin!

Still another scarlet symbol was placed on the flap of the side pocket of the car, indicating certainly, to Manning, that he would find a letter tucked inside. It was infinitely galling for him to recognize the probability that either the Griffin or one of his agents, perhaps the very man who had found the chance to affix the seals and place the message, was watching him from some nearby point of vantage to make sure he received the letter. He denied them that satisfaction, got in, and drove to Pelham.

Not until he was in his own garage did he take out the envelope, again with the signet of the Griffin, sealed in wax, on the heavy handmade gray paper. The address was in the too familiar bold hand that, to a handwriting expert, revealed eccentricity of mind and also force of character and purpose.

GORDON MANNING ESQUIRE ADDRESSED

Manning's face was grim as he broke the seal in his library, after deliberately filling and lighting his pet briar and waiting until his Japanese butler brought him a highball.

MANNING:

Still you serve to amuse me and therefore I again invite you as antagonist. The board is set, I have planned the gambit in which I may lose a pawn but only to win. I realize that you have been eagerly expecting my challenge. Last time we almost became closely acquainted, but, even if the cloak had held, I had not played my final trick.

You may be glad to know that I am succeeding admirably in restoring the organisation you and the authorities so ruthlessly destroyed—for which you will some day pay in full. I have another Headquarters that it will take all your vigilance to discover, my dear Manning. I believe you called my last my "aerie" though it is by no means certain whether the griffins, who were the steeds of the sun and drew the chariot of Nemesis, nested or used a lair. It matters little. Things shape well. The next to be eliminated will be that persistent prig and self-publicist, Evans Cooke, who claims to be building the true type of young American manhood by his interest in and contributions to the Olympic Games, the Amateur Athletic Association and other "body-building organizations," as he styles them. He considers himself a philanthropist and his chief enjoyment is to read about himself in the press. The man is a stench in my nostrils.

He may have an opportunity of recommending himself, as a shade, to Zeus, on Mount Olympus itself, since he will most certainly shuffle off this mortal coil at some swift second during the twenty-four hours calendered as the nineteenth of this present month. May you, my dear Manning, be there to see. I may be a spectator myself. The method employed is ingenious and I confess to a slight curiosity to observe how well it works, though, as you know, I never repeat myself.

(There was no signature but only a delicate pen drawing of the demi-griffin, couped.)

Manning knew of Evans Cooke. He was himself an amateur athlete of high standing with one record which, while not included in ordinary programs, was spectacular and interesting—the underwater long dive, "fetching." Cooke had inherited money and large interests on leaving college and had shown good capacity in handling his business.

He was always willing to give funds to true athletic promotion, however small and humble might be the attempt, however provincial. To greater projects he was equally liberal, once assured of their sincerity. He endowed gymnasiums, donated swimming pools, paid for running tracks and basketball and tennis courts, and bestowed numerous trophies every week of his existence.

It was this man the Griffin proposed so lightly to destroy, and Manning knew well that the monster considered his plans perfect before he announced his fell intention.

Manning had been given the date—seven days distant—but only in mockery. It was as if the Griffin, in this "game" of his that he likened to chess, had granted a lesser player a bishop or a castle. The main advantage still lay with the Griffin.

As for Manning's moves, they were clear enough—to enlist the police in providing protection, to himself mount guard over Evans Cooke, whether Cooke was willing or not; to exhaust every precaution and to be alert to discover the diabolical preparations, to prevent the kill. The Griffin had suggested he might himself be present. That must not be overlooked. He was mad and therefore he might make a false move out of sheer grandiose dementia.

Manning put in a call for the police commissioner. He was sure of full cooperation there.

"There's a dinner at the New York Athletic Club to-morrow night," said the commissioner. "Given to some of our Olympic winners. Cooke will be there. He'll speak, distribute special awards. I shall be there. You're a member, aren't you? Good. Then we can talk with him. He's not going to be easy to handle."

I V

COOKE WAS not easy. He did not pooh-pooh the danger. No man could do that against the Griffin's scarlet record; but Cooke declined to take special means to protect himself.

"Look at this last chap the Griffin killed," he said. "Shut himself up with you in vaults, Manning, wouldn't eat or drink. And he died. If my time has come I can't stop it. I suppose I'm a bit of a fatalist. They say the Griffin is also. He reads the stars and uncovers fates. He may have uncovered mine. You chaps can take all the precautions you want to, so long as you don't interfere with the fête I've arranged.

"I'm opening my new pool at my country place. No sports program except that a few record holders have kindly promised to christen the pool with the spray from their dives and sprints. It's built just the length of my own record underwater dive and I'm going to see if I'm still equal to it."

He looked it, Manning fancied; a man in his prime at something over forty, deep-chested, powerful. A fine specimen, a model for the type he hoped to develop.

"That's one fine pool," he went on enthusiastically. "I'm trying out, demonstrating rather, the new method of purifying swimming pools with ultraviolet rays instead of using chlorine to sting the eyes out of you. It works wonderfully. And I'm jing-ding-damned," he added, half humorously but evidently in dead earnest, "if I'm going to let the Griffin put off that event. The invitations have been sent out. It's a private affair so I haven't announced it to the press. They'll probably scent it and be on the job, however. Now, I suppose, I'll have to add you and the commissioner to the guest list?"

"We'll both be there," said Manning grimly. "Invited or not.

What's more, Cooke, I want a list of your guests. I want to know very precisely who will be present, as guests or employees. I don't propose to annoy any of them at all unnecessarily. We'll check ninety-five per cent out inside of twenty-four hours. But we've got to know; and I want to go to your place to-morrow and look things over. I'll drive there, may be there continually."

Evans Cooke looked at Manning more attentively. There was a manner about the crime investigator that was as evident and compelling as a flow of magnetic current. His eyes were cold with purpose.

"You're welcome, of course," said Cooke. "I wish it was only as a guest, Manning. I should like to know you better. Like to have you interested in my movement. You're the sort of chap could stir up enthusiasm."

"I'm interested right now in *you*," said Manning. "Take this threat seriously, Cooke. It's more than a threat. It's mighty likely to become a certainty."

Evans Cooke looked into Manning's eyes and there was laughter in his own. Not merriment, not derision, but the gay humor of a man who is unafraid. Manning gripped his out-stretched hand with genuine liking. A man of this caliber was well worth preserving. Cooke made a gallant gesture.

*"Te morituri salutamus,"* he quoted, and turned to greet some of the guests of the evening.

"What was that he just said?" asked the commissioner who had come up from the ranks and lacked a classical education.

"It was a slogan of the Roman arena," Manning told him. "The gladiators stood in front of the imperial box and chanted it to Caesar or Nero or whoever happened to be imperator. 'Hail!' they said. 'We who are about to die, salute thee!'"

"LUDONIA," EVANS COOKE had named his place. It was after the Latin verb indicating "sporting pastime." The place was on the level land of Long Island. The house itself was well designed but not unusual. There was a separate sports building with as complete an equipment, lacking the amphitheater, as Madison Garden. There was a quarter of a mile track encircling a space for field sports. The tennis courts were perfection.

Cooke practiced what he preached to the extent of his own capacity, and his guests were frequently amateurs and sometimes professionals of the top rank. The fête on the nineteenth was, however, largely a social affair. The new tank had been completed and was to be the last word in swimming pools.

Manning surveyed it approvingly. It must have cost plenty of money, he imagined, looking at the tiled interior, now empty, slanting from eight feet to three. The tiles had been specially designed. Fresh water was emitted through a bronze dolphin's mouth, made exit through an overflow shaped like a giant conch shell. The tiles were specially designed to represent fishes in action, luxuriant growths of weed. The globes that illuminated the tank of a night, beneath the water line, were concealed behind shades of actual nautilus shell. The ultra-ray lamps that would automatically keep the water pure were not yet installed. Manning idly watched the man in charge of the work and passed on to his minute survey of the grounds. They were fenced and could be efficiently guarded.

The police commissioner was working on the list of guests. None seemed even to suggest suspicion, but the Griffin was wealthy. Aside from the society end there would be athletes, male and female. The game was none too lucrative professionally, expensive from a purely amateur standpoint. The Griffin had unlimited funds. He had bought his way out of Dannemora. He might buy an assistant murderer. There would be plenty of men in plain clothes to look out for everyone who might be doubted. The employees were checked. Evans Cooke vouched for them.

During the late night of the eighteenth the trained, picked men of the police commissioner came quietly to Ludonia to take up their vigil. At midnight the place was dark. Evans Cooke believed in moderation, his entertainments were never carousals. The sound body needed sleep and he set the example and not merely expected his guests to follow it, but had all lights switched off at twelve. The estate, with neighboring ones and the village, was served by a subsidiary power line from high tension wires of the main power plant, reduced through a transformer.

Manning had a battery lamp. He had also a powerful electric torch. He had been there, day and night, for a week, and he was convinced that he had built up a good defense.

Now the zero period had commenced, he had little fear that the Griffin, for all his deviltry, could pass the cordon established about the grounds and the house. Inside, Cooke slept in the room next to Manning's. Close by there were vigilant protectors, eager and alert.

The Griffin was certainly not within the grounds. He would strike later, devise some means of delivering the blow in the open. It would fall like a bolt from the blue, it would be spectacular.

More than once the Griffin had boasted to Manning that, in order successfully to murder a man, one had only to study his habits to find the weak spot.

Manning had bestowed a week's extensive research upon the habits of Cooke, feeling sure the Griffin had done the same.

Now, prepared for twenty-four hours of tireless vigil, he went over his notes, his deductions, instructions he had issued and was yet to issue, working like a field marshal on the eve of a decisive battle by the light of his battery lamp.

The police commissioner would arrive in the morning. The guests would begin to appear shortly before noon. An elaborate luncheon was to be served and the waiters would be chosen members of both civic and private detective forces.

He went over once more the roster of the guests. Their records were flawless. Yet Manning believed that someone would be on the spot who was prepared to carry out the Griffin's diabolical plot.

At two in the morning he made his grand rounds. The one

exception to Cooke's ukase of "lights out" was by the pool, where they were testing the globes that, underwater, lighted the pool after dark with colors that could be combined, changed into varying effects. The switches were in a small cement building, an addition to the dressing pavilion, where also the valves for the intake and outflow of the pool were controlled.

At the pool the program of the day would center. Three girl champions, two of them Olympic winners, with two male stars, would display their speed and grace. Cooke himself would try to repeat his record. Manning believed he could, having seen him try it the day before, marveling at his host's prowess.

V

THE POOL was empty now and a corps of men was busy under the brisk direction of a gaunt New Englander who had undertaken the contract and was, Cooke said, a genius in the rough. He lacked education so far as books went, but Cooke proclaimed him another of those talented products of the northeastern seaboard who begin as tinkers and wind up as Edisons or Fords.

Sentinels had challenged, and then saluted Manning in his inspection. It was inevitable that these workmen must know that special precautions were being taken for some purpose. But the master electrician seemed concentrated on his job and its success, and on that alone.

He answered Manning curtly but not rudely and showed him how the work had been planned and carried out both for the illumination and the purification violet rays. Manning saw the purple rays flash on and off. He noted the inlets and outlets for the current, inspected the switchboard. Much of the work was completed, underground. Manning was not a practical electrician, but he knew the general theory and he could see nothing wrong. Yet he suspected that tank; he dreaded the moment of Cooke's underwater dive.

Still, it seemed as if the barricade was invincible. He could find no flaw in it as he returned to the house and sat on the terrace beneath Cooke's window, smoking pipe after pipe until the dawn came.

The water flowed into the pool. Final tests were made, the lights were shut off. The workmen left, checked out at the gate, the contractor remaining to see his work approved, collect his money.

"I wish," Manning told himself, "that Cooke hadn't made that gesture and used that quotation."

He meant the *"te morituri salutamus,"* the "I, who am about to die, salute thee," phrase that Manning had explained to the commissioner.

Half a dozen times, as he tapped out his briar, refilled it and sent the aromatic smoke into the still air, Manning deplored that little speech. "Confound him," Manning muttered. "I wish that had not come into his head."

The sun rose, the day wore on without sign of trouble. Vigilance was maintained. The forenoon passed, the guests arrived and were entertained, unconscious of the keen-eyed sleuths who served them deftly but watched everything, waiting for any sign of the unusual.

Manning sauntered about, introduced by Cooke as amateur handball champion. The strain was terrific, but Cooke appeared serene.

The attempt at tragedy, Manning told himself, would happen before sunset. At three in the afternoon, after the elaborate luncheon and some speechmaking, the guests assembled about the pool. Manning kept close to his host, a service gun holstered under one shoulder, his leather-covered steel cane in his hand.

Now, with a sudden quickening of inner alarm, he felt that the supreme moment of the Griffin's would-be fatal move upon this animated chessboard was imminent. But there was no sign of it. There was no unaccredited person upon the estate. The guards were all upon the *qui vive*. The waiters, relieved of their pseudo duties, added to the ranks of the protectors. Manning saw the commissioner himself, vigilant, experienced. The only outside employee, if the man could be so styled, was the electrician who had installed the lighting.

A shadow drifted over the sparkling pool as the first of the guest exhibitors came from the dressing rooms and started to climb to a diving platform. Manning looked up and saw an autogyro hovering overhead. He remembered the Griffin's hint that he might be present. But there were other planes close by. They had passed in circling patrol ever since sunrise. Two of them came racing up now. Police planes, armed with quickfirers, far speedier than an autogyro, if that turned out to be anything but the machine of a casual spectator out for a flight and attracted by the crowd. Someone was looking out of the gyro's cockpit. Manning caught the gleam of binoculars. If they were merely looking on, they had a commanding position.

The body of the girl Olympic champion leaped, poised in the air with exquisite grace, making a perfect swan dive as the spectators applauded heartily. The others followed.

Cooke had gone to the dressing pavilion. Manning watched for his appearance, with his pulse gone up, his blood tingling, his tension strained to the limit. He could not foretell what would happen, but he knew it was imminent. Yet he was sure there was nothing connected with the pool, with the lighting, that was out of the ordinary, that was harmful.

He looked about him and caught the eye of the commissioner, grimly watchful. He did not notice the electrician in the crowd about the pool. After all, the man was a mechanician, not a guest. He glanced up and saw the autogyro still hovering. The two police planes were close by.

COOKE APPEARED and the applause heightened as he took his stance. In his diving suit he was a really magnificent figure as he acknowledged the greeting with a smile and a gesture that brought the Latin phrase flashing again into Manning's mind.

"I who am about to die...."

Manning half started forward to stop the dive, but he was too late. Cooke crouched, his arms back, then forward, as he lanced in a flat trajectory into the pool. His body glided beneath the surface, his head came close to it but did not break the water.

He was going to make it, to equal his record, and nothing had happened. The onlookers stood ready to cheer him, Manning stood staring, waiting.

Cooke's hands grasped the rail that ran all about the pool. He stood up in the shallow water and moved to the steps, coming out of the pool unscathed, smiling and bowing to his applauding guests. Manning almost gasped with relief. Still he could hardly believe that Cooke had passed the ordeal Manning had believed the pool somehow constituted, though he had not been able to detect anything amiss. Cooke pressed through the crowd, walking erect in a little triumphant progress to the dressing pavilion. Manning followed him. He was not going to let Cooke out of his sight until midnight.

The swimming guests had watched Cooke's performance and remained outside. Now they were all in the pool, disporting there in an impromptu program of their own.

The dressing pavilion was empty. There was a row of cabinets, with one lettered with Cooke's own name, reserved for his private use. His hand was almost on the handle of the door when Manning entered. Cooke turned to see who had followed him, grinned in recognition.

"You see, I did it, and I'm still alive. I'll be out as soon as I've changed."

The water dripped from his bathing suit about him in a little puddle. His feet were in it as he took hold of the handle.

The smile on his face turned to a grimace. His features were contorted and his body convulsed as he clung to the metal handle in a grip he could not relinquish. Then, with his expression frozen to a mask of horrible pain, he was released, and fell backwards.

The pavilion was filled with a curious odor, sour, metallic as

Manning leaped for him, made a brief inspection, then dashed outside.

The pleasure seeking crowd fell back before his stern face. The commissioner came forward to meet him. They exchanged a glance. Manning nodded.

"Mr. Cooke has had an attack. It looks like heart failure," he announced, for the benefit of the crowd. "Better get a doctor and have the place cleared, Commissioner."

He spoke with his eyes on the little shack with the green door at the end of the pavilion. The door opened slightly and a man peered out. It was the New England expert.

The commissioner issued sharp orders, a man revealed himself as a physician. The electrician closed the door again as he saw Manning hurling himself towards him. There was no inside bolt, he had no chance to lock the door before Manning plunged through and found the man at bay.

He had connected wires with two electrodes and held one in either hand. If they met, even while they were a little apart, Manning knew that a terrific current would unite its poles. They were sputtering now, flinging off blue light. There was the same metallic smell and taste of tremendous voltage in the air.

"Keep away," the man yelled. "Keep away, I tell you."

"I want you," said Manning steadily. "You killed Cooke, for the Griffin!"

"For the Griffin? For Satan himself! The devil drove me. Stand back! I will not surrender."

THE KILLER was beside himself, foam flecked on his lips, and his eyes were wild. Manning lashed out with his cane and the end of the rod struck Cyrus Allen on his elbow. It was a risky blow. It had to be precise, to avoid contact with the wires. Allen dropped one of them and then the other. They coiled sputtering on the cement floor like burning fuses. Manning glanced round for a main switch and the murderer leaped for him, grappling with mad and desperate force that took all of Manning's strength and experience to offset. They struggled about the place, the gaunt man striving to trip Manning and Manning trying to get at his gun. He had been forced to drop his cane to grapple with the other.

Allen was like a mad dog, snapping with his teeth. They brought blood from Manning's shoulder, they grazed his jugular, breaking the skin. Manning got an arm under Allen's leg, tore loose his hold and tossed him in a heavy throw.

Allen struck the floor in a heap, lighting on top of Manning's steel-cored cane. He slid upon it towards the crackling wires, and the cane completed the circuit. There was a flash, a frightful stench of burning flesh, the body of Allen jerking in the midst of it, then still. Manning staggered back from the sheer impact of the discharge.

The shocked guests were departing when Manning came out of the green door. The detectives were handling the crowd ably. The pool was empty. The commissioner was in the dressing pavilion, with the doctor. The body of Cooke had been laid upon a lounge, covered with a blanket found in a locker.

"We'll have to have the official examiner, of course," the commissioner said to Manning. "But Dr. Drake here says there is no question as to the cause of death. He was electrocuted. There was no chance of bringing him back."

Manning nodded.

"I was afraid of something like that," he said. "I suspected the pool. The contracting electrician stepped-up the voltage and connected it to this handle with a switch in the control shack. He threw it when he saw Cooke going in to change. He could tell when the contact was made, and, when he was sure Cooke was dead, he shut it off."

"Cooke's hands are burned. There are ruptured veins. No doubt an autopsy will reveal deranged organs. Death was probably instantaneous, if that is any relief," said the doctor.

The commissioner and Manning both thought of the same thing; the penitentiary autopsies of those who die in the chair. The cause of death would be verified.

"Is there anything else I can do?" asked the physician.

"Nothing, Doctor," Manning answered quietly.

When the doctor had gone he turned to the commissioner and told him what had happened behind the green door. "It will come out soon enough," he said. "The doctor could do nothing for him, less than he might have done for poor Cooke. It was not a pleasant death, for he knew what was coming before he died. I only wish it had been the Griffin. He said he'd be looking on. Come outside."

The autogyro had vanished. The police planes still circled, waiting orders.

"He was in that gyro; did you notice it?" Manning asked the commissioner.

"I saw it. I… what's that floating in the pool, Manning, over at the outflow end?"

Manning fished out a black, wooden disk. A weight at the end of a string anchored it, had steadied it for a straight drop. Part of the center had been carved out into a shallow receptacle that was filled with sealing wax, scarlet as blood, in which was sharply imprinted the seal of the Griffin.

# DEATH HAS ITS FLING

*Up at Nitamo Lodge Sportsmen Hunted Game,*
*but Gordon Manning Went There to Hunt a*
*Savage Beast of Prey—the Diabolic Griffin!*

**N**ITAMO LODGE, named after a famous Sachem of the Mahikanders, is an exclusive fishing and hunting lodge in the Adirondacks. The stream is the Wiequaskeck and the man once privileged to cast a fly over its lively, well-stocked waters, speaks well of no other river. The club has its own hatchery and breeds its replenishment of feathered game. As for the deer, they have to be kept down.

It stands in the wilderness, almost as savage today as when Peter Stuyvesant made his treaties with the Katskils, the Mahikanders and the Indians of the Esopus. The land is beautiful, a happy hunting ground.

Membership is limited and expensive. Its privilege is rigidly guarded by a grave and severe Board of Governors. You must have right to it through family inheritance. If misfortune makes it impossible for you to meet the dues, you are still a member. They are true sportsmen who make up the gatherings at Nitamo Lodge. They never refer to it as a club.

They are liberal with guests, but a card is extended only twice a year to each one, once for fishing and once for shooting, a week at a time. If a man wants a deer he must forego trout or birds. And he must be proven. His sponsor not only guarantees his gentility, but his sportsmanship. He must know and love rod and gun. He must cast his fly with skill and proper selection. He must be able to pick off dodging bobwhite, or rocketing

*"Looks like he's stalling," Burke murmured to Manning, too low for the man in the stream to hear.*

pheasant, with reasonable accuracy and bring down his buck with one well-placed bullet.

Above all, he must not be a braggart, or selfish, and must be as good a companion about the big fireplace as he is in field or stream. If a man does not come up to these matters his sponsor is fined his guest-right for a month. Therefore, it is not easy to be a visitor at Nitamo Lodge and a man will speak of it proudly.

As for the Lodge itself, it is convenient, it is supremely comfortable, but it is anything but luxurious. One man and his family of one son and two daughters, besides his wife, manage it completely; the plain cooking is incomparable, varied with game in season. Men do not take their private servants to the Lodge, neither do they rough it. It furnishes a happy medium and—aside from the wife and daughters of the manager—it is strictly stag.

No woman has ever cast a fly on the Wiequaskeck, or fired a shot within the coverts of the club. Nor will they, with the consent of the owners. The place is a sanctuary from everything that reminds them of everyday life and affairs; the members are like the herd bucks that leave the does and camp in seclusion on the ridges; not that they love the females less, but their own, intimate communion more.

I T  WA S  the first week in May and the season fairly opened, but the weather had been unkind. The night before, frost had lightly revealed itself on the porches, again in the morning; not nipping, but enough to prevent any hatch of flies, to keep the water too cold for early fishing. The trout might rise in the late afternoon as the sun went off the pools it had warmed all day. Meanwhile only a Simple Simon would hope for fish.

On the Wiequaskeck the lusty trout were given an even break. You fished with flies only—the mere mention of bait was anathema. You matched the hatch, and some tied their own flies. It was lovely water, rapids and riffles, stretches clear as gin where the big fellows just dimpled the surface when they rose and you had to put a dry fly over them just once, and that perfectly; or they flipped at it with broad tails in disdain. There were cascades and pools and everywhere it was wide enough to be waded, to cast in comfort between the trees that thickly ranked it most of the way.

It was a fast stream, and, in places, a deep one. You had to be careful, even when you knew it, and guests were warned of the bad spots where a slip, with waders on, might mean death. But there were no records of casualties since the old Indian days, when the Mahikanders and the Katskils waylaid each other and the warwhoop drowned out the shrill whistle of the arrow, the rustle of the warriors from ambush, and the Wie-quaskeck ran streaky pink at twilight.

The seven men gathered at the Lodge occupied themselves in various congenial ways. Some overhauled tackle already in perfect shape but always a joy to go over, to compare, exhibit, and discuss. Others swapped tales of earlier seasons, of prize fish. In mid-morning someone organized a friendly casting contest. There was no wind and a target was set out on the lawn, a circle of white cardboard at which they deftly cast their flies from various marked limits.

None of them was a duffer, some were more than merely expert. The best known, and best loved, man among them was Governor Thorpe. Ex-governor, for the time being, since party domination had swung in the State; but nevertheless always known as "Governor," until the time when his friends and followers believed he would be called "President."

A genial man, a just one, ever alive to the interests of his home State and its citizens. He was emphatically the People's Choice in his own party, a man of education and family, but a thorough patriot. He had fought for water rights, for reforestation. A fine figure of a man, not far from sixty, he spoke with the conviction of an honest mind, he gave out the sense of power and dignity and humanity.

The governor threw a pretty fly. Time and time again his tapered cast of silkworm gut, chosen and tied himself, allied to the line of oiled silk, plaited and also skillfully tapered, sent the lure to touch the target.

But the wizard among them was a guest, sponsored by one of their eldest members, Derrick Blythe, himself debarred from being with them and his guest by a bad attack of asthma.

The guest's name was Anthony Bostick. He was tall and gaunt with a black shock of upstanding hair and a wiry, trimmed mustache. He had caught more trout than any of them, so far. They had noted the absolute delicacy of his casting, the flirt of his wrist at the last second that let the lure down upon the surface with the exact imitation of a fly.

Now he took his honors modestly. He had been trained when he was a boy, he said, by his father's gamekeeper, who taught him how to tie flies and how to cast them. Under persuasion, he gave an exhibition of unusual flycasting, including the famous Spey, or underhand, throw. His rod and his arm seemed to combine as one and when, time and time again, he flicked the target, they spontaneously applauded him.

They were still at it when the gong sounded. The midday meal was ready. It was laid in the trophy room. Plaster casts and stretched skins of fish were on the walls, with beautifully preserved birds, heads and antlers. A fire burned in the hearth, though the windows were open to let in the breath of Spring, balmy and promising, telling of rising sap and mating creatures. Trout did their breeding in the fall, but the other wild things were choosing lovers. Bird songs came in.

The table was laid, as usual, with the service plates face down and a clean napkin of red and white check atop each one. Linen, crockery, and silver were spotless. In the center was a great bowl of daffodils.

Only one end of the long table was set. The governor's place was at the head. He took his seat, arranged his napkin over one knee, and turned his plate in expectation of the first course. He stared at his plate. The dishes were of plain design, white with lines of green and red about the outer edge and the emblem of the club on the border.

This was an heraldic dolphin contrived into a ring with the club motto within it.

*Simon Peter said: I go a fishing.*

Now, Governor Thorpe was gazing with changing and conflicting emotions at the inside of the platter, which should have been plain.

It held a scarlet splotch, red as blood, a lozenge of bright crimson, an *affiche* that was embossed in a design that, at the first glance, impressed Thorpe as sinister before his brain swiftly gathered and aligned the data stored there.

The design was that of the upper part of a griffin in heraldic device, showing the lion's claws and tail, the eagle's wings and beak of that mythical creature.

The Griffin!

## II

I T WAS the title taken by the evil, murderous genius whose killings had amazed and terrorized the continent. A madman whose stupendous egomania prompted him to hate all that was good, progressive and wise. The monster who had slain a score of men who could hardly be replaced, men who stood for advancement, philanthropy and wisdom. He had thrown society and finance into temporary panics until he had been captured by Gordon Manning and sent to Dannemora.

Manning, ex-Military Intelligence, scientist, explorer and adventurer, had been called in when the police failed. He had now a commission from the governor, endorsed and renewed by the present incumbent, besides full police powers in the city.

Over Manning's protests, though he knew the judgment was within the law, the Griffin had not been executed and he had escaped from the institution for the criminally insane to pursue his bloodthirsty career.

He had slain more than once since his reappearance. Also Manning had managed more than once to circumvent his fell plans, but not to lay hands on the mocking fiend who openly proclaimed the name of his intended victim and the date on which he should die.

These things flashed through the governor's mind as he tossed his napkin on the plate to cover the *affiche,* and, leaning forward, pried at it with his knife as he told the rest an anecdote in his usual brilliant manner, that kept the girl, who was waiting to serve the consommé, in the background.

This thing might be a hoax. Certainly not a practical joke on the part of any of the men at the table, or the employees. But— the table had been set for an hour or two; there were the open windows....

The governor, making the point of his story, glanced through them at the new green of grass and trees. He saw nothing, yet he felt as if a shadow had passed over the lawn, as if a chill wind had trailed it, entered, congealing for a moment the marrow in his spine.

He was a brave man, of a brave line, but he believed he had received his death warrant. As the waitress brought his soup he removed his napkin, and with it the scarlet lozenge, palming it, putting it into his pocket, achieving the jesting tag of his tale, smiling at the others as they laughed at his wit.

Half an hour later, in his room, he looked again at the red symbol.

He had enemies, naturally enough. He had been threatened by the friends of men he had refused to pardon, by cranks. This might be one of these, masquerading as the Griffin. The latter's diabolical methods had been often enough exploited in the press after his satanic victories.

But this did not tie up with the Griffin's invariable method. He had taken up the appointment of Manning as a challenge. Likened it to a game of chess, wherein he played with living men, and studied out his moves before making the first one. Always he had notified Manning beforehand, never the man he hoped to annihilate. He might have changed his methods.

It was significant of Thorpe that he took it calmly, filling and lighting his pipe with steady fingers. He wondered if Manning knew of this. If so, why had he not communicated with him? There was no telephone at Nitamo Lodge. They purposely cut themselves off from the world. The nearest instrument was at the small railroad depot, whence telegrams were sometimes brought, thence despatched, in emergency.

He resolved to try and get in touch with Gordon Manning. He knew him personally. Manning had once been the governor's guest at the Lodge. He could be so again, if he would. But there was no date set, only the scarlet lozenge with the imprint of the ravening beast upon it....

A knock came at the door. The manager's son appeared.

"I beg pardon, Governor. You and Mr. Bostick have drawn

the Maple Pool. It should be good, 'round sunset. I've seen some good 'uns rising there."

"Fine, Tom!" said the governor. "But I'm afraid he'll wipe my eye."

"He can fish—but so can you," said the other. "Mail just got in. Dad brought it. One for you, sir."

Thorpe surveyed it dubiously after the man had left. No one should write him here. Only intimates knew where he was. His secretary had orders—but this was addressed plainly to him, at Nitamo Lodge.

HE DID not know the bold handwriting, purple ink on a thick, gray, handwoven paper. He turned the envelope over. On the flap the sinister symbol was repeated, sealed in red wax. It was from the Griffin.

A brief note. The note of a man whose mind was warped, perverted by dementia grandiosa, but infinitely crafty, infinitely evil.

> The stars decree your downfall. You deem yourself destined to rule a Nation but your House of Nativity proclaims your presumption shall be taught a lasting lesson. You, who think yourself a leader among men, shall be dust. The same immutable horoscope proclaims me as the Divine Agent who shall announce in your elimination that all men are grass when, in its next verdure, it shall be nurtured from your dust.
>
> Know then that on the Ninth of May, wherever you may be, however you may strive to avert the inevitable; you die.

There was no signature, only a well-penned drawing of the same device, the upper body of a griffin, rampant.

Thorpe read it without flinching. He knew how often the Griffin had succeeded. If it had to be, he would take it in the open; but reflection persuaded him that this wilderness place might be safer than many others, with due precautions.

He was not minded to forego his holiday. For one thing, he needed it. He had not stopped working for the public weal because he was no longer governor, nor because he might be nominated for president. He was a widower, and childless, who had simply and utterly devoted his life towards the betterment of his fellowman and the firm establishment of his country. He was not afraid of death but he enjoyed life, as he employed it.

The Maple Pool would not be ready to fish until about four o'clock. He had his own car, driving it himself. If the Griffin ran true to his satanic form, Thorpe had three days of leeway. The Griffin probably got unhallowed satisfaction over the thought that his prospective victim would cower through the hours before his predicted execution. Thorpe was not that sort.

He drove to the depot and waited for the always protracted connections between that outland place and New York City. He tried Manning's office, where he plied his profession as consulting attorney, he tried his house and his clubs, only to find that Manning was out of town on a mission he had kept private, but would return by the next morning.

Thorpe got the Commissioner of Police, personally, told him briefly what had happened, read also the letter.

"The ninth, you say?" answered the commissioner. "I'll get in touch with Manning the moment he returns. I may be able to locate him to-night, this afternoon. I think you're safe in the meanwhile, Governor, but for God's sake be careful. Where will you be for the next few hours? I'll send up some men."

"Better wait until you see Manning," Thorpe replied. "There is no danger here. The place is well patrolled. Send your men if you want to but choose them carefully. I'm on a holiday with my friends. I don't want us overrun by dicks. Get hold of Manning if you can. Meantime, I'm going fishing. May send you some trout. I expect to get some good ones this afternoon. This thing may be only a fake, Commissioner."

At the other end of the wire the commissioner grunted.

Thorpe himself was not as confident as he sounded, but he forgot it, absolutely, as he worked a Parmacheenee Belle in the riffles and felt the tug of a strike, the plunge of a big trout at the end of his gossamer line.

He was at the end of the tickles, above the pool. Bostick was at the lower end. He had creeled some good ones and Thorpe was on his mettle. The governor acknowledged the other's supremacy when it came to close casting, but he felt he was as good when it came to manipulating the artificial fly to copy the actions of a natural one.

This trout should tie the score. Thorpe was on to a record fish. He gave it line and braked it. It broke water, resplendent, iridescent, fighting like a bulldog against the barb in its jaw. He checked it, tip up, the splitcane bending like a bow.

Then Thorpe's footing slipped on the weedy boulders and he went down, instinctively holding his rod up but rolling in the current, swept down into the pool. His waders filled with water and he went deep, thrashing as he came up, plummeted down again, struggling. Vaguely he heard a shout, saw Bostick plunging, lurching out to the bank.

He made the shallows, but got no hold. The stream gripped him, conquered him. He was a fair swimmer but the water in his waders was like lead. He wallowed, taking water into his lungs, choking, wondering if this could be some infernal trick of the Griffin, his bewildered reason even now rejecting that....

Then someone gripped him, raised him, dragged him to safety.

It was Bostick.

"A close call, Thorpe! You need hip-waders here. Now, you're all right. And the trout is still on—"

"Don't lose him," said Thorpe, spewing water. He had held to his rod. Bostick knelt beside him, raising him, giving him a drink from his flask that Thorpe choked on but appreciated. "I'll handle him," he said, sitting up, feeble but determined. The line on the reel was almost out, but the trout was still hooked.

Ten minutes later Bostick had the fish in his net, jubilant.

"You're a sport, Governor," he said. "And you've landed the record!"

"You landed me, Bostick," said Thorpe. "I'd have drowned if it hadn't been for you."

"It wasn't your day to die," said Bostick. "Have another drink?"

Thorpe took it, gathered himself together.

"No," he said slowly. "It wasn't my day to die. You deferred it."

Bostick laughed, making light of it, weighing the big fish.

"All right to make it back?" he asked. "They've quit rising."

"I haven't," said Thorpe and proved it by getting to his feet. "That's mighty good Scotch, Bostick."

"Don't forget to shift to hip-waders," said the other. "If you haven't got any with you, I brought an extra pair. We should wear about the same size. They're rubberized twill, made in England, keep you dry to your waist and they're not a quarter the weight of the all-rubber ones. And much safer. It doesn't take much for a man to drown in swift water, once his waders hold him down."

### III

THE POLICE COMMISSIONER finally located Manning at his own house in Pelham Manor, late that evening. He drove out there rather than confer over the telephone, and found Gordon Manning just at the end of a delayed dinner served him by his Japanese.

"You look fit," said the commissioner. "You need to be. It looks like the Griffin!"

The two had gone into Manning's library. Tanaka set out liqueurs and highball materials. Manning, standing by the fireplace, filled his pipe and lit it as the commissioner bit off the end of one of Manning's imported cigars.

Manning was lean and brown and tall, physically in the pink

and mentally alert. The little lines that had registered on his face since he had first encountered the Griffin stood out sharply now. His keen eyes showed a trace of bewilderment. But he made no comment.

"Tell me about it," he said simply and listened to the end, smoking serenely enough.

"It isn't the Griffin's usual procedure," he said. "It's not easy to imagine him giving up the pleasure of baiting me—and you as well—by his boasting preannouncements. I've heard nothing, seen nothing. The Griffin always has left it to me to inform the prospective victim. What do you make of it, Commissioner? The letter, paper and all, may be a forgery."

The head of the Police Department sent out a vicious puff of smoke. His veins were congested, his face suggested apoplexy. If the pursuit of the Griffin had incised lines of care on the features of Manning it had affected the commissioner far more deeply. For a man like Thorpe to die might well mean his job and his future reputation.

"It looks like a crank to me," he replied. "Whether it is just a plan to see if the thing gets into the papers or not, or whether he may try an actual attack, it's hard to say. We can't take any chances."

"Of course not," Manning answered. "I'll go down there, to-night, and look the place over. I've been there, as Thorpe's guest. Offhand, I'd say it wouldn't be as hard to guard a man up there as in the city. The Lodge can be handled easily enough and the stream patrolled efficiently. I'd be with him all the time, of course. But I want to take a thorough survey. Thorpe, of course, will welcome me as an expected guest. I'll take my tackle with me, fish, at that."

"Thorpe don't want any of the guests or members tipped off," said the commissioner. "I'd rather see him down here, myself. I'd like to keep him in solitary until the ninth is over, but you can't budge him. He's up there to fish and he is going to fish, come hell or high water...."

"Or the Griffin," said Manning gravely. "That fiend has killed in places as remote as a solitary cell before now. Thorpe is a brave man. He's proven it many times, morally and physically. A sensible one. We'll try and not spoil his holiday or that of the rest, but we'll have to connect with the employees. The others may wonder at the sight of so many keepers, but we'll have our men placed during the night of the eighth, and once those chaps get casting a fly, they won't notice the banks except where they come ashore occasionally. The Wiequaskeck is a wading stream. I'll get in touch with you to-morrow. Let you know what I propose to do."

"I'd like to kidnap the governor, just the same," growled the commissioner as he stood up and got ready to go back to the city.

"That would be a confession of weakness," said Manning. "Besides, he wouldn't let you do it. You've got a closed car. I see it's started to rain."

The commissioner nodded. The rain broke on the window in sharp bursts and when the front door was opened the weather looked as if it had determined upon a night of storm. It was common enough this time of year, with thunder and vivid display of lightning.

MANNING STOOD watching it as the commissioner drove off. By the time lapse between peal and flash he fancied it was local. If they had one like it up at Nitamo Lodge it would spoil fly fishing until the waters cleared and subsided. He closed the door and went in, thoughtful but swift in his actions.

His senses, naturally acute, long trained against danger and emergencies, were swift to respond to the threat of evil when it was sent out by the Griffin but he felt nothing directed towards him now, nothing that might he called definite. There was a premonition of disaster that might or might not be inti-mately associated by the thought that Thorpe was in danger.

It did not look like the Griffin. There were cranks enough who might have real or fancied grievances against the governor, beloved as he was. A crafty criminal might well try to avert suspicion by asserting that he was the Griffin.

Only, unless he had the exact, diabolical twist of the Griffin, mentally, why warn the victim? That was the Griffin's perversity, born of his belief that the horoscopes he cast made his fiendish triumph certain.

Manning's roadster had a California top. He was not waiting for the storm to end. He would probably drive out of it. And, whether it was hoax or terrible tragedy in the making, he meant to lose no time getting to the bottom of it. He wanted to get there when day was breaking, to look for possible signs of preparation for murder.

If it was the Griffin, Manning knew that the plan had matured, had been worked out as a chess master works out his game, providing for every possible combination against him. But even chess masters lose, Manning told himself grimly.

Above all, he wanted to look at that scarlet *affiche* Thorpe had found on his plate. At first thought that suggested inside work, but Manning remembered the layout of the Lodge, the open windows at this time of the year, plenty of chance for someone to steal out of the woods, climb in, affix the seal, and get away again.

It might even be that fantastic creature of the Griffin's, Al, the legless freak of humanity who walked and ran on his hands with incredible agility, who looked like some grotesque thing out of a nightmare.

Manning waited upon himself. Tanaka was a perfect valet as well as butler, but Manning was self-serving. He packed rods, tackle, flies and boots, filled a bag with clothes and an extra automatic and shoulder holster, adjusting one now by his left armpit. He hunted up his creel and returned to the library, meaning to fill his flask.

Tanaka was there, clearing away. Manning's sleeping quarters were above the library and a stairway of wrought iron connected the two. The house was his own design and he often spent more than half his nights with his books.

He was halfway down the stairs when the telephone rang. Tanaka moved towards it. There was nothing extraordinary about a call. Plenty of people would want to know if he was back—yet there was something in the sharp vibrance of the bell that communicated itself to Manning like an actual magnetic contact.

He knew that the Griffin could cut into his wire by a special device. This might be only his highstrung nerves. He called to Tanaka.

"I'll take it...."

There came a great clap of thunder overhead that seemed to jar the house. Lavender light flared in through the tall windows, eclipsing the shaded lamps, flinging the shadow of Tanaka sprawling and enlarged upon the far wall.

Tanaka looked up. He lifted the receiving arm as Manning, inspired by instinct, vaulted the rail and landed lightly on all fours.

He was too late.

There was a hideous smell of burning rubber and of flesh. Tanaka lay crumpled. His brown flesh was curiously veined with blue as if Death had used his skin as parchment on which to write a hieroglyphic message. Dead—utterly. Nothing could restore him though Manning let his grief-stricken countryman and fellow servant do what he could until the doctor came, and the coroner.

It was an hour before Manning got away. The storm had passed as suddenly as it had risen. This death might have been its cryptic purpose.

Manning could not tell, but he believed, that he was the intended victim; that the storm was merely coincidental, that the Griffin had meant him to receive some frightful charge he had transmitted over the wire. The Griffin owned men, body and soul, who were supreme in their crafts and sciences, prisoned by his knowledge of their secret crimes. He had achieved this sort of thing before, using a man's radio.

Always he studied a victim's habits, used them to slay him. He had expected Manning to answer that phone, at that hour. If Tanaka had been killed instead, it was like a rabbit tripping a deadfall set for a panther.

Nothing certain, all offset by the question as to why the Griffin had ignored his regular routine. On the very day that Manning had been sworn in and commissioned by a distressed police commissioner as a special agent to hunt down the Griffin, the monster had written, congratulating him as a worthy competitor, always letting Manning know the name, the fatal day, taunting him beforehand. It did not seem likely he would forego such anticipatory gloating.

Unless his madness had changed since he had fled Dannemora.

These thoughts shuffled through Manning's mind as he drove the car at headlong speed over the long hills and around the sharp curves to the north. Twice a motor patrol hailed him but fell back at the sound of his police siren, a glimpse of his special license plate.

It was early dawn when he reached the reserve. Birds were twittering, tuning up, the air was vernal, the sky serene, the scene absolutely peaceful.

The lodgekeeper was up and recognized him.

"I didn't know you were coming, Mr. Manning," he said.

"Didn't know it myself till yesterday. You know how it is," answered Manning.

"Yes, sir. Got to grab the chance. They sure are catching some beauties. The governor broke the record yesterday. Nigh got drowned doing it. But he'll tell you about that, sir," the man went on, abashed at having talked too much. Governor Thorpe might not like it known.

Manning drove on slowly. There was dew on the grass and the foliage was fresh, dustless, the air was perfumed with spring sweetness. But back in the city, Tanaka lay hideously dead. Death might be couching now in these coverts where the ferns were beginning to uncurl, where rabbits gamboled, young broods cheeped and does nuzzled their young. The Wiequaskeck murmured. There had been no frost and already flies were dancing in the early sunbeams. A trout broke the shaded surface of a pool like the flash of a diamond.

He was remembered, greeted, at the Lodge, registered, with Thorpe's name in the sponsor column.

"You might tell the governor I am here when he gets up," he said. "I am earlier than he expected, I imagine. I'm going for a stroll."

## IV

IT WAS early morning on the ninth. The aroma of coffee and bacon greeted the men as they assembled for breakfast, jesting with each other, drawing for the favorite pools, making wagers for the best catch.

Five hours of the dreaded twenty-four had passed. Manning had seen the scarlet *affiche* and the letter. Both looked genuine but both had been shown in newspaper illustrations from time to time, when the Griffin and his last enormity took the headlines. The writing paper was handmade, Japanese. Both letter and seal might be false, a clever man might have contrived to have them forged, to divert suspicion from himself.

The main thing that bothered Manning was that he had no message himself from the Griffin, unless he might count Tanaka's death as a warning, unless that death had been meant for him. There had been times when the Griffin had grimly suggested that if Manning ever ceased to amuse him as an adversary, he might eliminate him. Yet hardly without notice. The Griffin loved the cat and mouse game.

It was possible, he thought, that someone might have got hold of one of the actual seals. The Griffin used them freely enough. Things were mysteriously lost from police records now and then. A letter might have been filched to match the paper, serve as copy for the forger.

It was hard to imagine any of those sportsmen committing a murder, hard to imagine any outsider getting through the lines Manning had established and which would be rigidly maintained until the twenty-four hours were over.

As for Thorpe, he took it lightly.

"I place my burden upon you, Manning," he said. "I suppose the place is swarming with plain-clothes men, badly disguised as keepers. I think the affair is a fake. Everyone here is vouched for. And as for myself, if I've got to die, I'd prefer to die in the open."

He spoke jestingly, but Manning saw he meant that last sentence. He managed to get the governor's promise to stay away as much as possible from the banks and all overhanging trees. Manning had checked up his watchers before sunrise. They were picked detectives from the Manhattan Homicide, Loft and Robbery squads, all with marksman badge above their shields, though these were not now displayed.

There would be a relief at noon. Until midnight not a rabbit could get past them, day or night. Others would watch the Lodge, inside and out, after nightfall.

He had checked the credentials of the guests. The hosts of two were with them. Derrick Blythe had wired from a private hospital.

BOSTICK ONE OF THE FINEST STOP LOOK OUT OR HE WILL TRIM YOU ALL STOP TREAT HIM WELL

BLYTHE

Club rules allowed two men to a pool. Intermediate waters were open. A pool once relinquished was open to the first to claim it.

There was mild rivalry between Bostick and Thorpe. The governor had the biggest fish but Bostick ran him close.

They paired off and drew the pool known as the "Sachem."

Bostick appeared good naturedly rueful. He had had an accident the day before when his line snagged and his tips had broken on the Leonard splitcane with which he performed such casting marvels. He produced a steel rod as substitute.

"They're not bad when you're used to them," he said. "But they can't take the place of hexagonal splitcane, made by a master."

Manning elected to be a rover. He announced that he liked fast water and meant to try out some new flies, fishing them wet. So he expected to stay close to Thorpe during the day. He intended sleeping in Thorpe's room that night, whether the governor liked it or not.

Because of Bostick's intimacy with Thorpe, Manning kept him also under close surveillance—and saw nothing suspicious. He saw Bostick put on his waders, high-waisted, duplicates of the ones he had loaned Thorpe. He watched him don creel, landing net, flybox and oil jar. A weapon would be impossible for him to use, trussed and hampered, with one arm, often both, constantly occupied.

There was no sign of any weapon. The thought seemed an insult. Bostick was a gentleman, hail-fellow-well-met; above all, he had saved Thorpe's life. He had a right to be regarded as a bodyguard rather than a possible enemy.

Also the Griffin—if it was the Griffin—sprang or swooped from unexpected places.

The morning wore on. Fish continued to rise, as flies still hatched and fish rose at them, more and more lazily, as the sun mounted. The anglers would go to the Lodge for lunch, come back again for the evening hatch and twilight fishing.

Then, when shadows deepened, was the time for crouching death to come out of covert. Not now, in the bright light.

Governor Thorpe was above the pool, flogging the riffles. Bostick was above him again. Manning was below the pool. In the deep water the big fellows had sunk to the cool bottom, ground-feeding. Manning started to leave the water and join Thorpe and Bostick on open water.

A man appeared, in khaki with leggings and a nondescript cap. There were signs of the officer to an expert eye. Moreover, Manning knew the man from previous experience, Inspector Burke, of the Homicide Squad, a good man.

"There's a stranger fishing up above," said Burke. "He came down a small stream. We're not interfering with him, in case he happens to be a bona fide guest, but he's not one of those staying at the Lodge. Three men are watching him and they'll stop him if he comes too close. He's about two hundred yards away, fishing the white water. Just landed one. Knows how to handle his fly."

"I'll see him," said Manning. "Come on, Burke."

THE STRANGER, properly accoutered for the sport, was in midstream, casting cleverly, covering the water. A trout rose short and he reeled in, examining his fly, wading slowly to shore. He was a tall man, dark complexioned. Manning met him as he left the water, asking him politely if he was a member or had a guest card.

The other was inclined to resent the interference.

"Who the devil are you?" he asked. "I don't poach. I imagine I have as much right here as you have."

Manning did not disclose his real identity. He parleyed.

"You have only to show me your card, member or guest," he said.

Burke and three others stood concealed. The man did not appear to be armed, but he was taking an injured attitude, inclined to argue.

Burke sauntered out of the bushes.

"Looks like he's stalling," he murmured to Manning, too low for the man to hear.

Manning had the same idea. It linked up with others. Why did the man refuse to show permission to fish the Wiequaskeck?

He might be an ignorant trespasser, or he might pretend to be. But why waste time? It was suspicious....

And then Manning suddenly remembered something, irrelevantly, shocking—Bostick's use of a steel rod that morning! It was not plausible that such an expert should neither carry an extra split-cane rod nor an extra tip to the one he had wielded.

"Take care of this, Burke," he said.

"Hold him if you get anything on him. Frisk him."

With that he started running down stream, his hunch presaging evil, even then in process.

It was with infinite relief that he saw the two above the pool. He had feared the stranger's intrusion might have been carefully timed. The stranger wore a wrist watch and Manning fancied he had glanced at it. Bostick also had a watch. Now he was busy with cast and flybook, either changing his lure or quitting. He called out something to Thorpe, who turned towards him. Bostick was getting ready to cast again.

High brush and trees obscured the view momentarily as Manning pressed forward to the stream. He heard a loud shout and thrust aside a bush to see Bostick throw his rod away, and stride through the riffles, slipping now and then. His face was towards Manning, now emerging from the undergrowth, and it registered horror.

Governor Thorpe had lost his footing on the brink of the deep pool. He toppled and slid into the deep water with the current, going down. On the bank Manning saw him sink to the bottom like a plummet, without a struggle. Bubbles of air streamed up, from his lungs and from the borrowed waders that, with their great length, now sealed his fate.

"My God!" cried Bostick. "He's gone!"

Manning was hauling off his own waders, cursing every precious second of delay. Plain-clothes men came bolting from the woods. Two of them dived in, but they were not experts and the pool was deep. Manning got his trappings off at last and made his plunge, swimming down. Thorpe was a big man, he was anchored with his waders. Manning could barely budge him on the bottom. The bubbles had ceased.

They got him out and worked over him, deflating and inflating his chest, one arm free, the other bent beneath his head. They tried everything that could be done before the pulmotor arrived from miles away and vainly attempted to succeed where they could not. Thorpe's lungs were filled with water. It seemed as if he must have struck something as he fell, before he plunged.

V

MANNING TRIED to flash back to that scene. There was a tiny bruise over Thorpe's right temple and Manning believed he had fallen backwards. He remembered something shining in the air, like a silver thread, like a spider's webline when the sun catches it. It might have been the gut and wet silk of Bostick's line in his cast or as he flung his rod aside and made for the man whose life he had already saved once from the same death.

It might have been....

Manning went apart, concentrating, striving for full memory. The Lodge was hushed. No one had left. No one attempted to. And Manning had given orders to that effect. The commissioner himself was on the way, flying by police plane, with him Manhattan's justly celebrated medical examiner, Dr. Morse. Manning had worked with him before.

There were one or two things. Thorpe was a vigorous man. He could swim. Why had he made no struggle, even though the fast filling waders would have dragged him down? He had surely been unconscious. But that tiny mark showed no great impact. It was a clean mark, no weed-smear about it.

One of the plain-clothes men had retrieved Bostick's rod, reel and line still attached though the gut leader was broken off as if the hook had snagged when he had tossed the rod away at sight of Thorpe, falling.

The rod, with others, stood on the porch of the Lodge in a rack. The anglers spoke in hushed whispers. Bostick repeated the story of Thorpe's first fall.

"He must have been unsteady on his feet," he said. "He wore nails on his brogues. Over the waders. He must have been subject to vertigo."

Manning walked to the outer gate, hardly knowing where he was bent, save that he wanted to be on hand to meet the commissioner and the examiner. The gatekeeper spoke to him with a shake of his head.

"A terrible thing, sir! A terrible thing! The country needed him. I've got a note for you, Mr. Manning. It was left here a little before noon. The gentleman said there was no hurry. I forgot it when I heard the news."

"Give it to me," said Manning. He knew from whom it came.

He was staring at the few lines in purple ink on the heavy gray paper. This was no forgery.

> You annoyed me, Manning, in our last encounter. Therefore I left you out of this gambit. You were lucky at Pelham Manor but I did not consult the stars for that. Now you are here, you have taken your precautions and you find that I, the Griffin, the Destroyer, am invincible. Read this riddle, Manning, if you can. In any case the answer would come too late.

Too late for Thorpe. Too late for Tanaka. Too late to catch the Griffin or his messenger, now leagues away. But not too late, perhaps, to discover the actual murderer, to take him.

Manning thrust the letter with its scarlet *affiche* on the bottom for signature into his pocket.

Manning was painstaking but it was not that which made him a genius. A light illumined his brain. He remembered the thin thread of light he had glimpsed, he remembered Thorpe's and the others' tales of Bostick's casting prowess.

The detectives had not left. Manning rounded up the man who had picked up Bostick's rod and set him with a dozen others to search every inch of the riffles above the pool, every crevice, telling them what to look for. It might be a fly, it might be something else. He was sure nothing had been flung into the pool, however small. Bostick did not, he thought, have it on him. He had not had time to conceal it. He would have wanted to get rid of it.

The commissioner arrived, the medical examiner with him. They talked aside with Manning, who stayed on the porch where Bostick sat with the rest, mute and grief-stricken. Then the two officials went in to view the body. The commissioner came out alone.

"Mr. Bostick, you were with him," he said. "Dr. Morse would like to talk with you. You suggested vertigo, I believe?"

Bostick went in and the commissioner nodded at Manning, who stood by the rack from which the rods had not been removed, Bostick's steel rod among them. A man came running, the one who had retrieved that steel rod. He saluted.

"Found it!" he said triumphantly. The commissioner indicated Manning, who took what the man offered with the thrill of the successful manhunter.

There was a length of gut, broken off at a leader knot. At the end of it, a small, pear-shaped pellet of lead, in all holding the equivalent weight of a thirty-two bullet; a light type of sinker for still water. Manning hefted it, looked at the knot.

"Bostick tied his own leaders," he said to the commissioner. "Used a silk thread buffer. The gut will match up at the break, under a micro lens. I saw him casting. He could hit a floating leaf at thirty feet with a small, light fly. With that steel rod of his, he could, with his skill and his wrist, turn that pellet into a bullet with a short cast. It would not pierce the skull, but it stunned Thorpe, sent him helpless to drown, unconscious, weighted down by the waders Bostick loaned him. Any wading boots would have anchored him, but Bostick made certain. It was a devilish scheme. That other chap was a decoy. We won't be able to prove anything on him except that he trespassed. This is the Griffin's work. Thorpe was murdered."

"Correct, Manning," boomed the deep voice of Dr. Morse. "He was murdered."

He stood in the door with his hand on Bostick's arm in seemingly friendly fashion. The medical examiner was a powerful man, but Bostick's lunge sent him reeling as the killer lunged towards the rod rack. His reel was still attached, the leader part of the line. The commissioner started forward and Bostick smashed him on the jaw. He was like a tiger, charging. A Norwegian knife, affected by fishermen, which released the blade from a wooden handle by a spring, flashed in the dusk and then Manning's gun barked sharply and Bostick went down cursing with a smashed knee.

"He figured it was safer to leave his rod with the rest," said Manning. "I didn't want to kill him. He might talk."

"He *will*," growled the commissioner.

There was no dissenting voice. Dr. Morse tended the wound and shrugged his broad shoulders. Manning thought of Thorpe—and Tanaka. Other detectives came up and they carried Bostick inside. It did not take long to get what they wanted.

"He admits he worked for the Griffin, under pressure," said the Commissioner. "The Griffin had something on him, found out the real Bostick was from California, not known here, snatched him, and this chap took his place. The Griffin picked him because he was a good flycaster. Tried him out with this pellet racket. We had to bear down on him a bit, and he passed out.

"It looks like a new commissioner, Manning," he added, aside.

"No more your fault than mine."

"Hell, you got the guy who killed him! I don't see how you figured it, at that."

"I fish myself," Manning told him. "Besides, there couldn't have been any other way. Thorpe was out when he started to fall."

Dr. Morse once more came out on the porch; stroked his gray goatee.

"They had him handcuffed," he said. "After he came out of the faint they gave him a cigarette. Yep, one of his own. One of those Spanish brands. He must have packed it today in case anything went wrong. Every end of them, inside the cardboard tip, had the dark brown tobacco soaked with cyanide. Anyway, he's gone."

*Once Again the Griffin Challenges Gordon
Manning—and Through the Night Creep
the Killers on a Terrible Mission of Hate*

THE MAN, who styled himself the Griffin, lounged on a balcony at the back of the old Colonial house. Lofty trees shut in the neglected garden, save where sunshine entered through the ragged branches of a blasted maple.

The golden gleam shone upon the form of the Griffin. His body was clad in a robe of sable brocade. A black skullcap covered his pate. His face was covered by a yellow mask of gleaming fabric, finer than silk, resembling goldbeaters' skin. It half-revealed the features, and made them hideous, seemingly leprous; clinging closely to the harsh contours; the high cheekbone, the beaked nose, the thin, cruel lines of the mouth. Black eyes gleamed through half-open slits. They were eyes without a soul behind them, the orbs of a murderous maniac.

The Griffin had slain, with fiendish ingenuity, a score of men who stood for the advancement of philanthropy, of science and art. Men hard to replace, whose death halted fine achievements.

Once he had been captured, after a failure to kill had inflamed his diseased, but subtle brain.

Gordon Manning, scientist, explorer and adventurer, ex-Military Intelligence; called in under special commission to uncover and arrest the monster, had succeeded; but the law had proclaimed the Griffin mad. Manning had protested, but the murderer was not executed; and, within a few months, the fury in his brain subsiding, he escaped from the institution for the

*He was wearing a gas-mask. As Manning appeared, he fired.*

criminally insane at Dannemora and went ahead on his diabolical career with added fiendishness.

Manning had unearthed the Griffin's secret fortress and
laboratory. The slaves kept there to carry out his satanic ends—
men of high accomplishments, held by the Griffin's knowledge
of their secret crimes—had been scattered. But the Griffin's
stores and sources of wealth had remained hidden. He had
regathered some of his workers, reëstablished himself in another,
hidden aerie.

It was here, in the old house, that the Griffin had set up his
latest stronghold. The spot had a sinister reputation. The gloomy

house, the private cemetery with its moldering vaults, the dark lake in the woods, where suicides had occurred, the impoverished soil, kept it off the market.

The nearest highway was miles away, and the neglected dirt road that tied up with it led to nowhere but the old mansion. Ostensibly, a dour farmer and his silent, withered wife were the owners. Actually, the Griffin had covertly bought the place, and they were his servitors; faithful because of their love of gold, too fearful of him to pry into his secrets.

From this place the Griffin emerged and killed; flushed with blood-lust, with his insane desire to eliminate all who dared elevate and enlighten the world he wished to plunge into darkness.

And then the Griffin had suddenly ceased to function.

A strange being, an anthropomorphous portion of humanity, came out on the balcony, swinging a legless body between over developed arms. This was Al, named after the gruesome, impure spirits of Persian mythology. The Griffin had found the freak with a wandering circus, bought its freedom.

Al was a deaf mute, but the Griffin had taught the limited intellect a method of communication. He patted the hydrocephalic head as he might have patted that of a pet baboon. The Griffin made swift signs and Al, balancing his legless trunk, handed him a tall staff of ebony that lay beside the bamboo lounge.

The Griffin rose, moving slowly but certainly, passed into the room behind the balcony. It was hung with black tapestries that had strange cabalistic designs woven upon them with gold thread. The thick rug was of the same malignant hue. There was a screen of black lacquer in which a disk revolved, emblazoned with the signs of the zodiac.

The Griffin seated himself at a carved desk of ebony. On it stood a plaque of bronze suspended between pillars, a gong, that now and then gave out a low, vibrant note without being touched. There was a gold-bronze griffin; half lion, half eagle, for a paperweight.

Al squatted in a corner, immoble as an image. His eyes glowed like a cat's in the dark angle he had chosen.

Out of a drawer the Griffin brought a list of names inscribed with purple ink on gray paper. Many of these were scored through with vivid scarlet. Dead men, these, perished in their prime. Opposite each name were brief notations, giving exact hours and days of birth.

The Griffin ticked off a name.

With the skill of an expert draftsman, his hands steady, the Griffin took a sheet of parchment. He set down a rectangular space, enclosed by a frame that held the zodiacal signs. Inside the space a diamond was precisely drawn, and inside that, square. From the four points of the square, lines went to the corners of the frame. So twelve triangles were formed, marked from the center of the left side from the prime sign of Aries, the Ram; into twelve houses, or domi. The houses of life, of riches, brothers, parents, children, health, marriage, death, religion, dignities, friends and enemies.

In the central square the Griffin set down the name he had selected. He began to murmur an invocation, calling upon the gods of the stellar pantheon; beginning with the sun-god Shamash, and the moon-god Sin, asking them for their aid.

"Oh, Marduk! O, Ishtar! O, Ninib! O, Nebo! O, Nergal!"

As he droned his mystic ritual, the gong gave out strange murmurs. The Griffin's slitted orbs glowed like black opals with their inner fires. The horoscope was shaping to his liking. At last he spun the lacquered disk that bore the symbols of the zodiac, checking up.

Then he stood up at his full height.

"The stars in their courses have delivered him into my hands," he gloated. "Now to communicate with my good enemy, Gordon Manning."

AT THE first tinkling of the telephone in his library, Gordon

Manning knew who was communicating with him. In his lengthy antagonism against the Griffin, his ego had become attuned to the approach of evil.

He had been worn, jaded in mind, in nerve and body, in that conflict. The morning after his appointment by the police commissioner, with its confirmation by the governor, the Griffin had called Manning and mockingly congratulated him. Then and there he challenged Manning to what the Griffin likened to a game of chess, with living pieces. Condescendingly, the Griffin averred that it amused him to play with such an opponent.

It was not a fair game. The Griffin always had the opening moves. He chose his own gambits, had his campaign worked out ahead. He professed to even matters by naming his next victim, and the day that he should die; but it was hard for a sane, well-balanced mind to cope with the deviltries of the Griffin's diseased but potent brain. There had been victories on both sides. Now Manning was rested, ready with renewed energies to give battle to the monster.

He picked up the instrument, with the blood tingling in his veins, the zest of adventure upon him; much as he had felt when he saw in the jungle the spoor of some man-eating brute.

He heard again the weird music of the gong and then the deep tones of the Griffin, sinister and sneering.

"Ah, my dear Manning. Again we get in touch. No doubt you thought me dead. Doubtless you hoped so. I hear you have had a holiday. I trust it has refreshed you for the fray. I am busy to-night, so I am sending you a message that should arrive at any moment. I need hardly tell you that in it you will read a name, also the date of the departure of its owner to that bourne from which no traveler e'er returns. Also, there will be a slight demonstration of the fact that the Griffin has not lost any of his power."

There came a chuckling laugh, dying away, lost in the eerie strains. Then silence—followed by a ringing of the door bell.

Manning rose from his deep chair without effort, moving as a roused animal moves, in perfect coördination. He slid an automatic from the side table into the pocket of his smoking jacket. Mati, the butler, was opening the door when Manning reached it. A lantern in the porch ceiling showed a sprawled body in the entry clad in the uniform of the local messenger service. A hand gripped a yellow envelope with a crimson, spreading stain in one corner.

It was addressed to Manning.

The boy lay face down, motionless and quite dead, and his blood pooled beneath him. The mark of entry from the missile showed as a slight snag in the cloth of his uniform, where a bullet had brought him down.

Manning picked up the yellow envelope, but he did not touch the body. Mati stood with his brown, Malaysian face the hue of putty, though he had seen sudden death before.

Manning spoke to him in his own language.

"I will call the police. The body must not be disturbed."

Manning knew there would be no clews. The bullet might bear distinctive marks, but they were useless without the weapon. And that, Manning was certain, would not be found. He opened the outer, bloodstained envelope. It enclosed a sealed letter. There would be a name, an address, of the sender at the office, but nothing would come of that. Some nondescript would have handed it in.

The letter was on heavy, gray, handmade paper. It was sealed with a splotch of scarlet wax, imprinted with the seal of the Griffin. A demi-griffin rampant.

At the bottom of the short note, written in purple ink in striking chirography, there was an *affiche,* a scarlet oval, with the same design.

The content was short. A name—and a date.

Manning's face became rigid as he read.

"My God!" he muttered. "Of all men—John Phillimore!"

Presently the police arrived, deferential to Manning, taking

the body to the morgue, going through the routine of inform-
ing the boy's parents, of questioning the messenger service. The
medical examiner gave his findings, plain-clothesmen took
measurements and photographs, reporters swarmed.

There were no results but flaring headlines, vague theories,
fantastic stories. The Griffin was out to kill. He had struck again,
at Manning's door. But the press did not learn what the note
had said. Manning did not mention it. The commissioner was
silent.

The issue was up to Gordon Manning.

## II

JOHN PHILLIMORE, M.A., M.D., F.R.S.,
D.S., etc., was scientist as well as practicing physician. His
residence was on lower Fifth Avenue, his clientele was exclusive,
and their fees served to not only maintain the doctor's establishment, but enabled him to prosecute his important discoveries.

Aside from his private, paying patients, Dr. Phillimore gave
two mornings a week to public clinics. He never neglected a
case that he thought he could help because there was no money
to give for his advice, and for medicines.

He had many friends, and he could have had a fortune, but
he did not care for it save as a means to his philanthropic ends.
His fame was growing, but he did not care for that, save as a
visible sign of his progress in behalf of humanity; to which his
life was devoted.

He was a bachelor, whose household was run by a housekeeper and two maids. He maintained an assistant and a nurse
for his consulting room; and two well trained aides for his
laboratory.

The laboratory was back of the paved court behind the house.
The court had two flower beds, always bright and gay according
to the season, fenced about with low iron hoops thrust into the
dirt. There was a small fountain between them, with a basin for
thirsty, dusty sparrows. Two ailanthus trees flourished, and there

were statues, of marble and bronze, gifts from grateful sculptor patients.

Altogether the yard was a pleasant spot. It could be reached from the ground-floor rear, or by a stair that led from the metal balcony that reached the width of the house, outside the windows of the consulting room and the dining room.

The house was a corner one. The wall on one side of the court was a high one, between the court and the street. The other barrier was lower, separating the yard from the adjoining one.

The laboratory was entirely modern. From it had come miracles of medicinal research, serums to prevent and check leprosy, and the hookworm. Here the germ of infantile paralysis had at last been filtered, and Doctor Phillimore, ever conservative and modest, had let it be known to a group of his fellows that he expected within six months to be able to announce that the scourge of children could be stopped by the use of his anti-toxin. That secret had leaked out, and the general press had seized upon it.

With this publicity, the name of Phillimore was added to the death-list of the Griffin. Where others admired, the Griffin, with his warped nature, hated and sought to destroy. He believed in predestination, in the influence of the stars; including his own; and men like Phillimore were meddlers, to be despised the more because of the esteem in which they were held.

Now Phillimore sat in his upstairs library with Gordon Manning. His face was grave but serene as he offered his guest brandy, and an excellent cigar.

"Mind if I use a pipe?" asked Manning. With the other's assent, he carefully filled his briar with his special blend, thrust the notched stem between his strong teeth, and lighted up.

Phillimore watched him with interest. Manning was a rather tall, lean man, tanned long ago by tropic suns. His gray eyes were steady and intent, one of them slightly puckered by a scar. He was dressed in rough tweeds, since he had dined in town, and had not had time to change before keeping his appointment with Phillimore. All of Manning's movements were precise but swift. He had the efficiency of a born athlete who has kept himself in condition. Phillimore approved of him.

"I have heard of you, of course, Manning," said the doctor. "Also of the Griffin. A purely pathological case."

"He should have been executed, like a mad dog," said Manning sternly. "He cannot be cured?"

Phillimore shook his head. "His fibers are rotten. He is a true paranoiac, and so incurable. A dangerous maniac, who should have been more closely conned. He is likely to end up in paralysis and epileptic fits, as deterioration leads towards dementia praecox. As a physician I may not agree with your belief he should be eliminated."

Manning shrugged his shoulders. He was not going to argue about the Esculapian oath. "Meantime, *he* does the eliminating," he said. "Your life is in grave danger, doctor. Two weeks from to-night he will strike. How, it is hard to predict. But he has never failed to attack, too often fatally."

PHILLIMORE SURPRISED Manning as he turned to a wall desk, and took from a drawer one of the gray envelopes with which Manning was only too familiar. He handed it to Manning, who removed the letter. The envelope was fully addressed but it had not been mailed.

"It was delivered by hand one morning when I was at the clinic, no doubt deliberately timed," said Phillimore. "He seems in earnest."

"He is," replied Manning grimly, as he read the distinctive script:

> The stars announce your downfall. You presume to change the courses of Destiny. I am the appointed Scourge of those who would interfere with Nature's methods. Who are you to ward off appointed death? You may not ward off your own.
>
> Some time between midnight and midnight on the eleventh of November, on the day of your birth, but not necessarily at the hour, you will surely die.

There was no *affiche,* but a clever drawing of the upper body of a griffin; wings spread, talons extended, fangs apart.

"He is ingenious in his suggestion that disease is part of general evolution, and the survival of the fittest. Ingenious, but false," Phillimore said, as Manning returned the letter to him after reading it.

"It doesn't seem to have disturbed you much," Manning suggested. "But I warn you that letter is not far from a death-warrant unless we can find means to guard you. I believe that if he fails on this date he will not repeat the attempt on you. He will think the stars have deceived him. And each failure will hasten the course of his disease no doubt."

"No doubt. I am willing to place myself in your hands, Manning; with the proviso that my regular routine is not interfered with. That day I do not go to the clinic. I shall have some visits to make. Certain patients will come here in the late afternoon and the early evening. I shall do some work in my laboratory, perhaps."

"You must do nothing that takes you outside the house," Manning said positively. "Not even to your laboratory. You must receive no new patients. That is essential. I shall be here for the whole of that twenty-four hours, and there will be other precautions taken. Even to your food."

"It is absurd to mistrust my servants. They are devoted to me," objected Phillimore. "I will consent to your terms, otherwise. Since it is only for one day."

"I do not mistrust them," said Manning. "Nevertheless, I shall provide your food, and my own, that day. Bring it myself, and prepare it myself. I am not a bad cook. But I have seen a man poisoned with one half of a melon that was sliced before me. The other half was innocuous. I have known that fiend to kill in a place apparently as secure as a safety-deposit vault. I admire your attitude. But I do not minimize your danger, or my responsibility."

## III

IT WAS "murder weather" on the eleventh of November. When Manning entered Phillimore's house shortly before midnight, after a personal round of the guards he had set in strategic places, the night was murky with rain and mist. Melancholy hootings came from the river. Street lights were veiled in vapor, and the air was raw and chill.

There had been no further demonstration from the Griffin, nor had Manning expected any. He entered upon his twenty-four hours' vigil in excellent condition to go without sleep. The plain-clothes men who were watching were picked men who would be relieved every eight hours, and during one meal. But Manning would have no break. He brought two men into the house, gave them their instructions.

Phillimore greeted him cheerfully. After a cigar, a high ball, and some chat upon places Manning had seen, and which the doctor hoped to visit, Phillimore went to his bedroom. He did not lock the door. Half an hour later, Manning looked in and found the other sleeping peacefully. Phillimore was up at seven o'clock, and enjoyed the simple but appetizing breakfast Manning served for them both.

The bad weather continued, the day dragged on. Phillimore spent his morning in his library, working over formulas and writing letters. Some of them were prepared in the event of his death. He was perfectly calm, without a trace of bombast. Manning envied him his nerves as the hours ticked off. His own were steady enough, but he was tensed, while Phillimore remained placid.

In the afternoon he received patients. His assistant was with him, most of the time, in the consulting room. He had been warned. No patients were to be received whose names were not on the appointment list. At dinner, Phillimore was cheery. He made only one allusion to the situation, when he pledged Manning in a glass of Pol Roger the latter had brought.

"I, who *may* be about to die, salute you," said the doctor with a laugh. "I know how Damocles felt, at *his* banquet. Five more hours to go. I suppose the Griffin counts on the stress of suspense as part of his punishment for my presumption."

"Perhaps," said Manning. He did not agree. He was sure the Griffin had fixed on his time, and had not changed it—that some minute of the three hundred remaining would see the attack delivered.

"Have you many patients for to-night?" he asked.

"Three only. None very serious. They should not take long. A woman with nerves, a man with arthritis, and another man who drinks too much, and eats too much."

"Will your assistant be there? And your nurse?"

"Only the nurse," said Phillimore.

"I would like to see her when she comes," said Manning.

The nurse was neither young nor old, self-possessed, and evidently very efficient. She had been with Phillimore for years. Manning liked her. She knew about the Griffin. Her eyes were brave, her mouth firm, and she made no comments.

"The doctor will leave the door of his consulting room open this evening," Manning told her. "I want you to never leave him alone, with any of these three patients, for more than three minutes. You can make some excuse to enter if your actual presence is not necessary."

She nodded. "They are all simple cases," she said. "I am really only here to-night in the event of an emergency."

"There will be *no* emergency cases to-night," said Manning. "Persons not belonging to the household will not be admitted. I have arranged for that. You will be in the office between the reception and consulting rooms. I shall be in the reception room myself, as a supposed patient, waiting to see the doctor after his appointments are over. That often happens, I imagine?"

She nodded again, chary of speech. But her eyes pleaded with Manning, and then she spoke.

"You will not let anything happen to him? He is so wonderful! He means so much to the world. If it was somebody like myself, it would not matter, but for him to—to.... I would gladly die for him," she burst out, after she had got a grip on herself. "So would many others."

Manning patted her on the shoulder. She did not often show emotion, he fancied.

"I'll do the best I can," he said.

Again he was in tweeds, to better play the part of patient. He carried an automatic in a shoulder clip, and he knew how to use it.

It was eight o'clock when he passed through into the empty consulting room and looked out over the court. At the far end, the windows of the laboratory were dark. He stepped on the balcony, returned and locked the French windows.

Two of his men were in the yard, lurking in the rain and fog behind the trees or statues. Another patrolled the street beyond the wall.

Manning switched on a ceiling lamp. The indirect lighting revealed the details of the room, with its examination table, its gleaming apparatus behind glass, all the precise accessories of such a place. Phillimore came in, took case-cards from a steel filing cabinet, and looked them over.

Less than two hundred and forty minutes now, until midnight.

MANNING WATCHED the patients as they entered. They seemed harmless enough—the nervous woman, the indulgent man and, last of all, a man whose face was drawn and haggard, who limped a little and seemed in pain with his arthritis. Inflammation of the joints appeared to have made him something of a cripple, as he hobbled through the reception room. Manning heard Phillimore greet him heartily.

The nurse had done her part. "Thank God he's the last," she whispered. "Mr. Manning, may I stay until twelve o'clock? I may be able to do something, though I hope there will be...."

Manning glanced at his wrist watch. "Three minutes," he said.

She picked up a tray, and placed a card upon it that had already done service that night. Manning watched her as she walked through the narrow office; took hold of the handle of the door.

Suddenly she swung about, her eyes bulging.

"It's locked!" she cried. "It's locked, and bolted!"

Manning leaped for the door; confirmed her statement. Not only a turned key, but bolts also held the heavy door. He thought he heard a light tinkle inside, barely audible. He was not certain of it.

"Call the man on the stoop!" he cried to the nurse. "There's another in the library! Break down that door!"

He had a feeling of nausea. He had no doubt that the doctor had been murdered, that the killer had fastened the door, and escaped through the long windows, closing them after him. He might yet catch him. The man with arthritis! Neither a new patient, nor an old one. But one who had been treated long enough to be so considered. The Griffin had planted him before he called Manning, or sent the doctor the message.

The nurse rushed for the front door, and Manning bolted to the dining room. He flung back the long windows and stepped out on the balcony. The lights in the consulting room were out. The killer had escaped.

The court was like a pit, silent as an open grave. His nostrils caught an acrid tang, vanished in a whirl of wind that swept the enclosed yard like a miniature cyclone.

Manning tried the windows of the consulting room. He could not see inside. They closed with a spring latch. He stepped over the railing to the balcony and dropped to the ground, a good twelve feet, calling to his men, whipping out his gun. Phillimore was dead. He must, at least, avenge him.

He strove to adjust his eyes to the gloom, still calling, getting no answer. He gulped another whiff of tainted air, closed his lips against it. He had an electric torch with a powerful lens and batteries. Its beam fought through the downpour, making rainbow gleams of the rain.

Manning saw the body of one of his picked guards stretched out by one of the statues. The man moved slightly, gasping for breath. The other was close by, on his back, legs drawn up. He too, might be alive. They had been gassed, as Phillimore must have been. The shower had given these two a fighting chance for recovery. Phillimore, in the consulting room, door locked, windows closed, must be dead.

Manning swung his torch, and saw an agile shape moving by the wall, flinging up a light rope ladder. He heard the *clink* of grapnel claws as they failed to hold.

The man turned. Manning knew this must be the murderer, the third patient, the man with the faked arthritis. It was dope, not pain, that had made him look so haggard in the reception room. He was far from a cripple now, spurred by a fresh dose of drug.

Now he seemed, viewed through the film of rain, like some strange beast, half man, half dragon. He was wearing a gasmask, with goggles, tube and strainer. He seemed unearthly. One hand went to his left shoulder, and as a weapon appeared, Manning fired.

This was, as usual, only an agent of the Griffin. A slave held because of the Griffin's private knowledge of some crime. A slave who might be made to talk, if captured alive.

Manning knew his bullet struck first, high in the body, to the right. It should have sent the other down with the impact, the shock of lead on bone.

But the other only staggered back, his left hand outspread against the wall for support. There was a bulletproof tunic next to his skin.

HE PULLED the trigger of his weapon. Manning saw no spurt of flame, heard no report. But something tapped lightly on his breastbone, broke and fell. He heard again the light tinkle of glass as he strove not to inhale nauseating, stupefying vapor that enveloped his head, flooding his nostrils, his mouth, his eyes.

Phillimore might have been shot this way, with gas contained in a fragile globe. It was more likely he had been slugged first, and a gas-pellet tossed back into the room as the killer fled—closing the windows, avoiding the lethal vapor, adjusting his mask before he jumped to the yard, where the guards had probably been eliminated already.

Out here, in the pelting rain, Manning had a show, if he could only—only—only—

Something came leaping, hopping like some enormous toad, a hideous shape that flung two arms, tremendous as a gorilla's, about Manning's knees. It was Al, his head made grotesque with another gas-mask, tugging at Manning with prodigious strength to drag him down, to settle him with powerful fingers.

Manning strove to break the hold, to club the misshapen freak with his gun, even to shoot. But the force had gone out of him. His arms lost all their energy as the poison gas slowly impregnated his blood.

He tripped over the border-hoops of the flower beds; buried his face in the chrysanthemums and in the wet dirt.

That saved him. He had not taken in much gas. It was not a heavy vapor. Close to the ground he found sweet air.

The freak had left him, making his getaway.

Three times Manning tried to get to hands and knees, and three times his limbs betrayed him. There was no pith in them. He groped for gun and torch, which he had dropped. He tried to shout, but his throat was seared. He found his gun, and aimed at a shape climbing the wall by the rope ladder, now fixed. The automatic seemed heavy as an anvil. He tugged at the trigger like an infant. The cartridge exploded, but he could not control his aim.

The freak was swarming up an ailanthus tree like a baboon. It leaped, legless but agile, swung along the coping, disappeared.

The other man was gone. And both had cast aside their gas-masks.

Wavering, groggy, his vision bleary and his knees weak, Manning got to his feet, like a fighter too badly punished to know his own corner.

The Griffin had scored. Phillimore lay dead. He, Manning, had failed in this encounter.

His own scorn spurred him, and he stumbled towards the wall. His two shots should have brought aid by now. The rope ladder was in place. The murderers had discarded everything in their flight, masks, ladder, even the pneumatic pistol.

It seemed to him he climbed a thousand feet, wearing the leaded shoes of a diver, before he reached the top of the wall, still dizzy, throat and nostrils raw, eyes smarting.

He saw the ruby tail-light of a black sedan that swung north into the avenue. His patrol was missing. Manning imagined him gassed, or slugged, or both; dragged into a doorway where, on a night like this, he might not be discovered for an hour.

Manning crept down the ladder, to make sure of the thing he was too certain of—that Phillimore was dead.

He would have the car chased, but he knew that was useless. He had pursued the Griffin's cars before. No dragnet would gill that eel.

IV

HE TROD on the pneumatic pistol, and picked it up. The fragile globes of glass it had popped out, like a Roman candle, had been filled with some product of the Griffin's secret, suborned laboratories, the discovery of one of his captive chemists; some gas akin to cyanogen, perhaps; but more efficient in action.

Those pellets had upset all Manning's precautions. Under cover of the night and rain, they had been shot at his two men in the court; perhaps from the top of the high wall or from the garden next door.

The freak must have been hiding somewhere, as an accessory, close at hand. As Manning went to the door in the basement he saw a big urn of stone half his own height. It stood beneath the balcony, could not be seen from it. It was empty as he flashed his light into it. But Al could have been in it, like the thieves in Ali Baba's tale, waiting for his accomplice. With his stunted shape he could have stayed there for hours without discomfort.

Coughing, Manning pounded on the door, until it was suddenly opened. A man thrust a gun into Manning's belly; dazzled him with a torch. There was another man behind him.

"Stick 'em up, you!" rasped the man with the gun, and then he wilted as he saw who it was.

"Think the murderer was trying to get in again, Burke? He's a long way off by now. Blair and Neill are out there, in the court. Get them in. Howell has been done-in somewhere. Find him, sergeant. We'll need pulmotors, surgeons! Get on with it, man. Hustle!"

Manning sped up the stairs from the basement into the reception room. The door of the consulting room had been burst open by the burly shoulders of the detectives.

The nurse was lying crumpled on the floor, but she was moving.

"She burst in when we broke through," said one of the men. "I tried to grab her, got a whiff of the gas. She flopped, an' I drug her out. We chucked chairs at the windows. But the doc is out for keeps."

The nurse was scrabbling to her feet.

"He's not, you fools, he's *not!*" she cried. Then she caught sight of Manning. "Listen—*you* know," she said. "I don't know what gas it was, but we've got to try methylene blue. Methylene blue—do you understand?"

Her voice rose to a scream.

"I understand," said Manning. He saw there was a chance.

Any poison that paralyzed the diaphragm, that stopped the blood from carrying oxygen, might be offset by the simple dye.

"You got any?" he asked. "Know how to use it?"

He had a fair idea himself, but the girl reacted. Her eyes blazed.

"I only got a little of the gas," she said, "I'm all right. Plenty of methylene blue in the laboratory. They use it to fix slides."

She snatched at some keys on a hook, raced through the court. Sirens were winding alarms now, police officials and executives arriving.

But the nurse and Manning paid no heed to them. The wet wind swept through the broken glass of the consulting room, cleared it of the lethal vapor. The nurse took the head of Phillimore on her lap as the police surgeon entered.

"If it's going to work, it works," he said, when Manning explained. "They brought a lad back, in California, half an hour after they thought he had passed over. Where's that methylene blue, nurse?"

It was ten minutes after the injection when Phillimore sighed. And the nurse sighed with him.

The surgeon looked at her with a mild disdain.

"He'll be okay," he said. "I'll take a look at the boys. You wouldn't want to come along, nurse?"

She did not hear him, and Manning motioned him out. A clock chimed, with ten strokes. Two hours to midnight.

"You'd better stay," said Manning to the nurse. "But I don't think he's in any danger—from the Griffin. He's shot his bolt. This time, he loses."

I T  W A S  midnight, and the weather, as if sensible to zodiacal spells, was now subsiding. It had, after a fashion, favored the Griffin, but the rain had served the right, rather than the wrong, in dissipating the gas.

Phillimore was fully recovered, able to prescribe his own

treatment, and that of the others suffocated by the gas, but resuscitated by a modern miracle.

A clock struck twelve.

"I'll stay until morning," said Manning to Phillimore, "though I see you are well cared for."

The nurse's face was rosy red. It had regained a not too long-lost youth.

"That's been one of my mistakes," said Phillimore. "I never thought I needed a guardian, until to-night."

"We all need guardians, including the Griffin," said Manning. He spoke a trifle shortly. There was a woman he wished would look at him as the nurse looked at Phillimore. But Manning's love was denied him while the Griffin lived.

It was long since he had slept, but he was in no mood for sleep. Absently, he turned on the radio. There came a rhumba, then a song. Then all blurred out. The instrument seemed dead as he moved the dials. Suddenly, it came to life.

There was the sound of strange music, barbaric and exciting. Manning was very sure he heard the voice of the Griffin, deep, and grating.

"This time *you* win, Manning. Next time you *lose*."

THE GRIFFIN RUNS AMUCK

*A Crazy Laugh, a Scream of Terror, and*
*Crumpled Bodies Strewn in the Night—*
*the Griffin Had Struck Again!*

MANNING CAME out of the private gymnasium down town, where he helped to keep himself fit with handball, and saw the panhandler. He had noticed him for the past three or four days hanging outside a liquor store close to the corner, where he could cadge the customers as they came out. It was a crafty idea, choosing such a pitch. Many men felt like a skunk refusing a poor devil the "price of a cup of corfee, mister," when they had just paid four bucks for a quart of whisky.

Manning had scant sympathy with such beggars. He knew that the experts among them could pick up three or four dollars in as many hours, and considered all contributors suckers. He was on his way to his office where the signs proclaimed him as "Consulting Attorney."

His private business had suffered severely since he had accepted the special City and State Commission to run down the Griffin, but there were clients who could not be denied, and the Griffin had been quiet since his last defeat. Manning wanted to get rid of certain important matters before that inhuman monster and murderer gave out once more his usual, boastful warning concerning his intended victim.

So far, the panhandler had not tackled Manning. But this afternoon he edged out from the doorway of the liquor store and sidled up.

He was a short man, shabby, shuffling in worn shoes, but he seemed, to Manning, spry on his feet. He was naturally swarthy,

*The car, hurtling at well over a*
*hundred miles an hour, was empty!*

with dark eyes that seemed all pupils, so bright, though opaque, they looked as if they were varnished. His color was unhealthy, the end of his long nose twitched as he approached.

He held his right hand almost closed, the fingers uppermost; curled about something concealed in the palm. This was an old trick. Manning was striding by, wondering at the cadger's picking him as a prospect, when he caught a glimpse of something crimson through the incurled, clawlike, dirty fingers.

"Something to show you, mister," whined the man, glancing up and down the street. Manning half-poised in his stride, cane in hand, a stick presented to him years before by a convict in a Western penitentiary. It looked like a supple, tapering, cloudy-malacca palm-rib, but it was made of a steel rod covered with rings of leather, shrunken close. Not a plaything, but a weapon. A terrible one, for defense or attack.

In the grimy palm there lay an oval of thick paper, about an inch and a half long. It was scarlet as a blob of fresh-spilled blood. The insignum of the Griffin. A small, crimson cartouche

*Ryan chanced the open curve in his attempt to escape the smash.*

embossed with the design of a demi-griffin, rampant—eagle's beak and wing, and lion's outspread claws.

Manning barely glanced at it. His perfectly conditioned body acted in instant coördination with brain and nerves. At that, he was almost too late. This was the trick of the true faker, the tiny instant of distraction to cover the real move.

The knife came upward, curved and keen, from the false side-pocket of the assassin's trousers, slashing at Manning's unprotected belly like a flash of light.

Manning felt the prick of it on the bone of his hip. But he had struck too, and faster; as the strike of a mongoose beats that of a cobra. The cane did not travel far, but it lashed hard and swift. The ferrule was merely the end of the steel rod. It smote the would-be killer's shin midway between knee and ankle; it plowed through the bone of the tibia; and the agony of that shock severed all nerve-connection, brought a yelp to the man's lips.

The blow worked exactly as the reflex tap of a surgeon. Involuntarily the other doubled up, standing on one leg, the knife falling from his unnerved fingers to the sidewalk.

Manning's cane rose up and down. It descended like a blunt saber stroke just where the other's skull rocked atop his spine, and sent him sprawling at Manning's feet.

A CROWD began to gather, fascinated, hypnotized, looking at Manning, calm and unruffled, at the prostrate panhandler, the curved knife that had skidded into the gutter.

There was a whistle from Broadway. A man pushed authoritatively through the onlookers. Morrell, of the down town deadline squad. He knew Manning at instant sight.

Manning checked the dick's half involuntary salute.

"Panhandler," he said crisply. "Tried to knife me when I turned him down. Get him away. It's important,"

"Okay. My partner'll be here in a jiffy. We'll handle him. Get back there, you!" Morrell addressed the crowd. A patrolman surged up, and Morrell snapped at him.

"Where was *you*, slugfoot? Turn in a call. We want the wagon. Turn it in."

Instantly the machinery of the police went into motion. Radio cruisers in the Wall Street district slid through traffic to the spot. A lone reporter at Center Street caught the scent. The news grapevine went into action. Legmen, newsreel operators, were like buzzards in the blue, swooping for a "story."

They got none. The unconscious panhandler went to Bellevue. Morrell pocketed the knife. Manning disappeared, after looking vainly for the scarlet cartouche. It had fallen from the pseudo-beggar's palm, had been trampled on, likely enough carried off stuck to the sole of somebody's shoe. He hoped it would be ground to dust before it was ever noticed. There was no need for him to see it again.

For the first time the Griffin had struck without warning. He had discarded all the rules of what he had called, satirically, his "game" with Manning, the agent specially appointed for his destruction.

"It was justa hophead, shot to the gills with coke, tryin' to slash a guy who wouldn't slip him an easy quarter," Morrell told the newshounds. That was his story, and he stuck to it. They got no more at headquarters when some of the veterans scented something deeper.

Manning's name was not merely a *sesame;* it could also close doors of information. The reporters were given an address supposed to be that of the man who had nearly been knifed, actually the street number of a vacant lot. That could be blamed upon the man, who was not seeking notoriety.

At Bellevue the panhandler was kept quiet, by approved medical tactics. He could be held for homicidal assault, probably as a narcotic case.

An inspector looked at the knife that Morrell turned in. It was curved and of odd, foreign design. A kukri blade, of the smaller type, as used by the Gurkhas of northern India. Its handle was bound about with silver wire, encrusted with small turquoises. It retained only the merest hints of finger-prints.

Its sheath had been sewn into the ragged pants pocket of the panhandler, the opening of the pocket a wide and slanting one, for easy access.

II

MANNING WAS closeted with the police commissioner. The faces of both men were grim.

"I saw the seal of the Griffin in the man's hand," Manning said. "There is no doubt about it. He is an agent of that fiend— and that is the least of it, Commissioner. It means that the Griffin will no longer play the game. It was a sinister, maniacal sport, born of a madman's brain; but at least he gave us some chance. That swollen, perverted ego of his made him notify his victim, name him to me, and also name the actual day when the Griffin would strike."

The commissioner nodded gloomily. "He's angry, of course, that you foiled his last effort. It has affronted his grandiose dementia. Doc Norbert told me that his paranoia would increase until it destroyed him, until his inflamed tissues rotted and ceased to function. Meantime, he would keep on destroying—unless we stopped him. Now...."

Manning nodded in turn. Norbert was the chief police surgeon, a man who had performed numberless autopsies on criminals' diseased brains. Norbert agreed with other eminent psychiatrists and anatomists. The Griffin was abnormal, a man without a soul.

"He's gone amuck," said Manning. "In Malay, amok. But the amok Malay is like a mad dog, without intelligence. The Griffin is crafty. He will strike right and left, at all those he hates. Their name is legion. Any one who stands for achievement, for advancement of the public good, is quarry for the Griffin."

"Not excluding yourself, Manning."

Manning grinned. "Me first, perhaps. Commissioner...."

The police head broke in, his brow furrowed. "You said just now, Manning, that the Griffin has, hitherto, always named 'him' to you. He has never yet killed a woman, but...."

Manning's shrug dismissed the question. If it were to become one of sex, that still lay in the lap of Time.

"About that man in Bellevue, Commissioner. With the Griffin striking in the dark, we must trace him to his lair. We did it once before...."

"*You* did, Manning. And the courts called him mad and put him in Dannemora, until he escaped. You called him a mad dog, just now. He is. The thing to do with him is to shoot him on sight and *then* have his head examined to see what sort of rabies afflicted him."

"I agree with you," replied Manning somberly. "If I get the chance my finger will not linger on the trigger. But this man is his agent. How closely he may have ever been in communication with the Griffin is doubtful. But it *is* a clew. We've got to make the most of it. So far, we've not been able to break down any of his agents. They have been more afraid of him than the methods of the law. This thing hasn't broken yet in the press. It must not. It may be best to let this man go, to trail him...."

A buzzer sounded. The commissioner pressed a button and the operator's voice came through, the phoning cabinet. "Bellevue talking, commissioner."

"Put 'em on." The commissioner glanced at Manning as the direct voice enunciated.

"The man they just brought in, charged with attempted homicide, is dead."

"What killed him?" Again the commissioner looked at Manning, who shook his head. The blow from his cane on the inion process had stunned the man, but it would not kill him.

"We wouldn't want to say, Commissioner, without autopsy. Man was an addict of some sort of drug. I'm inclined to *cannabis indica,* but...."

"I'll put Norbert on it," said the commissioner. He turned to Manning with a shrug. "There's your clew. *Cannabis indica,* same as hasheesh. Ties up with that oriental knife. Man might have been a Hindu. It won't get us far, I fear."

THE TELEPHONE buzzed again. When the commissioner responded it was not the operator who spoke. A voice asked if Gordon Manning were present? It was a voice that Manning knew well, though the commissioner had never heard it before. Even at his trial the Griffin had remained silent.

Long ago, the Griffin, or one of the men he kept as slaves, men of scientific and mechanical achievements, held by the Griffin's knowledge of their secret crimes, had perfected a process of projection that dispensed with regulation methods of telephony. Long ago, Manning, attuned to evil through his intimacy with the Griffin and his works, had been able to know when a message from that fiend in human shape was coming through. He knew it now, before the first raucous syllable was audible, before there came faintly through the receiver the sound of eerie, exotic music.

It was the voice of an enraged madman, kept only in control

by the force of a will that was erratic, but still functioning. The deep notes had lost the mocking tones, the arrogance, of other days.

"Ha! Manning! I know you are there. So, you escaped this time. But soon the stars will be set in their courses against you, and you will be cast off the board of Life as a useless and discarded pawn. From now on there are no rules, Manning; no rules but my own whim, Commissioner. You will get nothing from that fool who failed. I have taken care of that. And you will hear again from me before the planet Venus sets to-night. Ha! *Ha-ha-ha-ha-ha!*"

The burst of malignant, sinister laughter died, fading into the strains of music.

"He is a crank about astrology," growled the commissioner, enraged at the Griffin breaking through his private wire at Police Headquarters. "Damn his impudence! What do you suppose he meant with that crack about Venus?"

"I'm not sure," said Manning seriously. "He used to cast a horoscope, and choose what he considered a favorable day to make his coup. An *unfavorable* day for his victims, too often. When he missed out, he would blame it on the stars, I suppose. Saves his face for not having killed me, by hinting he did not consult the stars. As for Venus, I don't know, Commissioner, except that I don't like it. I don't like it at all. It ties up in my mind with what you mentioned just now, that the Griffin had never killed a woman, so far. I'm afraid he will—and without warning. And it won't be any one who's obscure."

"You mean that some time to-night that maniac is going to kill—or have killed—a woman, some notable woman? It's inconceivable, man."

"You can't preconceive what the Griffin may or may not do. It's my hunch, Commissioner. And we can't do a thing about it until after it has happened. If then."

## III

THE COMMISSIONER groaned. Lines of worry that had been graven in his florid face since he took office, and the Griffin began to operate, deepened until they looked like old scars.

"What *can* we do, Manning?"

The face of Gordon Manning, ex-Military Intelligence, adventurer, explorer and discoverer, eminent legalist, became so grimly set that it seemed carved from brown granite or molded in copper. Against the bronze of his skin his eyes seemed like insets of agate, through which determination and intelligence blazed their mutual purpose.

When he spoke, slapping his right fist into his left palm, gesture and words like piston strokes, it seemed to the commissioner that a dynamic explosion was taking place.

"What can we do? What we *may* do. Clews! We'll have to pick them up—afterward. But we'll close in. We'll trace his agents, one by one. And we'll keep in touch with them. Some day, supreme madman as he is, we'll be able to forestall some crime he contemplates. Then, with luck, we'll get him. *I'll get him.* I doubt if I'll bring him in alive. I'm doubtful if I'll be alive myself. But—*I'll get him.* I'm devoting myself to this, Commissioner. One could do nothing more worthwhile than to rid the earth of such a monster. I'll close out my private practice, turn over my clients...."

"I don't know about your compensation, Manning. There should be unlimited funds for such a purpose, but...." The commissioner's voice sounded troubled.

"To hell with that," said Manning quietly. "I've got enough. Give me the men I want when I ask for them. I'll talk to the governor. Long ago he promised me almost unlimited expenses, if he had to ask for a special appropriation. He hinted at the time that the President was more than interested. But I don't want Federal aid, as yet. It would only add the fuel of flattery to the Griffin's madness."

The commissioner grunted his approval.

"Too many hounds, too much cry," he quoted.

"We called him mad dog just now," said Manning. "That's too mild a term. He's a ravening, cunning brute who will have to be carefully stalked along a dangerous and bloody trail. He'll leave his spoor, like any other beast. Now he's gone amuck, he'll be careless—and we'll nail him, nail him with bullets, Commissioner."

Norbert called Manning directly, later, at Manning's residence at Pelham Manor.

"The chap that tackled you, Manning; it looks a bit like hyoscine. Only takes a small dose, and it's hard to trace after digestion sets in."

Hyoscine, Manning knew, was the same as scopolamine, an injection of which, blended with morphia, was useful in childbirth. A deadly drug. A man given a hypodermic dose of it, perhaps mixed with other drugs, might mistake it for the injection of a stimulant he craved.

Manning visualized the panhandler, cunningly stationed for a day or so, where Manning, always leaving the gym on schedule, would become used to the sight of him; but that day charged with something that would spur him up to and a little beyond a certain hour; and then, with cumulative action and reaction, would destroy him.

He put the question to Norbert.

"It's quite possible, Manning," said the Chief Medical Examiner.

HALF AN hour before midnight, when the amusement-seeking public thronged Broadway, reading the latest news bulletins that snaked in golden, dancing letters about the wedge-shaped building that dominates Times Square; when Venus was setting, as the earth whirled in its appointed flight, this message flamed...

Lorna Fulton, Celebrated Aviatrix, Found Murdered in

Her Own Garden on Long Island Under Mysterious and Amazing Circumstances.

The citizens at large had to wait until they got their morning papers to get the fantastic details of the murder. But Manning received them in his own library.

Lorna Fulton, famed for trans-Atlantic and South American flights, had been discovered in the night-blooming garden on her estate at Porthaven, on the north shore of Long Island.

There she had been found by her maid, gazing with eyes that no longer saw at the sky in which she had found her special element.

The cause of death had not been determined, but it must have been a swift dismissal. This time the Griffin was not to be denied.

A note was found beside the body, on heavy gray paper, in an envelope to match. Inside the envelope there was a weight of lead about the size of a silver dollar. This was stamped with the insigne of the Griffin. The message seemed to have been dropped, or pitched, to lie by the body. There was no address on the envelope. No need of any, when the script inside, characteristic and set down in purple ink, was read.

> To you, presumptuous one, who would seek the secrets of the sky, the stars decree destruction.

For signature there was a scarlet oval of heavy paper, embossed with the familiar seal.

The press had the news of this before the local police thought of concealment.

The Griffin would read the papers, listen to the broadcasts, chuckle at the thought of a cowering community, of the horror and terror that would stretch across the continent, flash around the world.

It was suggested in the news articles that the message had been dropped from a low-lying plane—sent, as it were, from the stars.

Manning did not accept any such inference. The maid who found her mistress had been sitting with another servant by an open window ever since the murdered woman left the house. They had not seen or heard anything in the air.

The weight, Manning thought, had been merely used to toss the message close to the body, and to ensure the lack of any footprints beside those of Lorna Fulton.

The garden was easy enough of access. It held shrubbery and trees that would prove perfect cover for the approach of an assassin or a messenger. There was no wound upon the body, not even a bruise. The flowers, the rich, soft earth in which they grew, had broken her fall.

The autopsy showed that she had died of strangulation, that for some reason her respiratory muscles and organs had ceased to work, the diaphragm had become paralyzed, and the hormones had ceased to carry oxygen to the blood stream; the lungs had collapsed.

It was barely possible that she might have been saved by an injection of methylene blue, but she had been dead too long before she was discovered.

At Manning's order, the soil of the night garden was carefully sifted, especially that about certain flowers which had withered unnaturally, their petals seared and blackened.

Minute particles of glass were found, exceedingly thin and brittle. A ball of glass, almost as light and frail as a soap bubble, had been tossed at the victim. What the gas was that had choked Lorna Fulton was hard to determine, possibly hydrocyanic, undoubtedly something concocted in the Griffin's private laboratories, wherever they might be.

And, beyond the broken glass, the diagnosis, no clew. The garden paths were of brick, they held no sign of an intruder.

One thing stood out, to Manning. The Griffin was repeating himself in his murderous methods. His rage against Manning had temporarily upset his sardonic subtleties for novelty. But Manning did not doubt they would return.

## IV

**T**ALL AND gaunt in his sable robe, the Griffin paced the chamber in his abode, hung with black tapestries embroidered in gold. The place was an old colonial dwelling, remote and solitary, though no more than fifty miles from New York. It had an evil reputation and was considered haunted.

In one corner crouched the monstrosity the Griffin had bought from an unsuccessful circus and named Al, after certain unsavory demons said to live in Persian deserts. Al had been born legless, mute and deaf, with a head of enormous size. The Griffin, who was his God, had taught him a limited sign language.

The Griffin spoke aloud as he strode to and fro. Al could not understand, but he knew that his God was aroused and angry, and he quivered in reaction as his master vapored.

"They shall see. This Manning, and those he would protect! He dares to offset the decrees of Fate, and he shall perish. But first I will show him, and all the myrmidons of law and order, that they are powerless before me.

"I am the Griffin, the fabled beast of Scythia! I fly, I swoop, I leap, I pounce! I am a mystery and a myth, immortal and invincible, the destroyer of the impudent and arrogant. I will raze them from the earth and utterly abolish them.

"So it is written, so it is decreed. The stars proclaim my invincibility!"

He swung out on a balcony as Al fawned in his corner. It was within an hour of dawn, dark and still. Ancient trees towered against the spangled sky. Beyond them lay a suicidal mere, source of neighborhood legend. Closer, the private graveyard and crypt of the family that had once held the estate through royal grant. It was all steeped in decadence, a fitting aerie for the Griffin.

He flung his arms to the heavens in a pagan conjuration, muttering the names of maleficent spirits. "Satan! Ahriman! Belial! Sammael! Shaitan! Beelzebub!"

His features were half revealed, and half concealed, by a mask of some membranous tissue that showed his beaked nose, thrusting against the leprous stuff, that clung like the half-shed skin of a snake. The heathenish nomenclature flowed from his lips through the fluttering screen as if he were telling a rosary at a Black Mass. His dark eyes glittered through the slits of the mask.

"Shedim! Asmodeus! Moloch!"

No longer did he apostrophize the zodiacal rulers. Sometimes they had betrayed him. Now, in his monomaniacal, murderous obsession, he believed himself supreme, one with the universal pantheon of fallen angels.

"Asteroth! Odin! Abaddon! Apollyon!"

The frenzy lessened, and he returned to the great chamber lined with black. From the desk of a carven table of ebony he brought a list where certain names were erased in scarlet. He read the others out loud.

"All, *all* shall perish, and swiftly," he proclaimed. "Then there shall be more, many more."

HE PUT the list away and tapped lightly a bronze disk that hung suspended between two pillars of the same metal. Its vibrations got through to Al. The freak raised himself, balanced on the palms of his hands, expectant.

The resonance of the gong still sounded when the Griffin touched a button concealed in the carving of the table, and there was a softly slithering noise as a section of the black tapestry slid aside, revealing the entrance to an elevator.

He entered it, and motioned to Al, who came like a distorted ape, swinging between his muscular arms, squatting by the feet of his master as the automatic lift descended into the extended cellars of the old manor house.

In one of many subterranean vaults, with roofs, walls and ceilings of reinforced cement, impenetrable as a fortress, a figure awaited the Griffin. It was a man, but it looked like an automaton, motionless, dressed in a brown denim overall stained with grease and acid.

The man's head was closely shaven. His flesh was like unbaked dough, his eyes hopeless, his face haggard and blank. On the front of his overall a number was stenciled in yellow pigment. The same number was tattooed upon the top of his bare skull.

"You have completed your experiments, Forty-One?" asked the Griffin of his slave. The human robot nodded. "If they succeed in the final test, you shall be rewarded. I will send money to your family. I will have conveyed to them a letter you shall write, stating that you are alive and content but still compelled—by circumstances that they will understand— to remain in retirement."

The Griffin's scabrous mask quivered with his silent mirth. The shackled and debased genius groveled in his gratitude. The automaton became a man, suffering, pleading.

"You will have them write to me, to tell me how they are? My wife, my babies!"

"We shall see. Now demonstrate."

The Griffin's voice was harsh, imperative. With a sigh Number Forty-One turned to a bench that was crowded, but not confused, with apparatus. There were lathes and elaborate tools, tubes and globes of glass combined with gleaming brass.

He picked up one of two models that looked like a child's expensive toy, and exhibited it to the Griffin, who nodded but did not touch it. The man without a name showed the second, set it down, touched a disk.

The low hum of a dynamo sounded, there was a flutter of blue light against the hidden lighting of the vault.

The Griffin watched the demonstration closely, hard to please, insistent upon perfection, suggesting various trials. At last he was satisfied. He chuckled.

"You have done well, so far, Forty-One," he said. He snapped his fingers at Al, who trailed him, propelled between his arms, his calloused hands padding on the stone floors, muscles flowing in the limbs that, covered with red hair, could strangle as easily as a gorilla.

They passed along narrow corridors, all silent as the grave, past doors where the slaves of the Griffin labored at devilish devices. At last they came out into the ancient crypt where old caskets had burst and fallen from their niches and moldering bones were scattered.

The smell of the charnel house seemed to awaken some wild spirit in Al. As they emerged into the graveyard, the moon flung long shadows from cypresses, shadows that wavered because of the clouds moving in a high wind; the freak uttered uncouth noises and commenced unhallowed capers, playing a grotesque and horrible game of leapfrog over the tilted slabs.

The Griffin watched him for a while, the yellow metallic skin of his mask gleaming weirdly. Presently the Griffin snapped his fingers again, and Al slapped along behind him to the front of the house where a dim light gleamed.

A man came to the door, the husband of the couple the Griffin hired to appear as caretakers.

"I am leaving to-morrow. I do not know when I shall return. See that all is in order when I do."

The man's weak chin wobbled under the wispy beard as he answered, and his pale eyes rolled fearfully at Al. The Griffin and his familiar went into a paneled room, where courtly dames and gentlemen had once posed and curtsied.

A panel slid at his touch, the automatic lift received them. Strange music ebbed and flowed through the Griffin's private chamber, his unholy of unholies; the scent of fuming amber sifted in the air. He drew toward him a hubble-bubble pipe.

The Griffin sat enshrined in his carved chair, the arms of which were supporting griffins, his eyes glittered as the smoke rose gurgling and bubbling through the perfumed water, inhaling the pungent fume through a mouthpiece of amber.

"I was hasty in the case of the flying woman," he communed

aloud. "But this next time, Manning, this next time, the Griffin shows his genius, and leaves you, poor fool, gasping!"

Dawn crept into the room above the trees and found him sitting there, tranced in his evil visions, while Al hunkered, doglike and devoted.

V

EVERY MORNING at ten thirty a car emerged from the private grounds of Dr. Arnold Sassoon, world-renowned psychiatrist, mender of shattered minds and nerves. The grounds were masked by a high hedge of interwoven hemlock, and the driver honked his horn as the gatekeeper swung the barrier and the car entered the highway.

Sassoon and his assistant, Moore, were bound for the private hospital for neurological diseases endowed by Sassoon himself. There wealthy patients, whose ills were mostly fanciful, were told certain truths and persuaded not to interfere mentally with their automatic physical functions; and poorer ones were treated with patient kindness.

Shell-shocked veterans had left the hospital normal men again, blessing Sassoon and all his works.

The highway ran north and south across Long Island. It was not much frequented, but in excellent repair, drained by open culverts, the brush kept trimmed below the oaks and maples.

There was a sign standing by the side of the road that proclaimed "Men Working" for the Light and Power Company. One man clung with his creepers to a pole carrying electric wires, the other stood idly watching the car, the closing gate. He looked south down the road as the car passed on. There was no other vehicle in sight.

A dirt road, once a wood lane, used now as a bridle path, joined the highway in that direction, about four hundred yards away.

Out of it there came a black sedan, making a sharp curve

north. It took more than its share of the road, and Sassoon's driver, Ryan, gave it room, silently resentful.

The black sedan did not straighten out. It was fairly in the road of the Sassoon car. It leaped forward with augmented and prodigious speed, bent for a head-on collision.

It could not be avoided, though Ryan chanced the open curve of the cement culvert in his attempt to escape the smash. His face was gray and sweaty with terror, not so much from the emergency as the fact that the other car, hurling itself at well over a hundred miles an hour upon them, was *empty!*

*There was no driver. No passengers.*

Like a torpedo, the mass of steel launched itself and hit. There was a frightful crash, rending, splintering, wrecking.

Sassoon's car was a good one, but far lighter than the other. It crumpled under the impact, like an empty tin can under the blows of a sledgehammer. Its engine and body were swept from the chassis, the frame itself twisted out of all shape. What was left of the car lay scrambled in the culvert, partly buried in the dirt beyond the ditch.

In the shapeless mass the three bodies of Sassoon, Moore and Ryan, horribly disfigured, lay in their own blood. Gasoline caught fire from ignition and started to turn the wreck into a pyre. The car that had attacked them was on its side, hood like a closed accordion, engine stripped and reduced to scrap. It was empty.

The crash had been terrific. The gatekeeper came running up the road, fearful, breathless and upset.

The sign, "Men Working," stayed where it was, but the man had come down from the pole, carrying with him a small wooden cabinet and a coil of wire. With the one who had watched the car he disappeared, plunging into the woods opposite Sassoon's hemlock hedge.

There was a slight movement in the tops of the trees above them that seemed to follow their passage. Then all was still. The breeze brought the reek of the fire. The gateman, distraught and sobbing with hysteria, came pounding back to the house.

Presently a State trooper on a motorcycle came tearing to the scene. A local policeman from Blueport followed in a car that had picked up the radioed news.

The officers started to put out the fire.

MANNING SAT in the library of his house at Pelham Manor in an unenviable state of mind and spirit. Without vanity, he believed himself the only one capable of coping with the Griffin, and the responsibility lay heavily upon him.

Now that the Griffin was amuck, the tension lay upon Manning night and day. To keep fit he had to offset it, to be relaxed and ready. Striking without warning, the Griffin would have to be surrounded with a net of clews and evidence. It was imperative that Manning discover his outside agents, not the wretched slaves the monster held in thrall.

Manning had once liberated those unfortunate accomplices. But the Griffin had gathered them again, or others. His resources were profound.

Manning knew that crime detection meant the painstaking investigation of nine hundred and ninety-nine blind alleys before entry to the one that led to apprehension and conviction. At times—rare times—brilliant deduction or a genius flash of intuition, might prove a short cut.

But every alley that Manning discovered to be a *cul-de-sac* was likely to hold the body of a victim. He would have to find some way to anticipate the Griffin's plans, to circumvent them, to tangle the monster in his net. Even now, though he did not know it, not one but three mangled bodies were added to the Griffin's ghastly tally. He did not have to wait long.

His telephone sounded, and Manning felt the premonitory thrill of evil committed before he picked up the receiver.

He heard the weird, barbaric music, and then the Griffin's demoniacal, triumphant laughter.

That was all. It was enough. Far more than if the Griffin had spoken. The laughter meant that the Griffin no longer warned him in advance, but advised him—afterward—that the fiend had scored.

Manning tuned in his radio on short wave, knowing what must shortly follow. He listened to the barked-out message that came within three minutes.

His car took him to Larchmont with his special siren shriek-ing, claiming clearance. Moments seemed hours while he revved up the motor and propeller of his private amphibian. It seemed a day before it threw off the suction of too placid water and soared to Blueport. There he dropped again to the surface and taxied to the dock where the car he had telephoned for was waiting.

He broke through the small crowd that had gathered. No officials had yet arrived from New York, but they would soon be there, with the reporters and cameramen. The Blueport chief of police was harassed, not recognizing Manning at first, but glad to acknowledge his authorities. Manning foregathered with the two officers who had first arrived, and the excited and bewildered gatekeeper. He found the State trooper succinct.

"It sounds phooey, the rest of it," said the man, after he had given a crisp report of what he had seen. "This gate guy is goofy, or maybe I am. It's mighty funny nobody got hurt bad enough in the car that did the trick; on the wrong side of the road, of course; so they couldn't get away. There ain't a sign of trouble, though the wheel's jammed back into the seat. No blood. No nothing. And Doc Sassoon and the two with him smashed like half-roasted eggs! He was one swell guy, Sassoon."

The trooper was trying to be hard-boiled. Manning gave him a chance to fiddle with his belt.

"Where does the gateman come in?" he asked.

"Claims he saw something like a big ape swingin' through the trees after the car left the driveway. Saw that, mind you, but didn't think much of it, he says. Only remembered it a few minutes ago. Can you beat it?"

"There is such a thing as registering an image without making a mental tie-up at the time," said Manning. "Like seeing a ghost. You put it down to imagination, subconsciously. Then something happens and it all clicks properly. What else?"

"That board, 'Men Working.' We called up the Light and Power Company. They sent a man. He's here now. Says they had nobody anywhere near here, an' that the board's a fake. Ought to have their name burned on the woodwork, branded in. The Griffin did this, Mr. Manning, and he pulled a fast one. Killing a guy like Sassoon ain't just murder. Why, he—I mean doc—he was a prince. Cured my brother—didn't charge a red cent. If I got a chance at that Griffin, I'd kill him with my bare hands. I'd...."

"What makes *you* think it was the Griffin?" asked Manning.

"I'll show you. There ain't much left but the rear end of Sassoon's car, but there's something stuck there. Looks like it was put there *after*, see? When the goofy gate guy beats it to the house; by one of those phony trouble men. I got it covered up. It'll be news quick enough, I reckon."

Manning knew what he was going to see before the trooper escorted him to the remains of the Sassoon car, still holding the half charred bodies until examination was completed.

THE CROWD, curious, pitiful and morbid, were being kept away. The officer had hung a dust-robe taken from the other car over the back of the death machine, as what was left of it lay on its side. The trooper lifted the light cloth and showed the sticker—the scarlet cartouche that was the Griffin's insignum, his *memento mori*, the blood-red token of his victory.

Manning conferred with the local chief and got the road roped off, all onlookers kept well away. Then he had a talk with the gatekeeper.

"There was men workin', all right," said the man. "I didn't see 'em when I run back to the house to give the alarm, but I wasn't thinkin' of anything but gettin' help, knowin' I was too late. All three was dead, mister, covered with blood, an' the fire ragin', an' stinkin'. Dr. Sassoon, he was in back, all mashed-like between the seats. Ryan, he had the wheel drove into his chest. Dr. Moore's head was nigh cut off with glass, or something. I'll not forget it to my dyin' day."

"How about what you saw in the trees?" asked Manning.

The man stared at him. His shallow brains were half scrambled. There was a vacant stare in his eyes.

"I dunno as I see anything," he said, half pleadingly. "It ain't easy, lookin' back, to remember. But it was something, mister, swingin' through the trees, like one of them chimpanzees. I was sober, though you might think me drunk or crazy, when I tell you that whatever it was didn't have any legs."

Manning remembered a stormy night when a legless *thing* had tackled him. "I wouldn't talk about it too much," he suggested.

He doubted if the gateman would ever be called upon for that evidence, vital as it was. Or that it would be believed that the attacking car was actually empty.

He reserved his own decision.

It did not take him long to find the dirt road that showed where a car, with the same tire treads as the one that had crashed into Sassoon's machine, had backed off the highway and reëntered it.

The road sloped upward, blank of anything but hoofprints for a while. Then Manning found the imprints of human hands, palm-flat to the dirt.

They led on, in an eerie trail, from where the legless monstrosity had dropped from a tree, until it joined two men and a car, that had come in, and left, the dirt road from the opposite direction.

Manning noted the tire prints until they struck a cemented way. The prints could be photographed, cast in plaster, but he did not doubt that the Griffin would see those tires disposed of promptly.

This killing showed that the ingenious working of the mad brain were once more in action.

Three dead men, and one woman, since the Griffin had run amuck. So far, not a tangible clew. The laughter of the fiend seemed to ring in Manning's ears as he returned, to find the scene of the murder swarming with those whose business it is to attend such grisly functions.

They went about their grim business of removing the dead, of carrying out official routine, while those who were to give out the news avidly covered their assignments.

An inspector saluted Manning.

"We're powdering for prints," he said. "They must have been wearing gloves."

"Looked inside?" asked Manning.

"Of course. There ain't a mark on the wheel, or...."

"I meant inside the hood," said Manning curtly. "They may have changed a tire. Powder the tools, look in the unusual places, everywhere. We've *got* to find somebody who bare-handled this car, Inspector, and pray to God his prints are on record. It must not be touched except by our men."

### VI

"YOU READ about Marconi steering a ship into harbor by radio beacons," said Manning to the commissioner. "It's not the first time it's been done with boats, up to battle cruisers; with cars, right here in New York; even with planes.

"That's how it happened. The Griffin's car, with all its numbers filed and eaten off—and no license plates—was empty when it shot out of that dirt road.

"The troublemen were fakes; one of them had plugged in to the power line. He was the control man; the other a lookout. If cars had come along they would have put it off, that's all. It was damnably simple, damnably impossible to foresee, to prevent, even if the Griffin had warned us."

"What about the thing in the tree, that legless freak?"

"Another lookout, to signal in some way when Sassoon's car was coming down his driveway. He had to be treed to look over the high hedge. The man on the pole had enough to do."

"So the Griffin wins, leaving us nothing to go on," said the commissioner grimly.

"There are the finger-prints we found on the radio car. On the spokes of the spare tire, under its canvas cover, on a wrench; and a beautiful impression on the only spark plug that wasn't shattered. Has the report come through?"

The commissioner touched a disk, gave an order to the man who answered.

He and Manning looked at each other while they waited. The commissioner tore the end off a cigar and thrust it into his mouth, chewing on it without lighting it.

Manning selected an imported cheroot from a pigskin case and lighted it, puffing quietly, but inhaling the strong smoke. It steadied his nerves. He did not expect too much from those prints that had been almost overlooked, but he did not want to draw a blank.

The head of the finger-printing bureau brought up his findings.

"Casey Flynn, alias Mickey Flynn, alias 'Croaker' Casey," he said. "Here's his record. Sent up for homicide, paroled, in again for manslaughter. When he left Sing Sing last he didn't come in to New York. The boys picked him up in Albany. They had nothing to hold him on, though he had plenty of money and was living high. He told them he had struck something good. They kidded him, asked him if he was going straight, and he told them he was going too straight for any dick to follow."

"Electrician?" asked Manning.

"No. Mechanic. Drove trucks for 'Alky' Simms. He could run marine engines. Claimed he was an aviator."

"Just an all round handy man," said the commissioner sarcastically. "Thanks, Cunningham. Leave that here. We can pick up that chap, Manning," he said. "He's an outside man for the Griffin. Might be hiding out, but more likely is not. Figures a roundup might create wonder why he disappeared; doesn't figure we found his prints. He worked on that death car. He's been mugged. Plenty of our men know him on sight. We'll get busy and bring him in."

"Don't do that," said Manning. "Let him ramble. But put your best under cover men and shadows on the job, to find out *where* he rambles, and get his connections. It's a slender thread, but it may be like the one that led to the heart of the Cretan labyrinth and the lair of the minotaur."

The commissioner grunted. He was not quite sure what Manning was talking about, but he understood his drift.

"It's our only chance," Manning went on earnestly. "To weave such threads into a rope, into a net, to trace the Griffin's agents back until we get in touch with him."

"Agreed. I'm with you, Manning, heart and soul, so long as they don't ask me to resign, or fire me. I'm none too keen to look at the evening editions. Can't you see the headlines? 'No Clews to Triple Murder. Commissioner Confesses Police Are Balked.' Not that I did confess it, confound them."

"I'll be blamed equally," said Manning. "I've no job to lose, Commissioner; there I'm ahead of you. But I've got to save my own face, and I won't look at myself with any satisfaction until the Griffin is in his coffin."

"Make it a triple one, lead, steel and solid stone."

"Amen," said Manning, and said it reverently.

*Poison Had Slain the First of Six Men*
*Menaced by the Griffin—and Before the*
*Moon Set Some New and Awful Engine*
*of Death Would Snatch the Second*

THE LATCH clicked, and Gordon Manning entered the hall of the old brownstone house in Chelsea, where the man who had been his friend—and his father's friend before him—had always lived.

Whenever it was possible, Manning visited the old professor once a week to play chess, in which intellectual tournament Manning was seldom the victor. Victor Harland, ex-curator of the National Museum of Anthropology; author, lecturer and explorer; had passed seventy and was no longer active in professional work, though his mental activity was unimpaired by advancing years. He had earned, and was enjoying, leisure.

He could, and did, play a dozen or a score of chess games simultaneously, and win ninety per cent of them, against crack opponents. Too often Manning saw a twinkle come into his friend's eye after the twentieth move or so, and knew that Harland had recognized a vulnerable situation. It was not for the chess Manning came to see him, so much as from sincere affection and admiration.

The big room at the back of the house was the same as Manning had always seen it, whether the gap between his visits was one of a week or a year. Walls halfway paneled between bookcases, a marble fireplace, where cannel coal burned cheerily. It was only early September, but the professor's blood was thin.

Tea things were on a table. Liquors on a sideboard. Harland

was a bachelor. The wife of the man who lived in the basement, and whose husband acted as janitor and gardener, was his acting-housekeeper. The professor liked to fend for himself. He was not over fussy, but he did not like to have familiar things shifted about. He owned the house and leased the upper floors to responsible, respectable persons who were quiet and orderly.

He greeted Manning cordially. The chessmen were already set upon the board. Manning was prepared to open with a Queen's Pawn Gambit if he won the first move. That opening would help to stall off defeat. But first there must be tea. The choicest buds of golden pekoe, that Manning saw was supplied his friend and mentor.

It was a rite with Harland. The infusion he made was perfect, to eye and nose and palate.

Plants, flowering and foliage, were inside the windows. The professor did not often use the balcony, or go outside at all. The long curtains of crimson damask were three-quarters drawn. Dusk was just approaching, and Harland had advanced the twilight by lighting the chess-lamp, with another on the tea table, where a silver urn hissed softly beside a priceless service of Crown Derby china.

It was very cosy. A canary disdained the professor's ruse and, looking into the garden, sang happily.

There was the usual interchange of talk. Harland knew of Gordon Manning's special mission and authority to capture the Griffin, but he did not mention it. At his age, he did not care to contemplate the spectacle of a monster in human form who deliberately destroyed, or attempted to destroy, the men who stood for advancement, men of achievement, of benevolence and enlightenment.

As he prepared the tea, Manning asked what had happened of interest to his host since the last visit.

"Not much. Save that I have met an opponent worthy of my sharpest steel, my boy. He may yet prove my master. He called first on Monday, introducing himself as a chess-player. He reads my column. He disputed a theory of mine and convinced me he was right. A strange character in some ways, but very keen. A brilliant mind. He was here again this afternoon and we had a match. He undertook to prove that Niemzowitsch was always right, and Steinitz wrong. And he could have proved it in that game if he had not made a slip that I saw, but naturally, did not inform him about.

"There is your tea. You do not take sugar. I should not. It destroys the fine taste. But I must have my sweetenings in my old age, my boy."

He chuckled as he passed the cup to Manning.

Harland was far from old age. He was still good for another decade, if not two. He helped himself to two lumps of sugar. Manning sniffed at the stimulating fragrance of the tea, sipped it. Chess-table and tea-table were close together. Soon the first moves were made, and countermade. There was silence in the room, save for the cheery chirping of the bird, with its occasional snatch of melody.

Harland had black, but he began to take the aggressive on the second move. On the seventh, he suddenly castled and sacrificed a bishop. Manning knew this was not weakness but some brilliance he must solve. Harland sat back and finished his tea. Manning closely studied the problem.

THEN, SUDDENLY, Harland was gasping for breath. His eyes bulged, his speech was harsh and incoherent. He glared at Manning; tears running from his eyes. The pupils were merely points. Sweat had broken out on his skin. His face and hands glistened with it as if varnished.

"Tarrasch does not take sugar," he proclaimed. "I defy either of you to dispute it."

He sank back in his chair with muscular twitchings that merged into a continuous tremor, as Manning jumped up, upsetting the chessmen. He lifted the professor as lightly as if the latter were a child. He loosened waistband and collar, stripped off coat and vest. He placed Harland face down on a lounge,

*Manning
grabbed the
man's ankles.*

doused his head with cold water, flung open both the windows—
wide. The canary stopped chirping. It was growing dark.
Manning felt the feeble pulse.

For a split-second he hesitated between applying artificial
respiration immediately, or telephoning for powerful stimulants.
It was touch-and-go. Harland's heart was blocked in its action,
his respiration was more and more labored. His lungs needed
oxygen. He was dying from both paralysis of the heart and
pulmonary edema.

Manning had studied medicine and surgery as a means of

self-preservation during his exploits in strange and remote places. He had an especial knowledge of plant poisons, many of them alkaloids known to native wizards but included in modern pharmacopoeias. Here were symptoms he recognized, though he did not attempt absolute diagnosis.

He called police headquarters and his voice rang sharply and with authority.

"Snap it through. Emergency. Gordon Manning talking. Is Inspector Sullivan there? Good—put him on.

"Sullivan? Manning. I'm at 349A West Twenty-First Street. Ground floor. Name of Harland. He's been poisoned. I want a police surgeon, in a hurry. Tell him it looks like pilocarpine, or jaborine. We'll need atropine. I'm administering artificial respiration. I want that surgeon in a hurry. Yes. It looks like murder. But the man isn't dead yet. It's the surgeon I need, more than your radio cruisers. Or an ambulance. You've got it straight? Atropine. Right."

He rang off. Harland's lower limbs were relaxed. His pulse still flickered, but his lungs had collapsed. His age was against him. Manning labored systematically. The police would send a pulmotor, he knew, but only immediate treatment could save the professor. If Manning could have got instant hold of atropine he would have had a chance.

The radio cruiser arrived first, and Manning waved the plainclothes men aside. They knew him and his special authority, and they remained, after a suggestion to search the premises, to question everybody. They figured it as murder. So did Manning.

"It's murder, all right," he said crisply, "but the murderer isn't where you'll lay hands on him. He hasn't been here for hours."

"You think—this is a friend of yours, Mr. Manning?"

Manning nodded, refusing the offer of one of the detectives to spell him, as he administered first aid.

"Then you figure it's the Griffin?"

"I don't figure anything, without the figures to go on,"

Manning rapped. There was more noise of official arrival. An ambulance was outside. The interne came bustling in. Another radio car. At last, the surgeon. Inspector Sullivan had got the chief medical examiner himself. The name of Manning was potent. The M.E. was a genius in his specialty.

"Pilocarpine, I think," Manning told him. "He had double vision, confusion of ideas, then tremors. If you don't mind a suggestion, atropine might modify the edema, asthmatic spasms and abdominal cramps."

"I'll accept it as my own diagnosis from you, Manning," said the M.E. They had worked together before, and respected each other. "Pilocarpine paralyses the vagus nerve. You saw sweat. Ah—profuse bronchial secretion! I'm afraid he was too old, Manning. We'll try, of course, but he's in the Shadow."

As the shadows gathered in the garden, tried to invade the room with their combined force of darkness, the Shadow of the Valley of Death received the soul of Professor Harland.

I I

## THE VOICE OF THE GRIFFIN

MANNING HANDLED the case. He combated the inquisition of the Press. He canceled the ordinary routine of police photography, of measurements and search for finger-prints. He knew them useless. And he rigorously resented all attempts to couple him, or the case, with a suggestion that the Griffin had contrived another murder, striking secretly.

"I know nothing about that, gentlemen," he said decisively. "Nothing at all. The professor was no longer active in any form of research. He is not the type the Griffin chooses. See the commissioner."

The reporters jeered a little, but not so that Manning heard them. The commissioner was hard-boiled as an egg cooked in a geyser. It was a good enough story, with Manning present, admitted a friend of the dead man. They saw that there might be plenty of motive for the Griffin to strike.

Once, he had named his victim and the day of death. But Manning had foiled him too often of late, and now the Griffin was running amuck, striking without warning. It was a wonder Manning himself was still alive. The Griffin was mad, but it was with the mania of infinite cunning. He deserved annihilation, but when Manning had managed to capture him, the law, because he was judged insane, would not kill him. They had placed him in Dannemora, and the crafty maniac had escaped. He was at large again, with the ingenuity of a fiend and the resources of a maharajah.

At last the death-chamber was cleared. The body had been basketed, and taken for the inevitable autopsy; of which Manning and the M.E. already knew the verdict.

Only Manning—and the canary—were in the room. For the first time, Manning was able to concentrate upon the cause, and also the manner, of the murder.

Harland was well when he arrived. He had talked of the man who had visited him, and played brilliant chess. Twice. The first time, a complete game, earlier that afternoon.

If only he had not taken the visit of a stranger casually! It might not have been the Griffin in person, but one of his many more or less enslaved emissaries. But Manning scored himself for having taken the incident too lightly. Harland was not big game for the Griffin, but he could stab at Manning through the professor.

He might also have stabbed directly at Manning.

It was a swift review and analysis that Manning made to an inevitable conclusion.

Harland had made tea. He had taken sugar. Manning had not. The Griffin might have known that Harland did so, from the first visit of himself, or his agent, and hoped that Manning did also.

Pilocarpine was the principal alkaloid of the leaves of the

Jaborandi plant of South America, akin to hyoscine, jaborine, scopolamine. The jinn of medicine. Faithful servitors, if one knew the charm that bound them; or destroying demons, when unbound.

They could all be dissolved in alcohol. The fatal essence could be set in sugar by transmission, with as simple an instrument as an eye-dropper. All done in a moment. While Harland's back was turned. No doubt the Griffin, or his agent, had been offered tea the first visit, refused it the second.

In a short time the alcohol would evaporate, leaving the tiny, fatal crystals.

Manning emptied out the lumps of sugar from the Crown Derby bowl and wrapped them in his handkerchief, for analysis. He had little doubt of his theory. He had none when he looked at the bottom of the bowl.

The Griffin—or his agent—had found time to set at the bottom of the container two scarlet *affiches*, ovals of stiff paper, red as blood, stamped with the Griffin's private seal, showing the mythical monster, half-lion, half-eagle, in heraldic device, rampant and demi—just the upper half of the fabulous creature with beak and mane, with wings and claws.

Two of them! One for Harland. One for Manning.

And Manning had escaped, merely because he did not like sugar in his tea!

Manning was inured to sudden, secret murder; but a light perspiration broke out on his own brow as he knew how narrowly, once more, he had escaped the infernal trickery of the Griffin.

He went to the open window as he wiped his forehead.

There was light on all the floors of the house, from basement to attic. It cast a suffused glow over the formal garden, faintly illumined the far wall. On that, Manning saw a swiftly moving shadow, as of a man in a cloak and Spanish hat. There was the profile of a nose like the beak of an eagle.

Then the effect, or the illusion, seemed to go out of focus, vanished.

Automatically, Manning's hand shot to his shoulder, touched the butt of his pistol. The shadow was gone.

The telephone was ringing.

He listened, knowing what he would hear. The exotic rhythm of barbaric, compelling music, then the mocking laugh of the Griffin. A final word.

*"To-morrow!"*

THERE WAS no use trying to trace that call. The Griffin had men in his power who knew how to tune in on wires with exact vibrations, defying detection.

To-morrow!

With that threat in his ears, Manning closed the windows; put the cover about the cage of a canary that would sing no more for its beloved master; and drove back to Pelham Manor, to his own house, in his own powerful roadster.

The Griffin knew that he had killed, and had also failed to kill. The next day he had threatened to strike again.

It was hard to sleep that night, but Manning compassed it. The Griffin had lately given him a bizarre sort of holiday, a chance to rest, to knit nerves that had come close to raveling.

Manning was ready to take up whatever challenge might be flung by the insane being, through whose brain surged the vagrant hallucinations of dementia grandiosa.

Yet, even Manning would not have compassed sleep if he could have foreseen what the morrow would spawn of evil.

III

ONE OUT OF FOUR

THERE WERE twenty-four hours in to-morrow, and they dragged for Manning. Aside from the shadow he had seen on the wall, which might have been only the projection of a silhouette pasted on the lens of an electric torch, he was inclined to think that the Griffin in person had talked chess with Harland, planted the poisoned sugar.

It was not very often that the Griffin acted personally, but Manning had a sturdy hunch that he was never far away from the scene of any of his crimes. Manning had seen him more than once. He might be more reckless these days. He would be enraged at Manning's escape, and anger had before this decreased the Griffin's cunning.

But, ever since the day after Manning's secret commission had been bestowed upon him, supposedly in secret, the Griffin had referred to the antagonism between them as a game—likening it mockingly to a game of chess. The metaphor was in some ways apt, since, as in chess, the essence of success or failure lay in the ability to see moves ahead, both of yourself and your opponent.

The Griffin always had the better of it because he invariably opened the game, but he had not always won.

Eighteen hours out of the twenty-four had passed. It was six o'clock, and Manning's man had just served him an exquisitely iced and balanced cocktail, when the telephone rang.

Manning knew that, this time, the Griffin was not on the other end of the wire. He missed the premonitory thrill of evil that always manifested itself on such occasions.

It was the commissioner of police, speaking over his private phone. His stern voice, the voice of a soldier, was agitated.

"I've got some news I want to talk over with you, in person, Manning. I wanted to make sure you were at home. I'm driving out, immediately."

"You'll have dinner with me?" asked Manning.

"Dinner? Good God, man, you won't feel like eating after you talk with me!"

Manning shrugged his shoulders as he hung up, not to minimize the weight of the commissioner's news, which he felt sure would be sinister enough; but because he had a fixed maxim

that a man, like an army, met danger better when his metabo-
lism was properly balanced, the human mechanism properly
supplied with fuel. It was the Griffin, of course. He had not
chosen to communicate first with Manning. He was going to
leave him to work in the dark.

In how much of darkness and complexity, Manning could
not dream until the commissioner arrived, his face grave and
lined, refusing the offered drink.

"That's a good cocktail," Manning demurred politely. "It'll
do you more good than harm." The head of the police grunted,
picked up the beaded glass, emptied it. He nodded his appre-
ciation.

"Manning," he said, "four communications, exactly the same;
with a cryptic message, each bearing the red seal of that infernal madman, have been delivered today. Two by messenger boys,
two by mail. The mailed letters were dropped at Grand Central.
We've traced the messenger service, so far as it can be traced.

"The police were informed reluctantly, and in a roundabout
manner, in two cases. One got through direct to me, another
came through a local captain. The press, by some miracle, hasn't
got on to it yet. If it broke, the city would be in a panic. As it
is, four families are terror-stricken. It's a marvel that chuckling
fiend hasn't given it out. I'm doing my best to prevent it. Coming
on top of Harland's murder, it would be the final straw. One
that would break my official back—though I'm not thinking
of that. It's the incredible craft and malice of that hell-spawned
ghoul!"

Manning heard him without seeing him, looking at the four
missives the other had produced and handed to him. Each was
a duplicate of the other. Heavy, gray, handmade paper, the
writing on envelopes and the single sheets in purple ink, in
striking script, the chirography of eccentricity, of pride and
conscious power.

*4–1 leaves 3?*

Then, for signature, the scarlet, oval seal, the cartouche red as newly-spilled blood, the demi-griffin embossed upon it.

Four seals; with the two in Harland's sugar bowl, six scarlet seals in all. One man already murdered, four more threatened, one of them doomed to die in some fantastic and horrible fashion—unless Manning could determine where the Griffin would strike, and how; which of his intended victims he would select for a strange and awful death.

The cryptic line could mean nothing else. It was refined torture. It said that one of four would be murdered, leaving three. Leaving meanwhile the hideous and grisly horror of uncertainty.

"Do they all know?" Manning asked. "I mean, have they been told of the other letters, the meaning of the message?"

"I thought it best," replied the commissioner. "I have taken precautions to guard them all. We may learn something from one of them that will save the other. But we've guarded them before," he added wearily, as the lines seemed momentarily to etch deeper into his face. "What do you suggest, Manning?"

"Strong guards, cordons that will not be evident, but of picked men, ready to act swiftly. The Griffin knows we'll do our best. He'll try to beat us with some fantastic device, as he has before. He may not have made his choice as yet. That may depend entirely upon his study of our plans. You know his ingenuity in basing an attack upon the habits of his victim. We must plan to trap him, to show some apparent opening. I have started to get together some agents of my own, but my private force is far from complete. I am trying to establish a chain that will give me some idea of what the Griffin may contemplate, ultimately lead me to him, perhaps. But this latest threat is satanic, Commissioner. He's going to play four games of chess at once, damn him, with his eyes open, and ours blindfolded."

Manning touched a bell. His Japanese butler entered. Manning nodded at the cocktail glasses. "Dinner for two," Manning ordered. The commissioner made no further objection.

He drank the second cocktail mechanically, seated to one side of the fireplace, laid but not lighted, scowling at the problem that confronted them.

Four minus one leaves three. And then the question mark. Which one to die, which to be left?

MANNING'S CHAIR faced the window that gave out to a path, bordered with grass and low shrubbery, an ivyclad wall beyond. That wall was topped with spikes. The path led to the garage, and was closed with a fence and a gate of steel. Manning knew his own life was in constant jeopardy and took his precautions.

It was dark by now. Dinner would be served soon. Then would come their council of war.

"These private agents of yours, Manning? How good are they? Under cover men, I suppose?"

"Men, and boys, some of them. I took a leaf from Sherlock Holmes' book, Commissioner. Newsboys and bootblacks are the best of shadows. And I've got some smart young men out of jobs who are good in their specialties. Limited, of course. They are coming along. When we get the Griffin, I'll turn 'em over to you. Some of 'em should be valuable."

"When we get him."

Manning studied the four addresses, the names, trying to find some clew as to which one the Griffin might select, especially if the way seemed open. It might be a dangerous guess. And to-night, from now on until the blow had fallen, or been averted, four families were shuddering, if not cowering, under the dread threat. As for the four principals....

They were all married men, with families. All men useful to the world.

Dinner was served in the library, an excellent meal, deftly served, eaten in tense silence. After it was cleared Manning took down the latest "Who's Who." He made brief notes, reading them to the commissioner—condensed biographies of the four men to whom the scarlet-sealed mandate of dread had been despatched.

Both men hoped, against hope, to find some hint of the Griffin's ghastly preference.

SHACKELFORD, NICHOLAS E. Botanist. Introducer of many valuable trees and plants into United States. Important factor in development of national forests and economic plant distribution and adaptation. Married, with one son and daughter, aged 58. Residence, Astoria, L.I.

CHANDLER, DOUGLAS L. Chemist; important worker in Chemical Warfare Research, in organic and engineering chemistry. Aged 47. Married, two daughters and one son. Residence, New York; Central Park West.

OSGOOD, CLIVE T. Law editor and publisher. Residence, Syosset, Long Island. Aged 61. Married, three daughters.

"It was he," said Manning, "who denounced the medieval aspects of the law at the time of the Griffin's trial. He protested against the code that sentenced him to imprisonment, instead of annihilating him."

"A likely lead," commented the commissioner. "The Griffin would never forgive him for that."

"I've no doubt he's on that devil's death-list," said Manning grimly. He set down his final notes:

BEALE, BERNARD B. Clergyman, educator. Radio lecturer for reform of charities, agitator for organized state and national insurance against old age, sickness and unemployment of all citizens. Married, five children, three sons, two daughters. Aged 51. Residence, Forest Hills.

"There is a practical philanthropist," said Manning. "Three of those children are adopted. You know what they call him. Not Bernard B., but 'Best Beloved,' Beale. He's got following enough to elect him President twice over. A man like that affects the Griffin like the sign of the Cross to Satan. I'll have to see all of them, find out how they live. We daren't concentrate on any lead until we know something. We've got to look out for all of them. I'll take Beale first. He's nearest."

He reached for the telephone. Presently he put it down again.

"The line is out of order," he said tersely. "Suppose you call the others, Commissioner. The books are under the stand. It might be best to do it through headquarters."

Fifteen minutes later, they stared at each other.

All the telephones were out of order. It could not be mere coincidence. The commissioner had issued orders to rouse the trouble-service of the telephone company for an emergency.

"They won't locate the fault," said Manning. "He tunes in, in some devilish fashion, as I've told you. No doubt he can tune out. How many men have you at Beale's place?"

"Four, continuously. Two inside, two out. It's a detached villa in a restricted district. About half an acre of grounds, land-scaped."

"You'll come with me?"

"Of course. Immediately."

Manning's telephone tinkled, rang more strongly, with a peculiar timbre in its sound, eerie, and somehow vicious. The commissioner was the nearer to it. He lifted the instrument. Instantly there stole into the room a strain of weird, exotic, barbaric music. Above it came the booming notes of a basso voice, incredibly sardonic.

"You're listening in with Manning, Commissioner? Splendid! Trying to pick the loser, gentlemen? Sporting odds, of three to one. I can't give you a tip. I haven't come to a decision myself. All four are meddlers. It leaves you slightly in the air, eh, Manning? You will admit I play a good game of, let us say, chess. Harland would admit that, if he were alive. Don't forget this, gentlemen; you can't avert the fate decreed by heaven."

Sardonic, hideous laughter ended the transmission. It broke

into madhouse cacklings, died away as the bizarre music took predominance, and, in turn, faded.

Manning slipped an automatic into the side pocket of his dinner jacket. The commissioner was already armed, his service revolver in a shoulder-clip.

"Let's go," said Manning. "I think my car's the faster."

I V

## THE FACE WITHOUT A BODY

IN THE chamber, lined with sable tapestries, where a golden pattern gleamed in strange arabesques, Al, the legless freak, squatted in a corner, fearful and fascinated.

The Griffin strode up and down, his body draped in black, his features hidden by a clinging mask that half veiled, half revealed his beaklike nose, high cheekbone, outthrust brow and chin. His eyes glittered through slits.

The mask was of some pliant parchment, like goldbeater's skin. It seemed like a leprous tegument, or the face-mold of a mummied Pharaoh come to life, inspired with supernatural vigor.

He spoke with malignant chuckles, using Al as a focus for his thoughts as a necromancer might address a familiar spirit. Al was a deaf mute, with whom his master sometimes communicated in signs. Now he hunkered, rapt, aware of evil in the making.

"A rare stroke, Al. To threaten four, and kill one! I have Manning on the hip, while he still mourns for that chess-playing fool, Harland. *I* play with souls. While they still inhabit their bodies, fearing death. Even the most enlightened. Their wives and children, Al, they also fear the Griffin, the Appointed Destroyer of the Arrogant.

"Which shall it be? And how? They will sit amid their guards, relying upon Manning. Ha! And the Griffin will pounce and strike, and utterly destroy. I shall give them time to cringe and pray, perhaps to hope a little—and then—"

He seated himself at a desk of carved ebony, supported by Griffins, and took from a drawer a list of names. Some were scored through in scarlet. The Griffin set down four on a separate sheet.

SHACKELFORD    CHANDLER
OSGOOD    BEALE

The mask quivered, as if the hellish hate engendered within him was being emanated in a wave of venom. He muttered the names of maleficent spirits.

Feverishly he set down a cantrip charm upon a strip of parchment, droning an age-old spell. Excitement racked him.

> Zaare! Zaare, Zaam, Zaare!
> Zaare ssleqer Bohorum, nabarayn
> Uessally—uessredaza—asseyan—Haurahe
> reamue—ayn latinum quene:
> draytery, nuyyeri, quibari, yeh ay
> hahanny ymkatrum hanitanery vyerym
> caruhe tahuene cehue beyne!

The leprous mask quivered, and puckered into his mouth as he lipped the gibberish. His glittering eyes shone red. He sat rigid in a trance, while the freak gazed timidly and made an uncouth whimpering.

There was a perfume of burning amber in that chamber, hid in an old Colonial house barely fifty miles from New York. Barbaric music, lilting, now of lutes, and now of strenuous trumpets and pulsing drums, drifted through the room.

The Griffin shuddered, stirred, came back to life, like an unhallowed Lazarus. Al, furtively and placatingiy, swung himself on his arms towards a hookah watching his master. The Griffin nodded.

The fumes rose through the scented water of the hubble-bubble as the Griffin inhaled the hasheesh-tinctured weed.

"There is but one way, the *certain* way," he said in a low voice. "Now, if the heavens will confirm the incantation, not Manning, not Lucifer, nor even Jahveh shall balk my vengeance."

He rose, and turned to a screen of inlaid teak where the signs of the zodiac were set in a circle that spun as the Griffin touched it. He watched the revolutions for a few moments, and then returned to his desk. With a pen made from the slit plume of an eagle, dipped in purple ink, he worked out his unhallowed problem.

BEALE RECEIVED Manning and the commissioner with unaffected composure in his library. "I do not underestimate the danger," he assured them, "but if I know this madman, it will not be easy to avert my fate. Not that I believe in fatality. I believe in my work. It must go on. I cannot consent to be made a virtual prisoner for an indefinite period. My projects cannot be blocked. There are too many dependent upon them. I am tying up loose ends, in case...."

He smiled at them serenely. Manning felt the innate goodness of the man. It was a hideous, but not an incredible thought that the evil plot of a madman, a man possessed of a devil, might prevail.

"I must go about my business," Beale went on. "Humanity in this country is aroused. At last we begin to understand what national economy means. Through tribulation, Truth prevails. But, of course, I shall try to help you in your efforts to once more trap this...."

A shriek of utter terror, of panic, bloodcurdling and horrifying, rang through the house. It came from above.

Beale came to his feet, his ruddy, placid and benevolent face blanched with fear.

"That is my wife," he gasped.

Manning was first in the room. The commissioner stayed to warn his outside men. It was still early. Doors were opening. Servants appeared, conscious of peril. Three youths, from twelve to eighteen, were on the stairs, with two girls, in their young 'teens. Manning sternly ordered them off. The two inside detectives drew their guns, and he bade them wait outside the door, whence the screams still issued.

Beale's wife was sitting up in bed, her eyes seeming enormous, rimmed with the whites, pointing with one shaking hand at the latticed casement, where vines clung, tapping on the glass with the light wind. The fingers of the other hand were thrust into her mouth, as if to quell her clamor.

She gazed at Manning.

"There, there!" she whispered hoarsely. "The face! The shining, grinning face! On the balcony!"

She sank back amid her pillows.

"Get a doctor," Manning snapped at Beale as he made for the window, struggling with a stubborn fastening.

The balcony was ornament rather than anything practical. It was vacant. The bough of a tree rustled, but the breeze might have caused that. Manning looked out into darkness. Nothing there.

And then he saw it—the face of the Griffin, lit with some livid fire, peeping at him between the branches of the tree, a little above the level of his face. The face of a fiend, with a nose like a beak, and a slitted mouth. Eyes that were luminous balls of fire.

Manning knew it was not real, that it could not be real; that the Griffin was not climbing trees. He got his gun clear and fired automatically, as a man might sneeze. Fired, and knew he had hit the target, though it barely moved.

A man shouted from below. The tree was shaking, then the one beyond it. Something was passing through the boughs, agile as an ape. Manning called to the detective who, in turn, hailed his fellow. Red stabs of flame bit through the blackness. Manning swung from the balcony and dropped to the lawn.

But whoever, and whatever, it had been in the trees, had vanished. The detectives had not even glimpsed it. They had shot at a sound, rather than anything visible, above their heads.

The neighboring houses had plenty of trees. It might well enough have been Al, Manning told himself, remembering past acrobatics of the apelike freak. And he had escaped once more.

The detectives got a gardener's ladder and retrieved the mask, made of papier mâché treated with luminous paint. It was attached to a lazy-tongs arrangement that had permitted it to be thrust forward, to press its livid horror against the window of Mrs. Beale's room. Likely enough the beaked nose had tapped there. It was sufficient to send any nervous woman into hysterics, when backed by the frightful history of the Griffin, and his threat toward that household.

The doctor quieted her with an injection, and was serious about her condition, present and future. Manning told him what had caused it, and he shook his head.

"I have been the family doctor for almost twenty years," he said. "So long as this threat is undispelled, there is grave danger, not merely to her health, but her sanity. That danger is far greater, with her type, than if the threat were aimed at herself."

Manning nodded understandingly. Here was a woman who was mother, not only to her children, but to their parent, to the man she loved.

"We'll make this place Griffin proof!" cried the commissioner. "There must be no loophole here, Manning!"

"The Griffin works from within, rather than without," said Manning. "He has killed in a sealed vault before now."

The commissioner said nothing for a moment. "Evidence of security may save her," he said. "We must make a show of it."

But neither of them was convinced. This menace of the shining mask might be only a feint; or the Griffin, reasoning they would so regard it, might return.

The odds were still three to one. In favor of the monster.

V

### THE HOROSCOPE

**B**EFORE MIDNIGHT they had seen Chandler, in Central Park West, where he occupied an eleven-room apartment overlooking the park. It was on the eighteenth floor and with proper precautions seemed murder-proof. The commissioner installed detectives in the elevator Chandler was to use. Two more men were always on duty to watch the corridor outside his rooms. There were six floors over his head. Manning gave instructions about food and cooking. Chandler, alert and highly intelligent, promised to meet these conditions.

"We'll be duly careful," he said, "but I think I'm just on the list to make it more difficult, like the Englishman's stork that barked like a dog."

Manning liked his attitude, but warned him that the Griffin was out for a kill, that he struck like lightning from an unexpected quarter to an undetermined spot.

"There is no cause for jesting when you consider him," he warned.

The famous chemist apologized. "I am not jesting here," he said, as he tapped his breast above his heart. "I have no wish to die. A wife and children do not tend to make one foolhardy. I have my career, also."

It was much the same at Astoria, where they roused Shackelford from sleep. He was a rugged man, sturdy as his forests. His son resembled him, a man of thirty, a civil engineer on vacation.

"I have fought savages," said the son. "One of us will always be awake, vigilant. This house sits in the open, as you see. There are your men to help us. My sister has adventured, also, and dad is, as you know, an old explorer."

"I have been in jungles myself," said Manning. "And felt

much safer in them than I do with the menace of the Griffin on my threshold."

The younger Shackelford looked at him, saw his bronzed, lean face, his steadfast eyes. He made a gesture that was a half salute. "I've heard of you, sir," he said. "I respect your warnings."

It was well after dawn when they drove into the estate of Clive Osgood. The commissioner's men were on the job, and reported all was well, but Manning was not content until he had spoken with the elderly but vigorous Osgood. Only one of his three daughters was living with him, but both the others had arrived, with their husbands; leaving their own homes to stand by their father and mother. Mrs. Osgood was a New Englander of old stock.

The jurist kept them for breakfast. More thoroughly than the three others marked for death he surveyed the situation, brain to brain with Manning and the commissioner.

"It would seem," he said, "that the Griffin might have more cause to rid his imaginary legion of enemies of me than the others. But his cunning might use me as a blind. Use me as a decoy, if you wish. It would seem to me a good plan. I shall go on with my usual habits of living, but there will be your men, and my own little army. I have three menservants, besides the maids. All have been in my service for years. I am not afraid to die, gentlemen, but I do not intend to make myself a too-shining mark. Every care shall be taken that we can devise, but let us leave some not too-obvious loophole, and see to it that there is a trap set within it."

Manning and the commissioner looked at each other. Here was their own plan, duplicated by a lively brain.

WHILE DRIVING back to the city, Manning was pre-occupied. The commissioner did not disturb him. The chief felt that all had been done that might be humanely contrived, and was like a general who had made the grand rounds, knew his sentinels on the *qui vive,* his forces ready for battle. But he watched Manning keenly, knowing his brooding might hatch a flash of genius.

Manning was driving swiftly.

The commissioner expected Manning to return to Pelham Manor, but once across the Fifty-ninth Street bridge, Manning swung south. The commissioner's car was still in Manning's garage. But he said nothing until they arrived at Centre Street. Both lacked sleep, but they were used to it. Manning had been in Military Intelligence, and the commissioner had also learned to banish fatigue in the war.

They went straight to the commissioner's private office. He gave orders not to be disturbed. Manning pulled the straw from a Burmese cheroot and lighted the fragrant roll, inhaling the powerful and pungent fumes for a few moments.

"I think I've got it," he said. "Commissioner, you've got a lot of fortune tellers on your file. Is there any one of them—he must be a man or woman who casts horoscopes—who takes himself, or herself, seriously?"

The commissioner cocked an eyebrow. "Taking you also seriously?" he asked.

"In deadly earnest."

The other said no more. As Manning sat smoking, the commissioner touched a button, made crisp inquiries of the man who answered.

"Ali Abdullah should be your man," he said at last. "He's a faker, of course. Some sort of Levantine who calls himself a soothsayer. He's predicted some rather surprising things. Gives the credit to his star-gazing. Probably uses clients' gossip to put two and two together. But he's not altogether a humbug. We've investigated him. He gets by through the practice of an alleged science. He actually casts horoscopes."

Manning rose to his feet.

"Good," he said. "Let's get hold of him. Bring him here. Reassure him, as I shall, commissioner. He's the man we want."

"You believe in the stars, Manning?"

"No, but the Griffin does. The birthdays of those four are in 'Who's Who.' We'll have Ali Abdullah do what I believe the Griffin did—what he certainly has done before. In all his communications, almost without exception—not counting these last four—he talks of the destiny proclaimed by the stars. Send for Ali. If one of these four is charted by the zodiacal signs to be in danger—there you have the man who is picked for death.

"I absolutely believe that I am the only one against whom the Griffin has moved without consulting the stars. He may have excused himself for his failure to destroy me on that account. Some day he will cast *my* horoscope—and he may realize that the ancient chart of the constellations, projected on the plane of the ecliptic, is no longer precise. Owing to precession, there is, these days, a discrepancy amounting to the breadth of a whole sign. The sign Aries of the ancients is now occupied by the constellation Pisces. But astrologers still stick to the old formulae. That does not matter. Get Ali Abdullah."

Ali was brought in within an hour, doubtless disturbed, but showing slight sign of it, reassured by the explanation that he was summoned as an expert, recognized as an aide to the law.

Manning spoke to him in the Arabic he had acquired in Malasia. Ali answered in the same tongue. His hooded eyes shone at the mention of a fee five times his usual charge for casting horoscopes. He had been required to bring his charts, and was prepared to answer some charge that might deprive him of his livelihood, relieved to discover that he was treated as a scientist.

It was a strange thing, in the private office of the commissioner, to see Ali, furnished with dates, sitting down seriously and solemnly his cabalistic diagrams. It was almost noon when he sighed, and thrust all his papers aside but one.

"THE MAN Osgood is threatened by adverse signs within his houses," he said. "He is in grave danger. By my calculations, which I have checked, this peril will destroy, or pass over, with the last appearance of Saturn within the phase of—"

"When?" barked the commissioner. The stars did not impress him any more than they did Manning, but they might make up the Griffin's calendar of death.

Ali Abdullah consulted an almanac. It was set down on a parchment scroll, but Manning knew that the same information was given in all the patent-medicine almanacs.

"It is today," announced Ali Abdullah. "When the moon sets. Saturn will not be seen, the moon will be like the fragment of a cloud. But the stars make their courses while the sun still shines. It will be this afternoon, before sunset."

Manning swung to the telephone, calling the Naval Observatory at Washington. The commissioner paid Ali from his own pocket, ushered the old astrologer from the room. He was fired with the conviction that Manning had read the mind of the Griffin.

Manning set down the telephone.

"The moon sets at three this afternoon," he said. "Ali was right about Saturn. And the Griffin will calculate as Ali did. We haven't got too much time."

"Time enough," said the commissioner calmly, though a nerve ticked on his forehead, "if the Griffin works on schedule. You and I will be either side of Osgood when that moon goes down."

Manning made a little gesture, not quite one of impatience. He knew that he alone realized the Griffin might kill, even if his victim were surrounded by a vigilant regiment. He had once held up an ocean liner to get his man, challenging and threatening from the air.

But they had found their clew. Manning had worked it out. He had used the Griffin's own tactics. The Griffin had boasted, more than once, and proved his point, that he could easily kill anyone after a study of his habits.

And Manning's knowledge of that part of the Griffin's madness that made the monster consult the stars, and consider himself the Appointed Dispenser of Destinies, seemed to lead them directly to Osgood. The others were still being guarded. The Griffin, for all his cunning, could hardly have foreseen Manning's move.

But he might. The odds were still three to one.

They would still have to outguess the Griffin's own subtle move at the last second. And that might be a move like Harland's sudden castling of his king, his seeming sacrifice in his chess game with Manning.

Because Osgood seemed the most likely prey, the madman might well think that Manning would consider him otherwise. An error would be fatal. By concentrating at Syosset they might miss the actual attack at Astoria, Forest Hills, or New York City.

But the horoscope appeared to Manning more than a hunch. For once he was inclined to believe in the stars. At least this gave them basis for definite action, released them from the devilish uncertainty the Griffin had planned. There was the chance that the Griffin's horoscope-casting might vary from that of Ali Abdullah; but Manning considered that a possibility that could be waived, and was not a great risk.

As he and the commissioner drove once again to Long Island, they saw the pale wafer of the moon, barely visible in the blue sky. It looked like a broken disk of ice, dissolving and melting. The life of Osgood might be also declining to a final dissolution as that moon vanished in the sunset, and Saturn shone malignantly below the horizon.

V I

THE  GUARDED  VILLA

I T  W A S  early fall on Long Island, the most beautiful month of the year, September; when the faint tints of orange and crimson in the oaks and maples, the warm gray of clustering bayberries, the touches of vermilion in the brush, seemed a culmination of the splendor of summer, rather than a hint of decay.

Now, with the prospect of action, both Manning and the commissioner were as fresh as if they had been rested with long hours of sleep.

It seemed utterly unnatural that on such a day a fiend should be chuckling in anticipation of a murder, that could only be conceived in a brain inflamed by disease. Some day the cells would break down utterly and paranoia destroy the intellect that now was merely stimulated by the first stages of cerebral fever, its delusions fantastic horrors the Griffin was still capable of carrying out.

In default of capture or death, the best weapon to use against the maniac was the frustration of his designs. Rage at defeat seemed to at least threaten to destroy his coördination. Once he had broken down, and Manning had captured him. Then the state had ministered to the diseased mind and it had re-covered sufficient balance to set the Griffin free again to carry on his reign of terror and horror.

His deeds had affected social, civic and financial circles. They had temporarily paralyzed industry, and now he had run amuck, like a *juramentado* Filipino; like a mad dog—save that there was ever method in his madness. In the death of Harland he had scored over Manning, and such a victory would prove a stimulus.

"If he doesn't pull anything off, or try to pull something off, at Syosset before sunset," said the commissioner, "that should eliminate Osgood as a victim, I suppose. But the idea is not much of a consolation. I have had extra men sent on, but I suppose there is little doubt that the Griffin is pretty well in-formed as to the disposition of those already on the spot, and may find out what we do with the extras. A cordon of dicks is likely to be entirely too obvious, more so in the country than in the city."

He glanced at the sky. Manning was intent upon his driving.

He felt in his bones that there was no time to lose. Ali Abdullah had been pretty vague about the hour of attack. It would be before sunset, some time that afternoon when the danger would culminate. And the afternoon was halfway gone. The sun would set in three hours. They might already be too late.

"That devil may be aloft in that plane, or another one," grumbled the commissioner. "So many are flying over Long Island these days there's no controlling them. He may have his spies in the air. They could fly low over a place and spot every move we were making."

Manning made no immediate comment. The Griffin had used exactly such methods.

"We'll be there in fifteen minutes," he said at last. "The Griffin knows we have always guarded the men he has named. No doubt he is keeping tabs on all four places. If he spots your extra men, he may get the idea that we think Osgood in special danger. And that idea may merely spur him on. In any event I believe he has his method of attack already figured out and will not depart from it. It is something based on Osgood's movements, customary or otherwise.

"Osgood is game. We might leave some loophole open for the Griffin to utilize and set a trap in it. But I don't think we could set any trap he would not smell out. I see only one thing to do. To keep Osgood where we can have our eyes on him until sunset, to have the men ready to close in on our signal or the suggestion of anything suspicious. You and I will have to be the best judges of that. A dick might think too quickly, or not quickly enough. There is only one entrance to Osgood's place— the gates in the high wall. Have those watched, but not closed. Let visitors and tradesmen come and go. He will have someone who can vouch for them. There's a little lodge just inside. Then it's up to the two of us, commissioner."

The commissioner gave a grunt that was almost a groan.

"I'm an amateur, with authority, Manning. It's up to you. I don't doubt your idea is the best. To have Osgood where we can watch him every second we would have to keep him in the open. That sounds pretty risky, to me."

"Remember that the Griffin never repeats his methods exactly," said Manning. "He has used bombs, death-rays; once, explosive golf-balls. Poison of several kinds. This, if the attempt is made, will be some unique variation. If we cannot forestall it, discover it before it is put into execution, Osgood is doomed. We'll do our best. Have your extra men patrol outside the grounds. We'll see what we can do inside. Here is where we turn off."

The commissioner roused himself from a feeling of hopelessness that seemed premonitory. He had been elated at first over Manning's stroke of genius in uncovering what appeared to be the identity of the appointed victim, the approximate time of the attack. It had seemed brilliant, but now it looked to him more like a flash in the pan.

They came to the high brick wall that ran along the front of Osgood's estate. It was not a very large acreage. Sides and back were fenced with galvanized steel wire of the type used by factories, heavily meshed, five feet in height, topped by a series of slanting angle-irons, strung with barbed wire.

It was a formidable obstacle to any trespasser. With men patrolling it, it was a virtually impassable barrier. Osgood had erected it more from regard for his valuable dwarf fruit trees than with any idea of personal safety. It was a comforting thing to see on an occasion like this.

THE HOUSE, of the Italian villa type, sat well back. In front of it the land sloped, and had been terraced, down to a lawn shaded by a few beautiful trees landscaped with well-ended shrubbery.

There was a pool with a carved stone fountain rising in the center, casting a rainbow spray in the afternoon sunshine. Goldfish swam about beneath the lily pads and water hyacinths.

About the pool four semicircular benches of marble were

arranged, the backs and seats made easy by cushions. There were lounging chairs, and two enormous umbrellas of vivid pattern.

The iron gates by the little lodge were not in the middle of the brick wall, but well to one side, so that the house and grounds might not be seen directly from the road. The drive led along an avenue of Carolina poplars. It ran about the house, with a right-hand fork for deliveries.

The gates were closed. Manning's car was challenged, not because of lack of recognition, but to show efficiency. The men saluted, reported all well.

"How do you know?" snapped the commissioner. "Where is Mr. Osgood?"

They pointed to the lawn, where Osgood sat reading in one of the marble benches, his back to the drive. Alone.

"He insisted on staying alone, that is, away from the rest of the family, ever since your message came, commissioner," said the homicide-squad sergeant in charge of the detail. "Of course we are watching him. There are six men within thirty yards of him now."

"Seen any planes flying low?"

"None you would call low, sir. Two or three have passed over since noon, but that's common enough."

"Ah! Manning, what are your moves?"

"Find out from Mrs. Osgood and the housekeeper what deliveries may be made between now and sunset, what visitors are expected. If any telephone calls are made, and Mrs. Osgood decides to receive, word must come to the lodge. Those gates were open the last time we came. Open them up again, but have men ready to close them, to stop anybody, on foot, horseback or in a car, who is not vouched for by Mrs. Osgood. I want her to look over the housekeeper's list. Put your new men outside, to help patrol the fence and the wall. Then you and I, commissioner, will go and sit with Osgood until the sun goes down."

"Going to tell him about Ali Abdullah?"

"I would. He is a brave and intelligent man. He has the right to know everything we know, what we intend doing. You know his reputation. He has never feared to speak out. He has just shown his determination by keeping his family out of danger. It's hard for them, but it is hard for him. A fine gesture of protection and manhood."

Osgood greeted them with perfect composure as Manning and the commissioner came towards him, after Manning's suggestions had been followed out. Still the sun shone, the fountain played, the light wind waved the leaves, and brought the perfumes of the flowers. Once a plane soared out above the Sound. It was high up, but not too high for powerful glasses.

Osgood listened to Manning's recapitulation with calm interest.

"Most ingenious," he said. "I never dreamed my fate might depend upon the stars, the malignant influence of Saturn. That was brilliant reasoning, Manning." He glanced at his watch. "Three-thirty, leaving about a hundred and fifty minutes of, let us say, uncertainty. Whatever happens—and I am not in the least degree ready or reconciled to death—I have completed one task. It took a good deal of tilling. This afternoon I shall see the first fruit. Thinking of fruit, will you gentlemen have some refreshments?"

Manning shook his head. "Nothing for any of us, meat or drink, until after sunset. Just what is this fruit you are talking about, Mr. Osgood?"

"The first copy of my book exposing the fallacies of medical jurisprudence as now practiced in the United States, with different practice in every confounded state, gentlemen. Some of our codes, the decisions handed down, smack more of witchcraft than of science. The abuse of alienists as contradictory witnesses, the arbitrary assumption of courts as to what constitutes rational responsibility in criminal procedure. It is high time that the law was changed to conform with the discoveries of science."

Manning nodded. "The case of the madman we are here

about is strongly in point," he said. "You are expecting this book? By special messenger? Mrs. Osgood did not mention it."

Osgood smiled. "She does not know about it, yet. I intended it as more or less of a surprise. My publisher is sending half a dozen complimentary copies. They will come by the usual delivery. I mean the Universal Delivery Service. It is used by many of the big stores. My publishers wrote me they would see the books got here today. I was a bit eager about it, I must admit. I telephoned them this morning."

He went on, presenting and discussing the high lights of his important opinion on the subject. It was, thought Manning, a somewhat macabre subject in connection with the threat of a madman who had been favored by the present laws; a threat that, to Manning, did not lessen with the passing of time, but became concentrated.

The Griffin had never failed to strike. But this time he had not mentioned an hour or a definite name. He might even now be delivering his blow elsewhere. Manning went to the gate to add the service delivery van to the list. There would be some household supplies from the village. No callers were expected, so far, but these were always possible. Known friends would drop in without warning.

VII

THE MOON SETS

IT WAS a little after half past four when the Universal Service's light truck drove through the gates. He excused himself abruptly and went swiftly towards the gate.

"Did any of you notice the tires on that car?" he snapped. Osgood's servant shook his head. So did one of the detectives, but the other spoke up.

"Yes, sir. The van had Fairgood tires, almost brand new. That's a Forge car and the tires are regular equipment."

Manning's eyes narrowed. At the end of the avenue he could see the van turning in after making the circuit of the house.

He saw a manservant coming across the garden towards Osgood with a package in his hand.

"Close that gate," Manning ordered. "Stop that car. Hold the men. They may show fight. Be ready."

"You think it's a phony, sir?" asked the man who had recognized the car.

"I know it is. I know the tires on all delivery-company cars of any importance. The Universal has a special contract for their rubber. They use nothing but Cupleys, even on new cars. Hold 'em."

He turned as the men came into the open, and the gates were closed. He saw Osgood beckoning to the servant, who began to hurry with the expected package.

Manning began to run, shouting to Osgood, the servant and, more specially, to the commissioner.

"Don't open that package! Don't drop it, man! Get rid of it, safely—quick!"

The servant stopped, startled, alarmed.

He almost let the package fall. Osgood stood stock still. Manning was still twenty feet away. The commissioner barked at the man:

"Hang on to it! I'll take it! It's dangerous."

The servant's eyes bulged. He came to a sudden decision, and dodged the commissioner, taking a few rapid steps. For a moment Manning thought him an agent of the Griffin. To kill the man might be fatal. He was passing too close to Osgood.

Then the man, with a manifest air of triumph, tossed the parcel into the pool. He turned, looking for approval.

"That'll fix—"

The ripples were still spreading when the explosion sent the water geysering upwards, with fish and weed; with fragments of the stone fountain, shattered to splinters.

It had received the full charge of the infernal machine. With his satanic cunning, the Griffin had doubtless arranged the bomb to explode on opening, but he had also determined that, if the parcel should be suspected, he would still get a measure of unhallowed joy, even if he missed his target.

He might have hoped to trap Manning. It is a common practice to drop a suspected contraption of this type into water. But the Griffin must have included metallic sodium or some element sympathetic to moisture, that acted instead of the detonator that would have worked by the friction of opening.

They would never know. They were all drenched. The servant was sent staggering by the air concussion. Osgood and the commissioner were thrown together. All three were uninjured, though they were drenched by the contents of the pool. People came running from the house.

Manning stumbled to one knee, recovered.

THERE WAS the crackling fire of a sub-machine gun at the gate. The van backed up, charged at full tilt at the iron gates—but failed to break through.

One detective was down, but the driver hung limp over his wheel. The man with him sprang out, shooting at another of the guards, wounding him. The man made for the wall, leaped into a tree, holstering his gun as he sprang. He was taking a desperate chance to gain the top of the wall, perhaps not counting on outside guards.

Manning came sprinting over the turf. He jumped and grabbed the man's ankles, swung on them with all his weight and brought the other out of the tree. As the man fell he grappled furiously with Manning, the two of them rolling on the ground as the others came racing up.

They dared not shoot. Manning, always in condition, hard as nails from hand ball, was a good wrestler. He knew the holds of the Japanese, but the desperate agent of the Griffin was armed with the triple strength of fear.

Manning wanted the man alive. He did not have much luck

questioning the Griffin's men when he nabbed one, but there was always a chance.

The man tore loose from a grip that almost broke his arm, driving upwards with his knee at Manning's groin. He managed to get out his gun. Manning, fighting against the nauseating agony, felt the barrel of the weapon against his ribs. He expected the searing flame and lead in his belly as he pushed back the man's chin and struck sidewise at his Adam's apple.

The man collapsed with a gasp, but his twitching hand pulled trigger. Manning's clothes were burned, but his skin was not scorched. His chopping blow had diverted the other's aim.

The bullet had gone upwards, through diaphragm and heart.

Even if the bullet had not been instantly fatal he would never have spoken again. Manning's jujutsu chop had broken his hyoid bone; would probably have killed him.

This time the Griffin had failed, but once more his agents had not betrayed him, could not have done so had they dared.

Manning rose, panting, regretful.

"It's over, so far as you and the other three are concerned," he said to Osgood. "They were never in real peril, of course, and the Griffin never tries to retrieve a failure."

"There is one thing I don't understand," said Osgood. "Where is the legitimate van?"

Manning smiled grimly.

"You may be assured the Griffin knew all about it," he said. "I think you will find that your publishers got a second call not to deliver today, for what seemed a sufficient reason."

"If I knew where to send it," said Osgood, "I'd present him with a copy. If he is ever tried again I hope some of the changes I advocate will be adopted."

"I doubt if the Griffin will ever be tried again," said Manning. "They might let him off. *I* don't intend to, next time I get within range of him."

# THE GRIFFIN'S GAMBIT

*A Legless Figure of Horror Climbs into a Locked
House to Start a Game of Death That Brings
Manning and the Griffin Face to Face*

I

## THE GRIFFIN'S KEY

THE LONG black car slid along the country road. The
purring of the engine was inaudible. The moon was
shining, though it was low in the heavens, and no lights showed
in or about the big sedan. It glided with the somber, sinister
aspect of a hearse.

Trees lined the road, which was a branch from a main
highway. It possessed no lighting, either for traffic control or
general purposes. It ran for about two miles before it linked
with another highway, and in that distance there were but four
houses, well apart; comfortable country residences without
especial pretense to display or size.

The car came to a noiseless halt where the shadow was thick.
Across the road from it ran a high hedge of osage orange, thorny
and impenetrable, backed by wire fencing that was invisible
from the road. There was an entry gate of ornamental iron,
swung between two pillars of cemented fieldstone, topped by
electric lanterns that had been switched off.

One figure remained at the wheel of the car, seated as rigidly
as an automaton. A door opened, and two weird figures descended. One was dwarfish, not more than four feet in height.
It was dressed like a man, but it appeared like a deformed ape.

It had no legs, but it moved with astounding agility, the trunk swung between the arms.

The other figure was almost as mysterious. It was tall and lean, wrapped in a black mantle of ankle length. On the head was a high-crowned, wide-brimmed sombrero. This man looked like some tragic figure of mediaeval Spanish romance. The collar of the cape was turned up, his features were not to be seen in the light. What was to be glimpsed of the face appeared ghastly and unnatural.

No words passed between them. What was to be done seemed to have been planned to the minutest detail.

The legless creature climbed one of the stone pillars as nimbly as a chimpanzee, hoisting its bulk with the strength of its arms, hand-over-hand, with fingers that gripped the crevices securely.

It was a fearful sight to see this object swarming up the wall to the lantern cage. It squatted there, like a gargoyle, motionless.

A dog came bounding and barking across the lawn. It was not yet enraged, its voice was a first warning, rather a general alarm. Its nostrils twitched to catch the strange scent that had roused it to duty.

The legless freak tossed a juicy fragment of meat. Here was a more inviting odor. The dog gulped it down. A sound, half groan, half howl, as the pellet inside the meat dissolved, and the deadly poison paralyzed lungs and heart, died away as the unlucky brute fell on its side, twitching, gasping, limp.

In the darkness the human gargoyle chuckled noiselessly. It was deaf and dumb. Such deeds as this amused it. Then it lowered itself inside the garden. No lights appeared. There was no disturbance.

Balanced on its torso, the freak juggled with the lock of the gate. It was not elaborate. The gate opened, and the cloaked figure passed in like a shadow, sinister and silent.

THE TWO strode across the velvet lawn, one on legs, the other on its arms. Still they moved with the fell and absolute

*The light showed her a horrible face, beaked like an eagle.*

precision of those who have spied out the land. Their evil purpose was manifest in their appearance, their approach, the silent hour, when vitality is low in sleeping folk, and courage has retreated.

A veranda ran about the building, once a Colonial farmhouse. The cloaked man stood between bush-cypresses, hidden, as the living gargoyle hitched itself up a post. The freak disappeared, entered a window opened to the night, festooned with clambering roses.

Swinging between softly planted palms, it passed through the sleeping chamber. It glanced at the fine four-poster bed where a woman lay, and almost halted. But the will of the cloaked man, who was its master, drove it on to open the unlocked door, to propel itself down the stairs.

The house had an odor of serenity, almost of sanctity. It believed itself secure. But this whimsy of a pernicious Nature left a taint behind it of perversion, almost of obscenity.

The front door opened. The freak made a hissing sound. The cloaked man passed through the door, ascended the stairs.

On the landing a faint night light burned on a small stand. The cloaked man gestured, ordering his slave to descend. Now a high-bridged nose showed, like a hook in shape. There was a glint of infinitely evil eyes, flickering like the licking flames of hell. They seemed to glow through a scabrous mask, as a leper's orbs might shine. The man's skin was dull gold, curiously wrinkled about features that looked like those of a long-mummied Pharaoh, resurrected from a sarcophagus.

The legless thing hopped down the stairs, awkward now, like a toad. It went out into the night, out to the car, where it took its place on the rear seat, without a sign from the chauffeur.

The moon sank slowly. The landscape lay dark, windless and inanimate. The woman awoke. She slept soundly, as a rule, without dreams; sane and healthy. She was a psychiatrist, without illusion, her life dedicated to those whose minds were too often filled with fear. Fear that she often banished, mental ghosts she laid.

But now fear gripped *her.*

Two green eyes stared at her. They were centered with black pupils. They did not move. Back of them, she felt a horrible, inflexible malevolence.

Her heart contracted. She was not sure if the vision were real, or conjured out of unsound sleep, by nerves that for the first time in her sound life had betrayed her.

The malignant orbs disappeared. They had focused upon her from battery-lit lenses in a contrivance suspended from the cloaked man's neck, like binoculars.

Now, in the dark, his own hidden eyes gloating like a ghoul's, the cloaked man shifted the green lenses.

The woman was brave, too brave. She had no weapon, no way of summoning help from servants who were faithful, yet might not be too ready to respond. But there was a reading lamp clamped to the head of the bed. She reached for it, fumbling and stealthy, still half-tranced by slumber.

The light showed her a horrible face, beaked like an eagle. It seemed to have a leprous skin, like that of a shedding snake, dully gold.

Her voice died in her throat as she roused, and tried to raise herself. The leprous face twitched to a derisive grin. A hideous chuckle was the last thing she heard as hands like talons clutched her throat, pressing, with deadly thumb-thrusts, upon her jugular vein and vagus nerve. Air and blood cut off, she thrashed like a landed salmon, subsiding with gasps as her lungs failed her.

The green lights played again upon her distorted face, lips twisted in the sardonic smile of death.

The chuckle sounded again.

The man leaned forward. He drew a small silver box from an inner pocket, took out of it a scarlet label, a small oval of stiff paper he licked beneath his skin-tight mask.

He affixed it to her forehead.

Then he glided from the room, down the stairs. The door clicked, with its automatic lock of false safety.

The car moved down the road into the farther highway.

There its lights went on, and it gathered speed, rushing through the night, with many other cars carrying men and women. Most of them were, or had been, pleasure bent.

But none experienced greater delight than the mad monster who sat with the freak Al beside him. The Griffin had made his first move, his gambit, in his latest game, the sport in which his perverted nature delighted; the murder of the worthy.

"We'll see what our friend Manning makes of *this* opening," he murmured. Al could not hear. The chauffeur, driving like an automaton, heard nothing.

He was not only servant, but slave to his master, who held him in unrighteous thrall, as the Griffin held all who served him, fearful of his power, his knowledge of their hidden lives.

## I I

## THE VOICE OF EVIL

THE LIFELESS, strangled body of Martha Everest, eminent psychiatrist, was found this morning by her personal maid when she brought her dead mistress her usual tray of tea and toast and orange juice.

On the brow of her mistress was the crimson insignia of the homicidal madman known as the Griffin; a red cartouche embossed with the design of an heraldic griffin, rampant, showing the upper half of the mythical monster, half-lion and half-eagle.

The maid, Susan Robinson, who has been in the service of Dr. Everest for many years, retained her senses long enough to call the police. They arrived to find the rest of the household unconscious of the tragedy, and the maid in a profound swoon.

Aroused, she stated, and the two other servants of the household corroborated her story, that there had been no alarm in the night. The doors of the house were found locked, the entrance gate fastened. A Belgian police dog was discovered poisoned, apparently by cyanide.

There were faint tracks on the lawn, but dew had plainly fallen later. The police....

MANNING, AT breakfast, tossed aside his paper as the telephone sounded. With its first tinkle he knew, aside from what he had been reading, that the Griffin had struck again. Without warning. Then the mocking voice spoke to him, with its inevitable, faint accompaniment of eerie, barbaric music.

"My dear Manning, you will have learned by now that I have made my opening move in a fresh game, and established my gambit. I attended to this matter with my own hands. It seemed to me quite a personal matter, and I must admit that I got distinct exhilaration out of it."

The voice paused, as if hoping to draw some retort, some

expression, from Manning. But Manning did not answer. He was pledged to destroy the Griffin. Manning had caught him once, and the law had judged him insane, placing him in Dannemora, where his fiendish ingenuity devised means of escape.

"That vaporing harridan, Martha Everest, had the temerity to refer to me as an outstanding example of dementia praecox. I sealed her lips and brain forever. She was a strong-minded woman, but I almost spoiled my own purpose. I almost frightened her to death before I strangled her. There have been times when I should like to strangle you, Manning, but I have thought of many other more ingenious ways of disposing of you. You were born under a lucky star, but some day the signs will properly assemble, and you will cease to bother me—though, mostly, you have amused me."

There had been times when Manning had actually lifted a chalice of death to his lips, others when he escaped by the breadth of a hair. It would always be so until he annihilated the Griffin or the Griffin played an unbeatable gambit and swept Manning from the board.

"I am reverting to previous methods in my next move, Manning," continued the Griffin. "You will hear from me within twenty-four hours. I shall send you the name of my next candidate for elimination, also the date of his demise."

Then came the taunting laugh, tainted with madness, tinged with infinite malevolence, laughter that would fit well in the horror-haunted halls of hell itself.

The laughter blended with the exotic music, died away.

Gordon Manning, ex-Major of Military Intelligence in the World War; adventurer, explorer and also counsellor-at-law, though he never appeared to plead a case, had been commissioned by both city and state to uncover and annihilate the Griffin.

But he did not now bestir himself to aid in the search for the murderer of the woman. He knew that once the Griffin had struck—given a clean getaway—he would not be traced by any ordinary methods. The police would do their best.

Manning was gradually gathering a force of under cover agents to offset the Griffin's slaves. Manning's recruits knew no age limit. He chose them for their aptitude. They included boys and men in all walks of life, one or two girls, and one woman. Not all of them knew to what end they worked, or even that they did police work.

A lot of them seemed slender threads to weave a net about such a monster, but Manning was the weaver. Slowly, but he hoped surely, Manning's agents worked to the final end of discovering the Griffin's lair.

Manning adopted the method of the honey-hunter, who, capturing a bee, let it fly and marked its direct flight to the hive. The ultimate crossing of the angles would locate the hidden spot, where the Griffin had regathered his forces since his escape from Dannemora.

SO FAR, Manning had gathered odds and ends of information that seemed to show that the Griffin's powerful car invariably headed towards a destination not far from New York. Such a car was fairly conspicuous, but not unmistakable. No doubt he shifted his license numbers, but there was a limit to that dodge.

Also, Manning had spotted a few of the men who had worked with the Griffin in the execution of his crimes. He might have discarded them, and they were watched, but Manning watched them also.

So now Manning waited to hear from these agents of his. In the hours before the message of impending doom arrived he meant to store up energy. He did not dismiss the matter from his mind entirely. That was a nervous impossibility. The Griffin's evil impulses broke through any attempt at assuming a genuine serenity.

Manning had breakfasted in dressing gown above his pajamas.

But he did light a Burmese cheroot and selected a volume from the handy shelves of the library.

The book was an early edition of Bunyan's "Pilgrim's Progress." He riffled the pages to the place where Christian encountered the "foul fiend, Apollyon."

> "So he went on, and Apollyon met him. Now the monster was hideous to behold: he was clothed with scales like a fish, and they are his pride; he had wings like a dragon, and feet like a bear, and out of his belly came fire and smoke, and his mouth was the mouth of a lion…. Then Apollyon straddled quite over the whole breadth of the way, and said, I am void of fear in this matter. Prepare thyself to die; for I swear by this infernal den that thou shalt go no further; here will I spill thy soul."

Manning did not liken himself to the redoubtable "Pilgrim," but he fancied that the Griffin might be comparing himself to Apollyon. And Apollyon finally got the worst of it.

That chuckle was not so confident in the late afternoon. He had a certain book in his hand when the Griffin's expected message was delivered. That might have been coincidence, but it was somewhat uncanny. In the light of what happened, Manning began to wonder about the intimate knowledge the Griffin revealed of his private life—if it were privy against the power of that perverted genius.

The message came at dusk, normally enough delivered. Manning considered the uniformed messenger boy genuine, though he would check up on that without hope of learning much. To trace the Griffin by such clews was about as useful as trying to trace the course of a fish in the water.

The letter, with its envelope, was on the familiar heavy handmade gray paper, the bold writing in purple ink. Its general style was the grandiloquent and autocratic manner the Griffin always affected. But the form of address had varied. The epistle was headed with the name of the Griffin's next victim.

It was a name that Manning knew well. A man he knew,

respected, and admired; with whom he had actually adventured along wild trails.

*Bayard Harding.*

In "Who's Who," Harding was set down as a zoölogist, but he was also an explorer and anthropologist of note.

His latest dictum had stirred not only the scientific, but the world at large. The gorilla, claimed Harding, had almost given up entirely its habit of living in the trees. Its nests were now made upon the ground. It no longer traveled by swinging through the boughs. Its arms were shortening, legs lengthening, and it maintained an upright position as its natural gait.

Soon, very soon, as science measures time, the gorilla would begin to follow the course of natural evolution, it would become a kind of man.

This statement of Harding's had provoked anger in some quarters. But the Griffin appeared to be more virulent than any other critic. To the Griffin, star-gazer, necromancer, caster of horoscopes, and ardent believer in zodiacal influence; Harding was a blasphemer, seeking to asperse the principle of astrology, to mock at the signs of the heavens. Therefore, Bayard Harding was to be eliminated.

The Griffin wrote:

> This man, seeking notoriety, would pretend that the positions of the heavenly bodies and their courses through the starry universe are linked up with the destinies of brutes. He offends the gods and I, their appointed arbiter and agent, shall destroy him.
>
> The date, my dear Manning, shall be on the seventeenth of this month. That give you time to prepare your important defenses. Nothing on earth may save him.
>
> I am also granting you a pawn. Here is a hint for you. If you ever read the analects of Lao Tsze you may remember the following:
>
> "To know the habits of your friend is not always wise, lest that make you despise him. To know the habits of your enemy

enables you to defeat him, even to easily compass his death against all opposition."

I know some of your habits, Manning, as well as those of Bayard Harding. Beware your own destruction.

There was no signature, only the heraldic device of a demi-griffin, rampant, showing the eagle beak and wings, the lion's mane and claws.

Manning set down the letter, looked at the book he had been reading when the telephone had tinkled, and brought to him the premonitory thrill of evil and peril.

It was a small volume, beautifully printed and bound in vellum. The title was deeply stamped in gold: "Analects of Lao Tsze."

There was small doubt that the Griffin did not boast when he said he knew some of Manning's habits, little question that Manning was being spied upon. Yet he would have risked his life upon the integrity of his two Japanese servitors. Soon, that was going to be proven.

As for the Griffin, despite his phrases, Manning knew that his main grievance lay in the suggestion that he, the chosen of the gods, an immortal of a thousand reincarnations, should be compared, however remotely, with an ape. That, and the fact that he was insanely jealous of anyone, or anything connected with progressive achievement.

Harding had to be seen, and warned. Manning knew how his friend would take it, victor over scores of desperate risks against savage men and beasts, and the forces of nature. None the less, Manning believed that he could persuade Harding to let him take every precaution that would not insult Harding's manhood.

He could not get a man like Bayard Harding to hide himself, to surrender his ordinary affairs. And the Griffin, when he killed, had penetrated even to the most modern of vaults and claimed his victim.

The clew was in that pawn the Griffin condescended to give

his opponent, it lay in the "Analects of Lao Tsze." Through some habit of Harding's that might also be a habit of Manning's, the fatal blow would materialize. And a man's habits were legion.

There was the commissioner of police to be informed, but not the press. Time enough for criticism if the Griffin's gambit won the game.

III

THE POISON IS TESTED

THE GRIFFIN, in his long robe of sable silk, embroidered with cabalistic symbols in gold, descended by the concealed elevator from his private chamber to the cellars where he had set up his laboratories.

His face was masked with the clinging stuff that looked like goldbeater's skin, half screening, half revealing his saturnine features. He looked like a pharaoh risen from his sarcophagus.

Al, the legless, deaf and dumb freak, ambled after him, like a familiar spirit. He knew to what such a visit tended, the rudimentary soul in him delighted in the horrors he would witness.

As they left the chamber it was redolent of burned amber, of hasheesh-tinged tobacco, filled with faint strains of strange music.

A man in denim overalls, whose face was bloodless, like something that had grown in a dungeon, a man with the cranium of a genius, but whose eyes were dull with despair, was waiting for his master. He had no name, only a number stenciled on the overalls.

"I am conducting an experiment," said the Griffin. "It is a dangerous one, Number Twenty-Four. I wish you to stand by, to use every effort to resuscitate any one who may be affected. You are to do your utmost. I wish you to gather your apparatus and your materials in readiness."

The voice of Twenty-Four was hollow as an echo in a tomb.

"I must ask the nature of the experiment," he said. "At least, what I must expect to combat."

"Asphyxiation covers it, broadly. *This* will be the agent."

The Griffin gave the ex-physician a slip of paper on which chemical symbols had been set down by another unnamed slave, once a famous chemist, whose disappearance had never been solved, though it was accounted for officially by the sudden death of his unfaithful mistress. The Griffin had offered him a haven.

Number Twenty-Four glanced at the paper.

"This is an intensely toxic, volatile and rapid poison, classed as protoplasmic," he said. "Employed in this form, which should prove difficult, I doubt if the victim could be resuscitated."

"Nevertheless, you will do your best," the Griffin told him, his tones like sharp steel, rasping on sharp steel. "Your mention of poison and victim is untimely, Twenty-Four. I do not know that an accident may happen. If it should, tell me your treatment."

"To wash out the stomach, using oxidizing agents, such as hydrogen peroxide, potassium permanganate, injections of methylene blue. The absorption of the poison will be terribly swift, however, and all antidotes may be ineffective."

"Go on," said the Griffin. His voice had softened now, but it was none the less suggestive. It suggested an inner chuckle. "What else?"

"Possibly hypodermic or intravenous injections of sodium thiosulphate. If I only knew how the poison would be administered...."

"Ah," said the Griffin, rubbing his palms together, "that is my secret, entirely my own idea, Twenty-Four; as to how, in the course of the experiment, it might be administered. Try all these things. If you are successful you will be rewarded. I will see that you are able to communicate with your family. There will be a monetary consideration. Kindly hurry."

Twenty-Four wondered wherein his success would lie. In resuscitation, or in failure. As for his reward, if he was given it, it would be like Dead Sea fruit, ashes in his mouth.

"I am in hell," he muttered as he went back to his special cubicle, "and the Devil is my master."

It was an hour later when he was again summoned, to find a man stretched upon the floor, naked, his body blotched red and purple. He showed no sign of life.

"Less than two minutes have passed," said the Griffin. "Get busy."

Half an hour later, haggard, wet with sweat, Number Twenty-Four gave his decision, not knowing how it would be received.

"There is no hope, there never was," he announced. "In that form there is no chance of revival. The man is dead, has been dead since I came in. His blood is jellied in his veins, his lungs, and in his arteries. I tell you, he is dead. And he does not look like an experimental chemist to me. His fingers are spatulate, roughened, they are not even stained with acid...."

His voice rose, cracked, became hysterical.

The Griffin's eyes surveyed him through the slits in his mask.

"Your personal comments were not asked," he said. "I fear this exhibition forfeits your reward, Twenty-Four. Al, see that he goes back to his place."

The Griffin spoke the words that Al could not hear but had learned to lip-read.

Twenty-Four shrank from this human gargoyle, skipping toward him, with his muscular arms for rope. He went out weeping and unnerved.

The Griffin looked at the dead man on the floor. A vigorous, but pleasant type, not long a serf in this inferno. Chosen by the Griffin, as a vivisectionist would select a rabbit or a monkey.

A crude person, promised sanctuary by an agent of the Monster. Now he had proved his utility.

"Excellent," said the Griffin with a chuckle. "It could not be

better. I promised you release if you proved worthy, Number
Forty-One. You were worth more to me dead than alive, and
you have your release from hunger, thirst, from all appetites of
the flesh. A healthy moron, serving my purpose. For I seek to
destroy the bodies of my enemies, to send them to the grave.
For you, Forty-One, there is an empty space in my private
cemetery. You will be fertilizer for the weeds."

WHEN THE GRIFFIN spoke of his private cemetery
he was somewhat arrogant. The old, remote Colonial estate he
had acquired possessed a graveyard, and a vault to hold the
bones of the owners and those who served them faithfully.

Most of those bones had long since moldered into dust. The
headstones leaned, the caskets yawned in the vault. And their
vacancies were occasionally filled by the Griffin.

It was Number Seventeen, the chemist, who profited most
by the Griffin's latest experiment. The man's soul had long ago
been eaten out. To him remained his skill, and his delight in
liquor, in well-spiced meals. Such matters were denied him save
at rare intervals. This was one of them.

He was served food that warmed his stomach, liquor that
flamed in his brain. For him, it was nepenthe. He had no doubt
of the sinister intent of the Griffin. He even admired the
madness that had suggested a method unknown to crime.
Always a cynic, Seventeen came closest to understanding and
appreciating the Griffin.

Seventeen had long ago bartered his soul. He doubted if the
Griffin had ever had one. If it were not for the precision of his
chemistry he might have subscribed to the idea that the Griffin
was a fiend in human shape. Nor did he care, as he guzzled his
curry, drank his burgundy and the brandy that the well-satisfied
Griffin supplied.

In his own chamber, tended by Al, the freak, the Griffin
supped less heartily, but as an epicure. After his meal Al brought
him his water pipe, and he sat in the throne chair behind his
carven desk, inscrutable behind his leprous mask, while the

bubbles formed in the rosewater and the fumes of the drug mounted to his brain.

Al squatted in his appointed spot, upon a cushion, worshipful. The eerie music vibrated, barbarous, voluptuous.

Now and then the Griffin chuckled.

I V

THE HOURS OF DOOM

"HOW LONG have you had this man, where did you get him from?" Manning asked his friend, Bayard Harding.

"About three months. I got him from the Elite Agency, the best in the city. I lost Itabe on my last trip. Enteric fever. But this chap has excellent references. He was with Furnell for six years. Furnell didn't want to take him to Anticosti. The chap's got poor lungs. But he's top-chop as a servant."

"Call Furnell?" asked Manning.

"Yes. He was just leaving. Gave Ali a first-class recommend. Commended him to me, and all that. Don't worry about Ali, Manning."

Manning was not especially worrying about Ali. The man seemed all right, but he was an Oriental, no doubt partly Arab, hailing from the Philippines. The day was the seventeenth, and Manning had taken over, greatly to Harding's amusement.

"Give Ali the day off," he said. "Tell him he won't be needed, any excuse you feel like. But I am telling you, Harding, that you taste nothing, eat nothing, drink nothing, that I do not prepare for you. I have brought in toothpaste and soap, with all other supplies. I know you like my cheroots, but for today you will smoke the regalias I just bought on the avenue."

"Stretching it a bit, when it comes to soap and toothpaste, aren't you, old chap? I hope you've included some Scotch."

"I've got the Scotch. As for the toothpaste, the Griffin tried that once. I have never known him to duplicate his methods, but I am taking no chances. Let Ali stay away until this evening. He need never know we cooked our own meals. We'll clean up. That is, I will."

"Have your own way," said Harding cheerily. "The Griffin is a crank. He can't beat the pair of us. You can be chief cook and bottle-washer, if you insist upon it. You're sleeping here, I suppose?"

Harding took it lightly. He was a big man, healthy and well-built. He was talking with Manning in the library, that was also a sort of trophy room, with many curios, strange weapons, modern guns, and mounted heads of rare specimens Harding had shot.

In one corner there was a mounted forest gorilla. It was a fine specimen of taxidermy, showing the "Old Man" upright, arms extended, as if drumming on its barrel-chest. It stood only four inches below six feet. The ferocious countenance, with its open jaws, was a fearsome thing to look at, even now.

Harding saw Manning glance at it.

"The Griffin didn't fancy being called a cousin of that, eh? I wonder how he'd like to have faced it, alive? I didn't want to kill the beggar. I had all the specimens I wanted. I was only studying their habits, but I suppose he thought I was too nosey. He charged—and he didn't die easily."

Manning was not to be diverted so easily from the matter in hand. He knew Harding was utterly fearless, but that did not armor him against the Griffin. The Griffin's subtle attacks were infinitely more dangerous than a charging male gorilla.

"I'm sleeping here to-night," he said. "In your room. Rather, you can sleep, I'll stay up. An hour from now you enter the time-zone of peril. To-morrow, at midnight, it will have ended. If you are safe, then I can go home with a light heart.

"The Griffin does not repeat an attack. If it goes wrong, he blames it on the sidereal almanac, or some shifting of the ecliptic that has made him miscast your horoscope. You may be sure he did that with you, and believes that the next twenty-four hours after midnight are unfavorable to you, that you are under the malign influence of the stars, of which he is the appointed agent."

"Bilge," said Harding. "Let's see that Scotch."

Manning had not yet unpacked the supplies he had brought, but he now produced whisky and club soda. Ali brought glasses and ice in cubes. Manning regarded the ice a bit dubiously. But he was sure of one thing. Even if the Griffin had somehow contrived to tamper with the cubes, he could also contrive to be certain that Harding did not die, outside of the time he had set. That would be a matter of pride with him.

"Mind if I take seltzer instead?" asked Harding. "I make my own. The club soda is a bit sharp for my taste. It spoils the Scotch, to my mind."

The siphon was empty. Harding unscrewed the top, removed the glass tube, and filled the wired container to the red line with water he drew from a tap in a lavatory that opened off the library.

He took a sparklet from a carton and tossed it to Manning. It was made of metal, the carbonic acid gas inside it hermetically sealed.

"You couldn't tamper with that," said Harding. He set the little cylinder in the charger, screwed it down to the pin, shaking the syphon until the water bubbled with the released gas.

Manning tried it instead of opening up his own soda, and agreed with Harding that it blended well with the whisky. It was still well before twelve, and he gave Harding a cheroot.

"You can have the day off, to-morrow, Ali," Harding told the man when he came to see if there were any more chores. "In fact, you can have to-night off as well. Mr. Manning and I are going to be busy on private matters. You need not come in until nine o'clock to-morrow night."

Ali salaamed and thanked the *tuan*. He seemed pleased with

his unexpected leave. They heard the outer door close. Manning, going over the apartment later, found Ali had departed.

They had plenty to talk over together on subjects of mutual interest and knowledge. Harding finally turned in and slept, while Manning watched.

H E  H A D  been watching Harding's habits, but they did not seem unusual. He noticed, however, that the zoölogist did not brush his teeth before turning in. The next morning Manning presented him with a new tooth brush, sealed almost as hermetically in cellophane as the sparklets were in their metal containers.

Harding chaffed about it all. The day passed without anything out of the way occurring, or being suggested. Manning's meals were simple but appetizing.

He and Harding cleaned up all traces of their culinary work. It did not so much matter about Ali knowing, save that he would not feel it became the dignity of the *tuans* to act as servants.

"Spoil his holiday for him," said Harding. "I've got a notion to change into lighter things, have a shower. It's a warm night. How about you?"

"I'll change after twelve o'clock," Manning answered. As the fateful minutes became more and more limited his responsibility and watchfulness increased.

It was like the monster to plan his murderous coups so that the victim might begin to relax, or else—according to his temperament—become strained to the breaking point.

While Harding took his shower and changed into his lounging pajamas, Manning again made his rounds. There had been certain deliveries made. Manning had taken them in and promptly tabooed them. A clock struck nine.

There was the click of a key in the latch and Ali entered, respectful, smiling, and sober.

He went to his room to shift into his service coat. Manning

went to Harding's bedroom, found Harding cool and comfortable in his loose togs and straw slippers.

"Ali's back," he said. "Better tell him you won't want him again to-night. We'll serve ourselves with what we want in the way of ice and glasses."

"You're not suspecting him because he's a Malay?" asked Harding with a laugh.

"I'd suspect him if he were the Prophet Muhammad, and could prove it," said Manning grimly. "We've got about a hundred and seventy minutes to go, and I'm not going to ease up until they are over."

"There's another bottle of that Mountain Dew left. Let's go into the library and finish it," suggested Harding. "Might take that grim look off your phiz."

Next he took up the ice cubes and got rid of them in the lavatory. He emptied the ewer and squirted out the contents of the siphon.

Harding shrugged his shoulders, but he knew Manning too well not to realize that he would not waste time on dramatic effect. The cubes had been all right the night before—but that was before midnight. They were in the danger zone now.

Ali's room was next to the kitchen. The door closed too tightly to show any light, but Manning heard the thin wailing of an Oriental fiddle. He let the tap run, after he had carefully wiped the orifice; he filled up a tray for fresh cubes, after he had cleaned it. He was leaving nothing to chance.

He set the switch for quick refrigeration, staying there, with one eye on Ali's door. It was not that he suspected Ali, but all things. Eternal vigilance might be the price of his friend's life. Even then....

Against the thin tones of Ali's fiddle, Manning heard Harding strumming an African marimba, with a good sense of rhythm. It was an eerie sort of accompaniment to the drama that might be unfolding its grisly plot at that very moment. The strumming stopped. Manning took out the partially congealed cubes. He did not like to leave Harding alone too long.

He shook up a fresh siphon.

It was nine twenty-five by the electric clock, with its scampering second hand marking the march into eternity.

Manning poured the Scotch for himself, after Harding. Both added ice. Harding squirted in the seltzer water, that fizzed coldly and cheerfully.

"Here's to the next to die," he quoted jestingly.

MANNING'S JUNGLE-TRAINED ear noticed something. Harding, raising his glass, missed it. Ali had stopped playing. It was a trifle, but the difference between life and death.

Harding had taken a long swig of his highball, expecting Manning was doing the same thing.

Suddenly he rose, strangling, stiffening, clutching at the air with hands that grew rigid. Harding dropped before Manning could reach him. Tiny bubbles of thick froth gathered at his lips, his eyes rolled up. His face was livid, then gray, splotched with crimson. He rattled in his throat, clawing at the rug; horrible, gasping for breath.

The Griffin had struck, almost at the eleventh hour.

But for the grace of the gods, Manning felt he would be lying there beside his friend.

The "Analects of Lao Tsze." The habits of your friends and enemies!

Ali had not tampered with the Scotch whisky. It was the seltzer that Harding preferred. But how?

Manning flung open the window. It was his full belief that Harding could not be recalled to life. He could summon medical aid—but there was also the necessity of seizing Ali!

Ali, with his fiddle, who had somehow poisoned the seltzer.

Manning made a dash for the door, entered the main corridor of the apartment, and saw Ali gliding for the entrance. Ali turned and a long knife flashed in his hand.

Manning tackled him bare-handed.

Ali had changed the carton of sparklets in the library. One of the Griffin's slaves in his infernal laboratories had charged them with some fatal gas, and Ali had bided his time. Manning meant to capture him alive.

He locked his left wrist below that of Ali, his forearm thrust through the bend of Ali's arm as he elbowed it back.

His right hand grasped the right wrist of Ali. The fingers of his left hand vised his own right wrist as he faced his opponent. It was a jujutsu armlock with terrific pressure applied to force Ali to let go of the knife or have his wrist dislocated.

Ali countered, falling on his stiffened left arm. He flung his legs about Manning's in a scissors throw, one leg above and one below Manning's knees, destroying his balance.

But Manning fell sideways, his weight lunging into Ali's crotch, both hands free again. Ali squirmed, seeking his knife as Manning went for his gun.

He struck with the muzzle at Ali's skull, and Ali's blade thrust upwards. It entered Manning's forearm; it grated on the bone. In the agony of the nerve shock Manning pulled trigger. The report of the gun thundered in the passage and Ali collapsed, a bullet between his eyes, ranging upward.

There would be no confession from Ali, even if one could ever have been wrung from him.

Manning was bleeding, too. Blood dripped from his arm as he called police headquarters, giving his name.

Every aid that the Griffin had tested on the unfortunate human guinea pig failed to resuscitate Bayard Harding.

The medical examiner bound up Manning's wound. Ali's steel had not been poisoned. The hurt was not dangerous.

"Nothing could have been done," the examiner said. "I'll take the siphon along. I see you didn't take your own drink, Manning. I'm taking that, too. You had a narrow escape."

Manning looked sadly upon the face of his friend. If his own death had saved Harding, had compassed that of the Griffin, he would have been content, he thought.

But the monster had scored again.

V

FACE TO FACE

IT WAS close to dawn when Manning let himself into his own house at Pelham Manor. He switched on a light and wearily went into his own library. His wound throbbed, but more poignant than that was the burden of defeat that clutched at his heart.

His favorite armchair invited him. It was by the side of the hearth, partly facing a lacquered cabinet that stood on high legs. Its paneled doors showed two scowling figures of Chinese gods.

He touched a switch and a shaded light went on beside his chair.

It was occupied by a shape of mystery, shrouded in a cloak.

It was the Griffin—here in Manning's own house! It meant that death must have come to Manning's faithful servitors, that death awaited him.

The Griffin chuckled.

"Face to face at last, Manning. I have been waiting for you. I won the game to-night, but I am tired of you as an opponent. I prepare to clear the board."

Manning's weariness fled. He jerked his gun and fired point-blank at the mocking monster. He knew the slug went true, aimed at the Griffin's heart. He saw the Griffin stagger from the impact, heard his jeering laugh.

The Griffin's knees struck the seat of the big chair and he fell into it. But he was filled with unholy glee. He was not wounded. Bruised, perhaps, beneath a steel vest.

Before Manning could pull trigger again, this time to send a bullet through that leprous mask, the doors of the lacquered cabinet swung silently apart and an apelike thing propelled itself through the air.

The arms of Al went about him. The fingers of Al clamped on Manning's throat with prodigious fury.

His wind was shut off. Hot flames seemed to fill his skull. His bulging eyes saw the Griffin, sitting forward like a devil in hell, watching a soul tortured to death, the mask wrinkled in his fiendish grin.

But this was Manning's house. He had built it, had planned it. The Griffin had his devices—and Manning was not destitute of some of his own.

He rolled over on the floor to the baseboard, hurled himself against it with the last remnant of his strength.

It gave way, swinging on spring hinges. This opening was not of wood, but steel. It gave into a narrow closet that opened on another room.

Al was scraped from Manning's back. A shrill contact alarm rang out as the panel snapped back and an automatic plunger held it fast.

Manning lay there, panting, choking, safe enough.

The alarm rang on.

It sounded at the nearest police station. But when the radio patrol cars arrived, the Griffin and his freak had vanished.

# THE GRIFFIN'S LIVING DEATH

*Doomed to Become a Living Corpse—This
Was the Fate That Awaited Manning as the
Griffin Prepared His Most Diabolic Trap*

## I

## THE MONSTER'S TRAIL

ALTHOUGH TIME was the one thing he could not afford to waste, Gordon Manning did not use the police siren allotted to him by the department. He did not dare in any way to make his progress conspicuous, despite the fact that he had made arrangements for a quick and secret shift from his own to another car, before he got out of the city.

For the first time it began to look as if the use of his peculiar type of agents to close in on the Griffin, to discover the secret lair of that homicidal mad monster, were about to be crowned with at least some measure of success.

But Manning was well aware that he himself might be under the constant surveillance of the Griffin's own men, and they would work as mysteriously, be as much under cover and hard to distinguish as Manning's own private corps.

One slip might spoil everything. At any moment that evil genius might become suspicious. It was hard to cope with the swift changes of an eccentric but brilliant mind.

It was best to strike the moment the iron became tolerably warm, rather than wait until it was hot and glowing.

For long, weary weeks, Manning had been receiving the reports of his unprofessional but efficient spies. It had seemed hopeless work, while every now and then the Griffin struck sometimes with warning, sometimes without.

When he warned, it was because of a belief in his own invincibility, the belief that the stars were in favorable aspect for the success of his crimes. Such warnings were intended to strike terror to the soul of the victim and those who loved him—or her. To fray the steady, strong nerves of Manning, always attuned to the thrill of evil, the expectation of hearing the Griffin's mocking voice announce a new murder of some one the world badly needed; or receiving a letter to that effect in the Griffin's characteristic writing, signed by his scarlet seal—scarlet as fresh-spilled blood, and stamped with his symbol.

NOW MANNING was on his way, summoned to a rendezvous where one of his men waited to point out the trail to the Griffin's den.

Such a job had been like the assembling of a mammoth jigsaw puzzle, handicapped by an intricate and confusing design, and the fact that the pieces had to be picked up here and there, scraps that seemed impossible to weave into the answer.

For weeks Manning had been plotting circles and triangles within which he would gradually narrow the limits of the neighborhood where the Griffin had his aerie.

That lair, Manning had concluded, was within fifty miles of City Hall, New York. That was a territory that included three States in its scope. None knew better than Manning how many places it held that were still rural, remote from the general lines of travel.

Radio and telephone may link up a house with civilization; a mile of dirt road and a lack of street lighting keeps it a place apart. The rapidly increasing mixture of cosmopolitan population, in both city and country, breaks up the old neighborliness.

Manning believed the lair was north, from the beginning; probably somewhere in Putnam, Dutchess or Rockland Counties, with the last doubtful. New Jersey had the handicap of too easily checked tunnels or slow-moving ferries. Long Island was

*Manning saw the bloodless countenance bending over him.*

not hard to scout and Manning had dismissed it before his first clews began to point to the north. Connecticut was, of course, a possibility.

But this tip, from one of his own agents, swung the needle of suspicion steadily north. There were hamlets in Putnam and Duchess where woods were still thick about them, railroads well away. They had been the centers for farmers before most of the farms went back to sumach and thornapple. Now they had dwindled to a disconsolate general store or so. The mills no longer ran; deserted houses stood about, reached only by wood roads. Houses that dated back to the days before George Washington wooed Mary Philipse at Philipse Manor, near Carmel, in Putnam County, and was refused.

There are, believe it or not, forgotten villages within that radius, where the main attraction for the winter is The Swiss Bell Ringer, playing the *Blue Danube Waltz*.

In such a place the Griffin lurked.

MANNING WOVE his way through traffic expertly. Near

the bridge that must take him out of Manhattan, he swung off the street into a garage. He stepped swiftly from his roadster into the closed van of a dyeing and cleaning establishment, and was driven off immediately to another garage, where he transferred again to another roadster, of different make and color from his own, but equally as powerful.

He had used this method of throwing off possible espionage before. He had no reason to think that he had been followed, even to the first garage; but precaution was paramount if the Griffin was going to be caught. Nothing would be learned at the garage. They knew who he was—Gordon Manning, special-service agent, commissioned to eliminate the Griffin.

Manning had brought him in once, and the clumsy law, working on medieval procedure, had called the Griffin mad, legally irresponsible for his hideous crimes. They had locked him up in Dannemora, and the Griffin had not stayed there long.

Next time—this time, Manning prayed it might be as he sped along the parkway—Manning was going to assume responsibility. If he closed in and the Griffin gave him the excuse, as no doubt he would, Manning meant to bring back a dead monster, eliminated beyond all recall.

Manning's present method, continued steadily, aside from the events furnished by some new crime of the Griffin, was similar to that of the old bee-hunters who roamed the prairies, catching bees as they went, letting them escape, marking their lines of flight.

Where those lines converged there would be their prize, a dead limb of some tree, dripping with luscious honey.

Manning's "bees" were the cars in which the Griffin, or his agents, escaped from the scenes of horror. Many times those cars were the same machine, and carried the Griffin. It was a long-hooded sedan of the most expensive make. It was black, shining with the rich luster of enamel. Many rich men had cars like it, and it was not easy to distinguish.

It seemed certain that the Griffin had a more powerful engine than the one originally sold with that make. He had left Manning's fast roadster behind, more than once. There was no doubt that the license number was frequently changed, that it could be shifted automatically as the car sped along.

The flight of these "bees" was of course broken by the very nature of the routes taken by the cars, by the odds of a deliberately twisted course; yet, little by little, they had converged to what should be a common center.

And Manning had established, within the narrowing area of his search, both key men and field men.

He had picked them from all ages. Some were learned and others could not spell properly. They had no headquarters; only few of them came in contact with each other.

Now he was bound for a key man, a good mechanic who had been glad to be placed in charge of a roadside garage and machine shop. There was not much trade, but the profits were all his, aside from the salary Manning paid him and the prospects of bonuses. Manning got a public telephone booth installed in the garage, which brought Farrell close to village gossip.

It was through Farrell, and a field man, Bishop, that Manning was making this play. His agents made themselves known to be in good standing with each other by the use of code words, changed every three days. A man not in possession of the last word was to be considered untrustworthy.

Though he picked carefully, paid well, and knew them grateful, Manning was careful. It was not that he mistrusted them so much, as his knowledge of human nature. The Griffin had unlimited means. He could offer a sum to a man that would, after months of poverty and distress, tempt him beyond his powers. Or he could threaten, he could strike. Once let him suspect one of Manning's spies and he would surely either bribe the man to be a traitor, or make away with him.

## 11

## THE FLYING DEATH

FARRELL WAS thirty-odd, unmarried, ambitious and straightforward. As garageman he did not play a hard rôle.

Bishop was over fifty. A man who had had much and seen it swept away. His wife was dead, his children scattered, all their prospects sunk in the depression.

But he had spirit in him yet. He had at one time in his youth been an actor, playing character parts. Money left him, and the breakdown of stock and repertoire companies by the movies had led him to business successes that the crash of '29 had ruined.

He could still act. It was Bishop who had reported, through Farrell, the present lead. He had seen the Griffin's car four times within the past two weeks. Its appearance in that neighborhood was like the hot scent of a fox to a wise hound.

Bishop posed as a down-and-outer, begging odd jobs, slouching about the fields. Sometimes he was a mushroom picker, with a few mushrooms in his worn basket. He trailed from farm to farm, and house to house, choosing hours when the Griffin's car was least likely to be on the road, mostly after dark.

He too picked up gossip and he compiled a sort of record, as did other field men, of the people in that vicinity, and how they lived. That was not easy. Many were of foreign birth, close-mouthed, especially to derelicts; many spoke only broken Americanese.

There were houses here and there that had been restored, or partly restored, from Colonial days. Some of these were vacant these hard times; others had caretakers of various kinds, often poor relatives, who shut the door in the face of any rover.

Manning analyzed these descriptions, set aside the most likely. In this locale, patrolled by Bishop, there was an ancient house that had fallen, with its family, upon evil days. Once it had been the stately manor house of a King's Grant, now it stood in a few forlorn acres, unpainted and decrepit. There were first growth trees, some dying, others blighted chestnuts, about a melancholy mere that had known more than one suicide. There was a private graveyard, with the stones tilted, the mounds heaved or fallen in, the inscriptions hardly to be read.

The natives called it haunted, not the only one on Manning's list. A surly man and his bitter-faced wife lived there, keeping to themselves, buying cheap and scanty supplies.

For the Griffin, such a place might be a perfect camouflage, if it provided certain conveniences. Such as a site for the laboratories where the Griffin kept his nameless slaves at work for him.

They too were derelicts, like Manning's men; but these slaves had sinned against the law, escaped from its penalties, and the Griffin held them in thrall through knowledge of their guilt. Most of them had been in high rank in the professions from which they had been banished.

MANNING TURNED off the State highway, through the forgotten and almost abandoned village, over a bridge and by a broken dam. The dirt road was poorly kept, the taxes raised in such a section were small and highway commissioners and supervisors ignored the byways.

Stone walls crumbled, hedges grew rank, fields lay overgrown with weeds and brush. Old red barns sagged, farmhouses stood forlorn on the hills, untenanted. The ditches were clogged. Once in a while he saw gaunt cows, trying to keep alive in worn-out pastures.

Poverty reigned, with neglect. The only merit to the district in the eyes of travelers lay in the fact that here was a short cut to the bridge across the Hudson, if the weather were good.

There was an unused schoolhouse, no better than a shack. The children were picked up and taken to a central school. Gardens were neglected, save for a few, poor vegetables. He passed few cars and those were relics, chattering and staggering along, keeping together by a miracle, a prayer, and baling wire. Few people.

This was called Cow Hollow. Less than fifty miles from New York, sinking yearly into worse condition. Gnarled orchards strove to bear a little bitter, wormy fruit, not worth the picking.

Manning stopped at Farrell's garage. He did all the business there was in the neighborhood, largely because he seemed inclined to give credit. Most of those who hung him up for gasoline or repairs on one of their rattletraps considered him a sucker.

He came out, and Manning ordered oil, not wanting to mix his own ethyl with the gas Farrell handled. The oil *was* his own brand, kept for such a time by Farrell.

There was nobody about. Farrell could talk freely.

"Bishop gave me the new code word yesterday," he said. "Before I telephoned through to you. He's seen that car three times this week, including yesterday. It comes through between three and three forty-five in the afternoon."

Manning glanced at his wrist watch. It was two forty-seven.

"He knows it's the same car," Farrell went on, "though it has a different number each time, because its been in a smash some time, and it's got a new rear fender on the right side. They did a good enough job putting it on, but it hugs the chassis a bit. I noticed that the time it stopped here and asked was this the right road to the bridge. That was a stall. They saw me outside and wanted to ask questions of me, see? I told 'em what you said for me to say."

Manning nodded. Farrell was a good man.

"So I tipped Bishop off. You only notice this when the car's passing you. They saw me looking at it but they didn't know why. I only really saw the chauffeur. He had a sour puss, looked like it was cut out of a turnip. The one in the back might have been the Griffin. The blinds were drawn and I could just see there was someone. I told 'em I didn't expect to see such a fine car out here and he said it was because of the short cut."

"Been by here since?" asked Manning.

"No. They must come in over Grimm's hill. But they swing in to the road where Bishop sees 'em. They can turn off that to get to the bridge, though it's not the best way. Still, folks often get mixed up on the short cut. If you don't turn off the road it leads to the place they call Manor House, the spooky dump you know about. Used to go on through to the river, I guess, but now the road peters out beyond the graveyard. Nobody uses it."

"Where shall I find Bishop?" asked Manning.

"You can turn in at Three Elm Farm. Nobody living there now. Only two elms left. You can see 'em plain from this road. They're by the farmhouse. No gate, and rough going, but you can make it. Cut right across the farm behind the house, down an old cow lane to where the mailbox used to be. Just the post there now. There's some trees and scrub where you can park out of sight if you want to. The fence is down along the Manor House road. Bishop'll be loafing round there to tell you if the car has passed or not.

"And he'll show you yesterday's tire tracks. It rained yesterday morning. If they ain't changed 'em. I doubt it. They're the regular tires for that car, and the rubber's new. Unless they figured you had spotted the car, otherwise they'd likely keep 'em on."

"Good man," said Manning. He looked at his watch again. "I'll be going." He handed Farrell a twenty-dollar bill. "Bonus," he said.

IT WAS two minutes before three. With luck, he would get in touch with Bishop before the car passed. But luck, he knew, was too often with the Griffin.

For some reason the Griffin had been making regular trips. And that meant deviltry.

It began to look as if the Manor House might be the lair. Three Elm Farm was not the place. The shutters hung crazily, the chimneys were tumbling down; there was not the track of tire or hoof, or even the pads of a roaming, hungry dog upon the place.

Manning drove down the cow lane, came to some street choked with wild grapevine. He was above the Manor House road, but hidden from it.

He braked, hesitant. To his left, a man shambled dejectedly along, using a stick, a basket like a fisherman's creel upon his back. A tramp, a mushroom picker—Bishop.

To the right, he saw a car advancing, a long, black car. It came on at a good fifty miles an hour, its weight—and the skill of the driver—seeming to ignore the inequalities of the dirt road. Now and then it swerved, or swayed a little, but it held a fair course.

It neared the shambling figure, which moved towards the ditch, humble and insignificant.

Suddenly Manning threw off his brakes, snatched a heavy automatic from a side pocket, and went rocketing down the slope. He made a beeline for where the fence was broken, distant from where a path had once led to the mailbox.

He dodged sumach, thornapples, plunged through a thicket, surged through second growth and saplings that made his passage a minor miracle. The gun was tucked under his thigh. He risked a blowout every second, but he trod hard on the gas. Now he could not see the road and every pulse-beat seemed to tick off the fatal message—that he would arrive too late.

The Griffin had been ahead of schedule, if there *was* a schedule. Bishop had been faithfully ahead of time. He was to pay for that faithfulness with a hideous death.

Perhaps the Griffin had suspected or merely disliked his presence on that road. It would take little for that monster to get rid of anything he deemed the slightest nuisance.

Manning had seen a thing that would have seemed unbelievable to any one not acquainted with the Griffin.

AS THE long car sped, it suddenly accumulated pace. A weird, incredible figure, like some nightmare fantasy, like a shattered gargoyle plucked from an age-old cathedral, swung to the running board. It clung there, legless, one apelike arm through the open window.

The lonely landscape held no other living things. The rushing car—Bishop—Manning, thundering, bounding down the slope, avoiding disaster by split-seconds.

Only a flock of somber crows cawed through the air, witnesses of Death, striking fiendishly.

It was Al, the legless freak bought by the Griffin from a traveling circus, a deaf mute with an atrophied soul and brain, corrupted by his new master.

In its free hand the freak held something that looked like a lance, or a sharpened pole. The big car raced, charging, hemming in Bishop against the fallen fence and the hedge that backed it.

The young trees blotted that out for Manning. He had all he could do to avoid them. He could not. His running board and fenders struck them, dented and crumpled. A buried snag tore a tire and he barely escaped collision with a stump. He held on, lurching on a rim, his arms and wrists wrenched.

He crashed through the tangled fence, smashed rotten rider poles, plunged into the ditch, skidding to the road, twisting and turning on the surface, still slimy with yesterday's rain.

He wound up with his back bumper bent against a fallen stone wall on the far side, leaped out, gun in hand.

The black car was out of sight.

Something lay twisted in the opposite ditch. A body thrust through and through with a lance, writhing in the last, convulsive agonies of death, bloody and distorted.

Manning stood over Bishop—what had been Bishop. He had seen death in many shapes but none worse than this. For a moment his blood ran cold.

Bishop was impaled upon a stake six feet long. It had been armed with a point of wrought iron, now clotted with crimson.

Al had held that lance, or had flung it. The latter was more probable. The car, with its tremendous speed, perhaps seventy miles or more at the moment, had provided the frightful impetus that had taken Bishop off his feet, as the spear sheared through belly and backbone until half of it stuck out behind; left him like an impaled beetle, squirming and gasping as he died.

The tire tracks were plain in the road. But here was the dead man, and Manning's car was stranded with a jammed brake, a bent axle, a blown tire and twisted steering gear.

The body that had been Bishop gasped its last breath.

The cawing crows came wheeling back, as if they saw or scented carrion. And Manning stood gun in hand, powerless.

### I I I

### THE LIVING DEATH

A L , T H E deaf mute, legless freak, squatted on a square hassock in a corner of the Griffin's private chamber. There was no morality in him. Killing was a delight, the instinct implanted in him as it is in some epileptics who commit homicide instead of having convulsions.

And now this abnormality, whose clothing was sprinkled with the blood that spurted from poor Bishop as the car rushed past, was enjoying his reward with complacency. He squatted on his legless trunk, with an all-day-sucker thrust into his mouth, blissfully absorbing it.

When Al had been in the museum of the circus, he had put on an exhibition of shooting arrows, hurling lances and flinging knives. It was this performance that had helped decide the Griffin to buy off the freak.

This afternoon he had made use of Al's accomplishments, staging it to suit his own love of the bizarre, adding the force and fury of the speeding car.

The Griffin had not been definitely suspicious of Bishop, nor of Farrell, but it had struck him that the lonely neighborhood had rather suddenly acquired an increase of population. He had noticed Bishop several times. He might be tramp or mushroom picker or he might be a spy. The fact he was an interloper on territory the Griffin reserved for himself, the merest thought that he might be scouting for Manning or the police, sufficed for his warranty of death.

The Griffin, seated in comfort in his car, had watched the killing with the sadistic delight of a Nero. Human lives meant no more to him than those of the guinea pigs, rats and mice used by scientists in their researches. But the Griffin experimented for no cause but his own. He was indeed like Nero, who encouraged Locusta, the poisoner, by providing her with slaves on which to experiment.

Now the Griffin sat gloating behind his carven desk as Al guzzled his sweet. The Griffin's features were screened by the mask of thin material that looked like goldbeater's skin, like the skin of a snake just before shedding. He looked like some ancient conception of Mephisto. The mask twitched to his grimace as he recalled the dying contortions of Bishop—who might or might not have been a spy.

He sucked at the amber mouthpiece of a hookah pipe, and the bubbles danced in the rose-scented water that cooled the smoke. The bowl burned to ashes and the Griffin rose, and began to pace up and down his chamber. He was clad in a long black robe of heavy silk brocaded with cabalistic designs. A sable skullcap was on his head.

There had been amber as well as hasheesh in the pipe, and now the fumes of the former gained ascendancy. From some unseen source music sounded in a barbaric strain of drums and cymbals, of pipes and stringed instruments.

THE GRIFFIN seemed to talk to the freak, with whom he could actually communicate only by signs; but the mad monster was really talking loud. Boasting to himself, loving the sound of his voice, the proclamation of his intentions.

"It was well done, Al," he said. "It was nobly done. He leaped and fell, like one smitten by the shaft of a centaur. Though you are far from that. But it was a good play.

"It has been in my mind that there are too many new and strange faces that follow me about. Gordon Manning on the trail. The fool! Does he think to trap me again and send me to that madhouse. Ha! Forewarned is forearmed, Al. He who strikes first strikes shrewdest. So—we shall strike. Manning shall be the victim. Long ago I promised him an unusual death. And he shall have one. This very day it is perfected. And, by Ahriman and Abaddon, not all the hosts of heaven, not all the fiends of hell shall save him!"

A bronze disk supported between pillars suddenly boomed sonorously. It was the signal that Griffin had been expecting. In the wall a space was suddenly revealed, the entrance to a lift that the Griffin entered, forbidding Al to follow by a gesture. The hidden door closed, the lift descended, going to the cellars of the old manor, now enlarged and converted into laboratories where the Griffin's evil genii worked his perverted will.

Left alone, Al sulked, then sucked at his candy. He set it aside and swung himself on his palms to the desk. He looked around, like a mischievous ape, at once curious and fearful. The booming of the gong made certain impressions upon his atrophied sense. He knew that it summoned the Griffin, that it announced events.

He balanced his torso with one arm, reached up the other hand and touched timidly the disk. Out of it there came a spurt and crackle of blue sparks and tiny lightnings. The shock of the discharge stung through the freak, bowled him over, his arms numb, his ugly face convulsed as he gave vent to a hideous, bestial cry that he sought to stifle by stuffing one sluggish hand into his mouth.

He rolled to his hassock and lay there while his flesh seemed stabbed with pins and needles. His God, the omnipotent, all seeing, ever present Griffin, had punished him for his sin. Al was cured of meddling. The more so as he had seen his Master touch and tap the plaque without harm; not knowing the Griffin had thrown a switch before he left the chamber.

Al moaned, with uncouth noises, drooling and gabbling. At last, finding himself recovered, he retrieved his sweet, and squatted once more on the hassock, educated and subdued.

BELOW, THE GRIFFIN stalked through cemented corridors just high enough for him to pass without bowing, and came to a central crypt. This was his theater—like the theater of a hospital. Here things were dissected, inanimate objects assembled, demonstrations made. A man awaited him, more like a robot than a human being. He wore an overall of yellow on which was painted, back and front, the numerals 67. His face was the hue of beeswax, bloodless, expressionless. His lips were without hue; the only color showed in his eyes, intensely blue, blazing behind lenses that enlarged them, made them goggle, glow with something akin to insanity.

Innumerable wrinkles radiated about his eyes and mouth. He was entirely bald. His shaggy eyebrows were white. But there was still a restrained vigor about him. Number Sixty-Seven had been a famous chemist, a toxicologist who had mixed up his subtle poisons with his own cosmos.

The Griffin had snatched him from the chaos that resulted. Here was a slave after his own evil heart. He had made a pawn of the other, rescued him from the death penalty to transfer him to a hideous servitude only mitigated by the fact that Sixty-Seven was given apparatus and allowed to use his alembics in experiments. The Griffin consulted him, and Sixty-Seven knew well enough why.

There had been a time when despair came to him, followed by a measure of resignation; of late he had been restless. This last task had pleased him, strengthened the perversion of spirit that he had gradually accumulated, as if partaking of the Griffin's unholy nature through association.

It was the Griffin himself who had suggested the source of the present experiment. Sixty-Seven had perfected it.

There were two draped figures on narrow tables. One sheeted form was quite still, yet not entirely rigid. There was something about it that suggested life was not extinct. The other covering moved slightly as if the unmistakable body beneath it breathed. Now and then there were twitchings.

The Griffin frowned at this and Sixty-Seven spoke swiftly. "This is the example in which the toxin was first used upon a human subject. It proved not to be sufficiently concentrated. You told me you did not mind how many subjects I used from the numbers you supplied me."

"True, so long as you succeeded. Those men have passed their utility to me. But why show me a failure?"

"I shall show you also a perfect success. I thought that you might like to see both phases. The first man will ultimately die. He has suffered frightful torments. He is now anaesthetized by pain. He can bear no more."

SIXTY-SEVEN STRIPPED off the coarse shroud. The body of the "subject" was emaciated—the Griffin did not feed his slaves too munificently—but it was also horribly swollen. It looked like something badly stuffed. The limbs were shapeless and blotched, the veins like black cord, twisted and coiled. The lips were drawn back, and the teeth showed between the bloodless gums like those of a skull. Only the blood-specked white of his eyes showed. They seemed to be staring inwards.

"This is after twenty hours," said Sixty-Seven. "I doubt if I could save him, even if I had prepared an anti-toxin. No one else could. They could never determine the toxin. There are no known tests for it."

"He looks as if he had been bitten by a snake," said the Griffin. "Let us see the other one."

Sixty-Seven covered the blotched man, whose body still twitched to the pain engendered by the toxin, though the worn-out consciousness no longer registered.

There were no such terrible stigmata on the second body that lay exposed and nude. The eyes were open but fixed.

They did not respond to touch or movement, but there was a horror manifest in the distended pupils, the narrowed irises.

Like the first, this body was ill nourished, but it showed no sign of violence, or of agony, beyond the haunting horror in the immobile orbs. The breath misted the mirror Sixty-Seven placed to the slightly parted lips and the chest rose and fell almost imperceptibly. The limbs were plastic, the flesh seemed normal but it was cold as that of a cadaver.

Sixty-Seven thrust a lancet into the nearer arm. No blood followed the withdrawal.

"The heart has ceased to beat, the arterial system is idle. This is after twelve hours. It is a perfect state of suspended animation. He will be dead, to all intents and purposes, within another hour. But there will be no decay. Not for many weeks. He is embalmed alive. While alive."

The Griffin frowned again.

"It is good," he said, "but not all I had hoped. He will die too soon."

"I can modify the toxin so that the subject will not lose consciousness, as this one nearly has, for days, for a week, perhaps more."

"Good. And the brain?"

"The subconscious cerebration will cease, but he will know he is alive. Until life—as we term it—finally passes, he will be able to think, he will remember, he will imagine the future."

The Griffin chuckled. He tapped Sixty-Seven on his shoulder, leaned on him and began to shake with ghoulish laughter.

"It is excellent," he cried at last. "I was not sure when you showed me the two which I might choose, after all. The torment or the peace, with perfect understanding. I select the latter. The living death. The torture in the brain. I shall bring you your subject soon. And then, Sixty-Seven, name your reward."

The magnified blue eyes flamed behind the lenses. "You mean—whatever I wish?"

"I have said so," replied the Griffin magnificently.

"Freedom, that is what I want. I want the sun, I want to mingle again with men—and women."

"Strange talk for a scientist. Yet you wizards are often very human. It was a question of women that brought you here, I remember. Would have taken you to the chair, if I had not intervened. If I gave you freedom you are apt to land there yet."

"Who would know me?" Sixty-Seven burst out bitterly. "Look at me, forty in years, seventy in appearance. Old enough, in seeming, to be my own father. But young enough to want to use my life. I could leave the country. I could...."

The Griffin checked him. "You shall have your freedom," he said. "Complete and absolute. After you have done this thing for me."

He turned away. Sixty-Seven gazed at him with an expression hard to interpret.

"What shall be done with these?" he asked. "The first will corrupt before long."

"Dispose of it. Have the other set aside for observation. Interesting things may be done with living death, if only for exhibition, and an object lesson."

"And I shall be free?"

"You have my promise, after you have served my purpose."

Sixty-Seven stared after the Griffin's departing figure. His lips moved as he muttered silently.

"Freedom, complete and absolute! I have his word."

The Griffin had disappeared. From the stone passage there came a chuckle. The low roof echoed it.

## IV

## RACE TO DEATH

GORDON MANNING, in the study of his house at Pelham Manor after dinner, preparing to enjoy a cheroot and a liqueur, was not surprised when Mizu, his Japanese butler, brought in a letter, instead of the Eau-de-vie de Dantzig.

One might never be surprised at a madman's whimsies, murderous though they were. The Griffin had struck the day before, though Al's hand had held the lethal weapon. The sight of blood, of death, had whetted the monster's appetite perhaps; or he might be merely boasting, not knowing Manning had seen the crime.

The letter was in the usual gray envelope of thick, hand-made paper. Manning could see it had been sealed with a scarlet *affiche*, an oval stamped with a demi-griffin in relief. The address was in purple.

How it had been delivered did not much matter, he thought, a trifle wearily. The Griffin was not to be so easily traced. He listened to Mizu's half apologetic explanation.

"The berring, verree, ritter ring, but I hear. I put on chain, open ritter bit. This retter come through, prease excuse."

"Excuse what, Mizu?"

"Excuse I no rook. You terr me be carefur. I pick up this, shut door."

"That's all right, Mizu. Bring in the liqueur."

Manning broke the seal, glanced almost casually at the few lines. Whatever this might be, he had already prepared a counter-stroke.

Farrell had taken his damaged car back to the garage, taken along Bishop's body, from which Manning had wrenched the lance.

Police regulations did not count where Manning was concerned with the Griffin. The medical-examiner could be dispensed with in his capacity of being the first to arrive on the scene. And the local authorities would be subordinate to those Manning summoned.

He wanted to fade out of the picture for the time. There had been no other witnesses but the crows. The tracks of the black sedan were still there, not to be traced immediately.

The Griffin was wanton enough in his slayings but there must have been some suspicion behind this one. He would be alert to watch for any follow up, though Manning doubted if he would return, in person or by an agent, to the scene of his crime.

That was, Manning fancied, perilously close to his lair. The Manor House must be investigated if, as Manning felt they did, the tire tracks led there. But it was best to let the Griffin think he had definitely succeeded. His madness must be growing for him to be this reckless. It was his swollen ego, inevitably leading him on to what he might consider a sort of divine immunity, granted to him, the appointed servant of the stars.

Manning had prepared the net to be drawn. He had consulted with the commissioner, made plans that would be put in motion at midnight. Then Manning, in his own roadster, would join the picked New York detail at Farmers' Mills. The commissioner would be there in person.

IT WAS a few minutes after eight. Manning drew the straw from his cheroot, lit it carefully, inhaled the first fragrant pull before he read.

> My dear Manning:
> This notifies you of my next elimination. But not of the date. You must puzzle that out. Briefly, I am tired of you. You do not play the game properly. You move pieces in ways the rules do not permit. You have won a game or two, but I no longer propose to lose.
> I am sweeping the board, so far as you are concerned. You no longer amuse me. The name of my next "victim," as the

papers style it, is Gordon Manning.

In this the stars are with me. Put your affairs in order, Manning, for you are about to die. And, as I promised, I have designed for you a demise both fitting and unique.

For the last time, for you, I sign myself.

The signature was a sketch of a griffin, excellently drawn above a blob of crimson wax.

It was not really news to Manning. He knew the Griffin had many times tried to kill him. This would be a special and concentrated attempt, but it did not disturb him. He was striking first.

The tire-tracks had been followed that afternoon, closely enough to know they led to the manor, beyond which there was no road. The Griffin had been traced to his lair. The place would be surrounded. Manning had heard the short speech the commissioner had made to his subordinates.

"The man who shoots and kills the Griffin will be promoted. He will be praised by the whole nation. The Griffin is to be treated like a mad dog. Major Manning will have charge of the detail, and I shall be along."

Mizu came with the square bottle, where flecks of gold danced in the liqueur he poured into the tubelike glass.

"Prease, I hope nothing wrong," he said anxiously.

"Nothing wrong, everything very right, Mizu."

Manning let the slick potion glide down his throat. He drank silently to the confusion of the Griffin, to his death. The world would breathe easier. This insane, satanic monster had disrupted social and financial circles, had destroyed the most worthy. His demise would be the resurrection of public confidence. While such a fiend stalked free, the very stability of government was threatened.

He picked up the letter again. The gray paper had changed color, or seemed to. So with the ink. The writing was no longer firm. Everything was fading.

And Mizu was standing, watching.

Manning fought with the lethargy that surged upon him. He forced his tongue to speak, his will to function, while swift thought rocketed through his brain.

The Griffin had not named the hour. He had not *meant* to give enough grace to Manning to "put affairs in order." He had designed a "unique death!" This was not it. It was only the preliminary. After all, the Griffin had struck first.

"Mizu," said Manning with his stumbling tongue, his thickening speech he strove to make distinct, "what have you done? What did you put in this drink?"

He looked at Mizu in a haze that grew denser. He heard Mizu's voice, mocking.

"Mister Manning, I verree sorree, but my honoraber nation not rike your American nation. You try keep us verree down. Pretty soon we fight. Pretty soon we take. Me, I am officer on staff of Imperiar councir. Here I am butrer, but rearry major. Pretty soon generar, I think. I rike money to back Japan. My famiry not rich. Money arways good for man with ambition. The one who sent that retter give prenty money to me and Yamato. Now we prenty rich. *Sodiska*."

The final sentences faded out like shadows in the sun. Mizu, and Yamato, smitten by dreams of grandeur, even as the Griffin, had betrayed him.

Manning slumped in his chair.

ALL WAS blurred until he felt himself reviving. The rim of a glass was between his lips. A man stroked his throat, inducing swallowing. He gulped, involuntarily, and his head cleared. But there was no vigor to his limbs.

He looked up into the masked face of the Griffin, gloating behind the screening skin, his eyes glittering through slits.

"False move, Manning. You thought you were a roving pawn, moving across the board to where you could move, as the queen moves, and close the game. But I castled. It is checkmate. Now I'll tell you what I am going to do with you."

Manning wondered what the time was. Not much more than

ten o'clock. Two hours until midnight. They would wait for him at Farmers Mills, delay indefinitely. Meanwhile—he was lying on a table in a crypt with cemented walls. He could not move. He was bound, hand and foot, and the drug still gripped him, though the effect was passing.

He saw the Griffin, robed in sable, masked with a leprous film. He twisted his neck painfully and saw Al, the freak, squatting like a creature in an obscene nightmare. Two figures in overalls, with numbers painted on them. One number was Sixty-Seven. The man was bald, pallid, wrinkled, with weird, mad, blue eyes back of powerful lenses. This one felt his pulse, nodded.

"I'll tell you about the fitting death I have devised for you," said the Griffin. "You have the distinction of being the first to experience it. You know, of course, of the Hymenoptera—the stinging and social insects. Bees, wasps, hornets, ants. In your travels you must have encountered them. Some of them, most of them, are carnivorous, cannibalistic. They feed their young and themselves upon the bodies of their victims which they sting into paralysis. That venom has the rare, antiseptic faculty of being able to preserve the meat they drag into their larders.

"Another case of the spider and the fly. I had a notion that you meant to come into my parlor, Manning, but I have forestalled that, and brought you here. Taking an advantage of the misunderstanding between Japan and America, of the perhaps inflated ideas of certain Japanese loyalists, who are overeager for a final adjustment.

"Bees have stung men to death. The digger-wasps possess a vicious venom. They belong to the genus Sphex. The *pepsis femoratus* stores its burrows with the great tarantula spiders, highly poisonous themselves, but less agile. As *you* have been less agile. Sometimes they kill, mostly they reduce their prey to a state of immobility. That is the method I have adopted, concentrating their venom with the expert aid of number Sixty-Seven, here present, who will now inject you with the toxin.

"I shall leave you a living corpse, Manning. Even if you were found, you could not be restored. Your brain will function for a few days, as you recount your sins, your follies, your stupidity in pitting yourself against the Griffin.

"The Zodiac declares that this is the time when the heavenly powers desert you. I am going to place you in the mortuary of this manor, in an empty coffin, from which I have strewn the bones that thought they claimed it. Later, I may arrange to have you found, exhibited, living but dead, until corruption slowly decays you.

"In the meantime, since you may have been too active, and be traced too soon, I am departing. For some time I have sought and found a better place for my righteous activities. But you"—the Griffin's mask quivered with the intensity of his hate—"*you* will no longer irk me. You will cease to exist, save as your brain knows you are doomed, like an envenomed larva. Inject him, Sixty-Seven."

Manning saw the bloodless countenance bending over him, felt the prick of a needle in his arm.

"You will stay here," the Griffin ordered his slave, "while I conduct the final preparations for leaving. Then you shall be freed. Manning, you have made your last move. The game is over."

MANNING WAITED for the paralysis to set in. A light burned low in the ceiling of the crypt. It was shadowed by the figure of Sixty-Seven, who bent over him.

"You are his enemy, the man who seeks to destroy him? You are Gordon Manning?" whispered Sixty-Seven.

Manning nodded. The blue eyes were glaring down. How did this serf know of Manning? As if he read the thought, the other answered.

"He told me who you were. His enemy—and mine. You represent the law. Now you are helpless. Never mind who I am—or was. If I free you, if I help to deliver him to you, will you help me?"

Manning made no compromise, though it was not his own plight he considered. Whoever this Sixty-Seven might be, might have done, he was an angel compared with the Griffin.

"What do you want?" he asked.

"I need money. I need clothes. Then I can escape. I did not inject you with the real venom. I will release you. We can both get away."

"I've got money with me," said Manning. "I'll change clothes with you. I don't know who you are, how you came under the Griffin's power. But we want *him* more than you. Do you know what time it is?"

"Night. But what day, what week or month, even what year, I cannot tell. Only let me go free."

"We'll change clothes," said Manning, "but how do you get out of here? As for the time, I've got a wrist watch."

"There is no ventilating system," said Sixty-Seven, "but I have studied the drafts. There is a way to the open. I have seen him and that unhallowed freak of his pass out, and smelled free air. If he leaves he will not bother with us who live underground. We are all condemned. We cannot tell who he is or where he goes. It's eleven-fifty, by your watch."

In ten minutes the commissioner would be assembling his forces, seven miles away. How long he would wait for Manning was hard to say.

Sixty-Seven severed Manning's bonds with a scalpel. They changed clothes swiftly, crept out to a corridor.

"The exit is this way," said Sixty-Seven. "I can feel the air. Do you want to come with me? I have freed you. There is an elevator to his quarters."

"It will be an automatic," said Manning, "I'll go with you. I suppose I'm compounding a felony in this."

"Listen," said Sixty-Seven. "I killed her. I admit that. She deserved it. When I'm away, it won't be where they'll extradite me. I'll write the truth. Not about this. But I'll give proof that she betrayed me. And, take this."

He pressed a small metal case into Manning's hand.

"This is the hypo, charged with the wasp venom. You may need it. Stick it into that fiend, if you get the chance."

IT SEEMED to Manning a fitting instrument, but he doubted if he would have the luck to use it. The place was a labyrinth. It was quiet enough. The Griffin was above, making his getaway. His slaves were asleep below, or seeking surcease.

Sixty-Seven, strange in Manning's clothes, his bald head topped by Manning's own hat, wetted a finger, held it up.

"The air current blows this way," he said. "We can trace it."

It seemed to Manning that hours and miles passed by in the dank silence of the passages. None accosted them. The Griffin believed him inanimate. But he might return at last, to give Sixty-Seven his freedom. For the slave had known what the Griffin meant by that. Those who served the Griffin were no longer useful to him once they achieved his purposes. The Griffin never repeated his methods. And, if this slave destroyed his greatest enemy, he would in turn be blotted out. Or left to his fate. The Griffin's word held more than one meaning.

The cold air-current guided them along the corridors. They came at last to a high grating where a figure stood on guard. Sixty-Seven stood back, and Manning, in the garb of Sixty-Seven, the numerals on his overall the clearest thing in the dim light, moved on.

"I've orders to set a body in the mortuary," said Manning, in a muffled voice.

"Well, I've had no orders," said the other surlily. He did not wear an overall. Manning saw he was belted, with a gun in a holster.

"Look at this," he said, and thrust forward his half closed hand.

The other stooped, and Manning's fist caught him in a swift uppercut to the jaw. As the man swayed, Manning hit him again and let him slide to the floor. He took his gun, searched him, found keys. One of them fitted the lock to the grating. Manning opened it, and there was a rush behind him. Sixty-Seven, who was Sixty-Seven no longer, was in full flight.

Manning bent over the guard. He was a typical thug, a hood. He snorted through his nose, knocked out. Manning bound his arms behind him, with his own belt, tied his feet together with the laces on his shoes, left him lying. He would stay out for a while.

The grating had closed off a mortuary. The inside bulb showed vaguely shelved caskets, others on the floor, broken and empty.

Here the dead, forgotten, owners of the manor had been set in their last sleep. Here the Griffin had meant to store Manning.

Ex-Sixty-Seven was scrabbling at another grille.

"Get me out of here," he said. "Let me out."

Manning sorted the keys, found one that clicked back the wards. There was moonlight outside, a medley of tilted headstones. Sixty-Seven was gone, vanished in the night.

He turned towards the house and saw the only light vanish. He heard the whir of a motor, and ran through the graveyard towards the front of the manor. Its back was to the cemetery. There was a sort of lane between tall trees.

GUN IN hand, Manning reached the driveway in front of the house. The moon glinted on the high varnish of a big car. Its headlights were turned on. It began to move, to gather speed, making for an exit.

Yet the graveyard faced the highway. Manning now knew that the Griffin had restored an oldtime road, that he had a perfect getaway. There was but the one car. He might have already transported his slaves. Or he might have left them, knowing they could not betray more than was already known, as he fled to his new retreat. Doubtless the caretaker and his wife had gone already. The big house was dark.

Manning shot at the car, aiming low for the tires. He was groggy and his aim was none too good. He realized that, as the car winked its red tail-light at him derisively before it vanished.

He had emptied the weapon. He was powerless. The Griffin had escaped.

But the Griffin had thought Manning left to a living death, and Manning was still very thoroughly alive, if helpless for the moment.

Something whimpered, leaped out of tall weeds, launched for Manning's throat. Hands clawed at him, at his windpipe. The fury of the attack bore him backwards. He tripped over a bush.

It was Al. The Griffin had discovered his meddling, had discarded him. Mute and unhearing, the freak could disclose nothing, knew little. But he was still faithful, like a dog that has been kicked, but still knows only one master.

He knew that this man had fired at the car, had tried to stop the exit of the God, his Master. Al was in a frenzy of fear and rage. His Master might come back, forgive him, if he found he had killed this man he grappled. This side of the house was in shadow. Al did not see the numerals on the overall. His dull senses blended to only one idea—to slay.

He slavered as he wriggled his torso on Manning's chest, his powerful fingers sinking deep. His thumb was compressing the jugular vein, the fingers of the other hand on the vagus nerve.

Manning, hardly over the drug Mizu had given him, strove with failing strength to release that deadly grip, knew that he could not. In his fall he had lost the emptied gun but he groped for it in the dirt, hoping to use it as a club.

With every slowing beat of his labored pulse he was losing energy. He tried to roll uppermost but the freak clung like a bloated leech.

Something prodded Manning's leg, halfway between hip and knee. A last, flaming flash of comprehension came to him. It was something in the outside extra pocket of the overall, used by mechanics for a rule, by Sixty-Seven for other purposes.

He clawed at Al's face and nostrils, got half a gasp of air, a temporary release upon his throbbing blood vessels, before the freak clamped down again.

His fingers closed upon the metal case, opened it, found the needle, jerked the plunger.

His brain seemed flooded with burning blood, the whole world reeled about him as he jabbed the needle into Al's neck, thrust it home.

THERE WERE lights all about him. Headlights, spotlights, moving flashlights. A police surgeon was kneeling beside him, saying something about a pulmotor.

Manning heard himself speaking faintly and hoarsely, felt his voice rasping his raw throat.

"Never mind that," he said. "Let me up. Give me a drink."

The liquor seared his gullet, but it revived him. He gulped air. Saw the commissioner in a sort of halo of intermingled rays.

"We waited an hour, then came on," said the Head of the Police. "Rounded up a bunch of beggars in the basement, but there was no sign of the Griffin. Then we found you in the bushes, with this Coney Island exhibit. What did you do to him?"

"What did he do to me?" Manning echoed wryly, gingerly feeling his neck. "I gave him the same dose the Griffin meant for me. And, if he spoke the truth, the freak will be well out of it all. He won't even know what it's all about, with what he has for a brain. They should have chloroformed him when he was born. The Griffin's got away. But it will upset him a bit when he finds out I'm still in the game."

"That's all that counts, with me," said the commissioner.

"Thanks," said Manning grimly. "But I think I'd be willing to pass out, if I knew the Griffin was ahead of me. Or with me. It's likely to come to that, some day, and, if it does, I'll be content."

IN THE GRIP OF THE GRIFFIN

*For Manning There Seemed No Escape*
*from the Den of the Griffin—It Was Either*
*Death from the Claws of the Hooded Fiends*
*or Death in the Flaming Tunnel*

I

THE TOOL THAT ATE GLASS

THE MAN in the mask worked swiftly and expertly on the side window of Gordon Manning's villa at Pelham Manor. He had a small blueprint of the interior of the house and he had selected this window for several reasons.

It was, as he knew, the window to the service pantry, from which he could gain easy access to the big, double-storied chamber that Manning used for living room, library and dining room. There were three other doors in the big chamber. One of them opened on a winding stairway that led to Manning's bedroom.

The lights in the house had all gone out an hour ago. All the inhabitants—Manning and his two Filipino servants—were inside.

The man in the mask was an expert at burglary. The one blot on his career, as he saw it, was when he had murdered a somewhat prominent householder. He considered the killing had been forced upon him. He had escaped, and the police had been baffled. But there was one person who had evidence that could send him to the chair.

That person was the driving force behind his present attempt. It was the inhuman, insane monster known as the Griffin.

The man in the mask, whose name was now merged in the number given him by his amazing master, knew there were no electric alarm fittings connected with this window. It was like all the other windows in one thing—the glass was thick, laminated, bulletproof; too tough to be tackled with a diamond cutter.

It was two o'clock in the morning, and the restricted neighborhood was sleepily silent. There were police patrols, but Number Thirty-Nine had discounted them. Manning's house was detached from its neighbors. Trees grew in front and broke up the rays of an arc-lamp half a block away. Trees masked both sides of the little estate.

Number Thirty-Nine had never speculated that there might have been some irony in the bestowal of his number by the Griffin. He did not possess much imagination, he was not especially superstitious, and he had not considered that thirty-nine was three-times-thirteen, and might be thrice unlucky.

He knew he was on a dangerous job. Reward had been promised him, if he succeeded. Failure meant death.

He was working well in the shadow. A buttress in the brick wall hid him from the street. He worked by the light of a compact electric lantern, strapped to his left wrist. He wore gloves of oiled silk.

First of all he attached to the center of the window pane a contrivance that was like the leather handle of a suitcase, save that the two ends were attached to rubber suction disks.

Above this he made a narrow gutter of specially-prepared putty. The gutter was to prevent the acid he was using from trickling down the glass and eating into the suction disks. He was a precise craftsman. He believed in neatness and efficiency.

He sprayed the acid from a device made in the Griffin's private laboratory. The whole affair was the combination of a once famous chemist—now Number Twenty-Three—a mechanic who once designed carburetors—Number Seventeen—and a suggestion of Number Thirty-Nine. It looked like a plumber's blowtorch. The vacuum chamber forced out acid instead of flame, but the acid was a fluorine compound that melted the tough glass under the fine spray as if it were ice beneath a jet of steam.

*Manning ran toward them, shouting*

There was only the slightest hissing sound, as Number Thirty-Nine directed the jet with the precision of a master etcher. He passed a fine blade of steel through the completed slit, and repeated the process below the leather handle. Then he made other putty cups, to catch the excess as he united the horizontal slits with vertical ones. He shifted his light to his right wrist, and used his left hand for the spray on the left side, his right hand lightly and firmly holding the leather grip.

A square of glass, almost exactly twelve inches in each dimension, came cleanly away. Number Thirty-Nine cleaned up the glass, put away the acid-blower in a luncheon box. He reached through and opened the patent catch. The window went up, noiselessly.

*A flashlight swung toward him.*

Thirty-Nine stood in the butler's pantry of the house of Gordon Manning, arch-enemy of the insane, homicidal genius whose fiendish murders had shocked the world with the fiendish destruction of those the world could least spare; benefactors of humanity that the Griffin conceived, in his grandiose dementia, should be eliminated from his realm.

Manning, sworn by will and duty to destroy the Griffin, had captured him, once; but the law, with its medieval conceptions of insanity, had sent the monster to Dannemora. The Griffin had not stayed there long before he escaped.

Then, once again, Manning had almost got his man, barely escaping his own annihilation in the attempt. The Griffin had fled, not unaware that Manning was closing in. Somewhere he was in hiding, preparing a new aerie where he could study the horoscopes of his chosen victims and supervise in his laboratories the labors of his slaves in preparing for new atrocities.

All the venom in him was now directed against Manning. He was like a frenzied scorpion that stings itself with its own tail. So furious was his resentment against the ex-Major of Military Intelligence and renowned explorer that he had forborne to consult the stars and choose the time when the astral influences were hostile to Manning. Manning must be swept from his path—at once!

Therefore Number Thirty-Nine crept through the house, his light now in one hand, in the other a pistol whose poisoned, dumdum bullet was discharged by highly compressed gas. The weapon made no report. The bullet need not be fatally aimed. Once let it enter the flesh of the target and the victim was doomed. A shot that scored an immediately mortal wound would be merciful. The poison meant an hour of supremest agony, of helpless, strangling, burning and convulsive torment.

Thirty-Nine tried the swing door from the pantry. It swung easily, and he advanced, the beam from his lantern darting here and there. He stepped towards the door that led up to Manning's bedroom, listening, smelling, tasting, looking; every sense alert.

He was like some feral beast, prowling from the jungle into an open glade, pad-footed, tensing for the kill. His face snarled and twitched back of his mask, puckered it into black wrinkles. Suddenly he stooped, his scalp crawling, while his heart missed a beat.

He had heard a slight *click* that seemed to come—as it did come—from several places in the room. It sounded a little like the cocking of a trigger, but he knew that modern weapons have hammers that rise mechanically, silent and deadly as the lift of a cobra's head.

He did *not* know that he had stepped into an invisible ray, that back of every door in the big chamber another door of steel had slid into place. Behind the drawn curtains the same thing had happened with the windows. That he was a prisoner.

He realized he had walked into a trap when he heard a calm, cold voice speaking. Behind him, somewhere.

"You are covered, my friend. Don't move a muscle. Your hands will do just as they are. Keep very still. It would be unfortunate—for you—if you should sneeze, or even cough."

Thirty-Nine stood as if petrified. He feared to breathe. The bland assurance of the voice was far more sinister than the dread pronouncement of a judge sentencing a convicted murderer.

It was the voice of Manning, but it did not issue from the lips of Manning. It had, once. Now it was merely a phonographic record, started when Thirty-Nine intercepted the eye that never slept, Manning's tireless protector.

The ray flowed from a photo-electric cell. An intruder's shadow would almost have sufficed to interrupt the flow and break the current. The impulse so created was magnified by a grid-glow tube, relayed in two directions. To the delicately-triggered mechanism that released the steel doors and the one that started the phonograph.

Thirty-Nine was trapped. He stood frigid with fear and suspense. Into his brain arose a tremendous hatred of the Griffin, who had forced him into this.

11

## THE PAWN MOVES

THERE WERE actually three relays to that electric impulse, though two of them were connected. Close to the ear of Manning, as he lay in bed, a buzzer sounded, its vibrations pitched to a key that instantly aroused him.

He touched a button and flooded the bedroom with concealed light. His blinds were drawn. He got out of bed with the ease of motion that told of perfect coördination and condition. He stood on the floor in one effort, as a panther rises from its lair.

His lips twisted in a slight grin. He was in contact with the Griffin. He did not doubt that for an instant. But he feared it was only an agent with whom he had to deal.

Dealing with the Griffin's agents had always proved difficult. But Manning had not given up hope of persuasion. In his last encounter, one of the slaves had turned against his master, or Manning would not now be slipping on dressing gown and slippers, with the grim smile on his lean, brown face, beginning to be lined a little these days.

The case of the Griffin was not so severe as the responsibility that Manning felt. It was a relief to realize that, this time, the Griffin was after *him*, and not some innocent, and invaluable, factor in the advance of civilization.

Manning looked through a masked peephole and saw the black-masked man standing motionless. He tucked an automatic pistol into the pocket of the dully brocaded dressing gown of cedar-green silk and twisted a bit of carving in the paneling that rose from floor to fluted ceiling. Manning was partial to paneling. This room was lined with the woodwork of an Elizabethan manor. The secret section that opened up had been designed by the original architect, in the years of court cabals and lovers' strategies.

Manning sauntered through it, leaving it open. He went down a spiral stair of steel. His main chamber had coved corners that concealed such avenues. They did not show on the blueprint that Thirty-Nine—and the Griffin—had relied upon.

The Griffin had the cunning of the madman. And, in his insane precocity, he was inclined to underrate Manning. Which was a weakness. But Manning did not underrate his erratic enemy.

To deal with the Griffin, Manning often fancied, was like stalking some wild and weird survival of the reptilian world; armored, alert, unknown; a creature that lived in more than one element. One never knew how it might act. Its retreat might be a ruse. It would be almost invulnerable, responsive to instincts incomprehensible to a normal man.

But this black-masked intruder was not the Griffin. Only an emissary, now at Manning's mercy.

He did not feel very merciful, as he went down the shipstairs, with which he had replaced the wornout treads of the English casing.

There was another panel in the library, of Manning's own devising. He stepped through it, noiseless in his un-heeled slippers, set the muzzle of his gun exactly over the right kidney of Number Thirty-Nine.

Thirty-Nine quivered from head to foot.

"Switch off your lamp," said Manning. "There's a lounge in front of you. Pitch it onto that."

The chamber had been lighted automatically when Manning entered. Thirty-Nine blinked through his mask. He had not realized his lamp was still on. His wits had stopped working. As a slave of the Griffin he knew nothing of invisible rays. He heard no news, read none. He was not even certain of the passing of the days, the months, the years. He knew that he was gray, and growing old, and that was all.

In his prime he had been a master-cracksman. He had rec-ognized a super-master when the laminated glass was shown

him, and the means of eating through it; easy to him, who had
petered safes with nitro-glycerine and putty gutters.

Now he was caught.

"The gun to your left hand, very gently," said Manning. "I'll
take it. It looks like a novelty. And now, sit down in that chair
to the right of you."

Thirty-Nine marveled as he watched Manning. He told
himself that if he had ever seen this man before he would never
have tackled the job—and knew he lied. Manning might be
the deep sea, but the Griffin was the devil.

Manning was mixing a drink of Scotch and seltzer in a long
glass. He was tall, and almost thin. His skin was tanned. He
was a little helmet-bald at the temples. He had the nose of a
hawk and the eyes of a hawk—questing, indomitable.

"You'll take this without ice, and like it," he said, with a smile
that was almost genial. "The room is temporarily sealed. You
couldn't get out of it, even if you got the better of me—and that
phase of the situation is negligible. It's good Scotch. Do you
good."

He mixed a short glass for himself, quaffed it with a nod at
Thirty-Nine. He shut the intruder's gun away in a drawer.

"LET'S TALK turkey," he said, as Thirty-Nine felt the
good liquor warm his belly. "The Griffin sent you here. You
think the Griffin owns you, body and soul—if you have a soul.
You rather wish you haven't one, in the light of some crime of
yours, through which the Griffin holds you. Possibly affecting
others, for whom you care. Mother, wife, kiddies?"

Thirty-Nine set down his emptied glass.

"You've got me," he said. "Why rub it in?"

"Have another drink," said Manning.

Thirty-Nine gulped it down.

"The Griffin has got what the police call 'the dope' on you.
But I've got considerable influence with the police myself. If
you were turned in as an agent of the Griffin, captured by me,

you'd be, to use the expression of the commissioner, considerably 'mussed-up' before you hit the line-up."

The throat of Thirty-Nine went dry.

"There has been no real lynching in New York City for the past fifty years," said Manning, "but there might be. Not having the Griffin they might take it out on you. If they didn't, a jury would."

"Gimme another drink," said Thirty-Nine. "I don't care what it is," he croaked, "so long's it's wet. I was forced to do this, see? You called the turn. Suppose I come clean, how about it? If I fix it so you get the Griffin, and you find something, or he tips you off to something that might give me the worst of it? How about that? Where do I get off?"

"I can't definitely promise you anything, legally. And I'm not a particularly wealthy man. But I'll bet ten thousand dollars to a shirt button that if you furnish the means of capturing the Griffin you'll get a pension rather than a penitentiary sentence—if I have to pay the pension myself."

"I can show you where he's moved to. It don't suit him. It's only temporary. You've got him on the run. Listen, Mr. Manning, I got a wife an' two kids, growing up fast, see? Mebbe they think I'm dead. Mebbe she's got no use for me. But I've got use for them."

He sucked down the drink Manning had given him. He seemed sincere enough, but even if he were acting superbly Manning knew that the mere thinking of such things would produce emotions that would fool the most blase, even as Hollywood actors supply themselves with synthetic reactions.

"Take off that silly mask," said Manning. "I'm going to ask you some questions. Don't lie to me, because I'll have it checked up before we leave. I won't stool on you. So come clean."

Thirty-Nine told a lot in the next few minutes. The location of the Griffin's lair, the nature of the crime the Griffin held over him, and the Griffin's especial grip upon him. The man could not tell the nature of the acid, nor explain the mechanism of the little gun that Manning had appropriated, but he explained their uses. The poisoned bullet could be analyzed, the glass solvent should not be too hard to discover; though Manning saw no immediate use for it, save as evidence against the Griffin.

And, when he landed the Griffin next time, evidence would be superfluous.

There were plans to be made before Manning could attack the Griffin's stronghold. He could not pull this off alone. But he must scout ahead alone. However carefully he moved, he would be in jeopardy.

Manning had deliberately stalked a Javanese rhino on a mountain trail, where there was no chance to evade its charge. He had gone on foot into the bamboo to finish off a wounded tiger. But such things were tame and safe pastimes compared to seeking the Griffin in his lair.

"You can't get out of here," he told Thirty-Nine. "Don't try it. I won't be long. Did you come in your own car?"

The man nodded. He was not going to try to get out of that place where he had been so easily trapped.

"The car's in the all-night garage, two blocks south," he said, a little sullen after Manning's inquisition. "It's best for us to use it. The Griffin has lookouts. Your own car 'ud be spotted, and they might toss a pineapple at the two of us. My car's a taxi, see? At least it looks like a taxi, though it ain't registered as one. They know it. They'll pass it through. They don't have to see you. They won't know what my job is to-night. The Griffin don't hand out information. So I can drive you right past the place. And then, mister, you'll have to take care of me, if you have to plant me in solitary in Sing Sing until you get him."

Manning nodded. It was like the Griffin, fatalist that he was, to choose a new, if temporary, aerie in the city, where nineteen thousand police waited to get a glimpse of him.

Manning took the acid-blower and poison-pistol with him to his bedroom. Through the peephole he saw Thirty-Nine pour himself half a tumblerful of Scotch, and drink it neat.

He made no attempt to examine exits, but he furtively lifted the French phone, testing it to listen in. He might not have known that an extension could be automatically made exclusive, as Manning now made the one on his night-table, with a switch.

HE FIRST called police headquarters. His name was a sesame, and he got the inspector on duty immediately, giving him Thirty-Nine's true name, asking for his record.

"It's just a check-up," he said. "I'll call back in ten minutes."

Next Manning got through to the police commissioner at the latter's home. The commissioner's sleepiness vanished as he listened, while Manning talked crisply.

"When I spot the place, I'll get through again to you, at headquarters. We'll complete plans then. We won't get the Griffin by throwing a cordon about the place. He'll have his getaways prepared. I want you to rouse out the right men in the city engineers department, so that we can get at the details of all sewers, conduits and subterranean works in the neighborhood. We want to stop all exits before we try an entry."

"I'll do it, Manning, but I don't like it," the commissioner said. "It seems too much like toasted cheese in a trap. A mouse ought to know it smells too good."

"I'm not a mouse. I may smell the cheese, but I won't sniff at it. I have no idea of trying to get into the place, now. Only to locate it."

"Right! But put a tail on yourself, from your end. We'll try and pick you up as you come off the bridge, but I'm not banking on it. The traffic is heavy these nights. And it's a bit foggy over here. Thick on the rivers."

Manning switched back to the inspector. Thirty-Nine appeared to have told the truth. He had actually told more than the department had against him. But Manning kept faith with him.

He took another look at his captive. He was still fiddling with the telephone. Manning called the local chief of police, found out that a sergeant named Tierney was then on night duty at the station, and arranged for him to be relieved.

"It's the Griffin, Chief," he said, and knew how the other would react as he held the wire. "I want Tierney to tail me in a private car, in plain clothes, from the all-night garage two blocks south. I'll be leaving there in a taxicab, fifteen minutes from now. Tierney is one of the few coppers I know who can wear civvies and drive a car as if he wasn't a policeman. How about it? He can hire a car from the garage."

"He'll be there. I'll phone him now, and I'll take over his trick myself, Major Manning."

Manning took his time to dress. Tierney had to be given his fifteen minutes. And, since there was fog in New York, it would grow thicker towards dawn. Time was not vital.

He put on a double-breasted suit of dark gray that fitted him to perfection. He chose his tie carefully, the plaid of a famous Scotch regiment, with whom he had liaisoned in the war. For all the fog, it was warm, and he decided against an outer coat.

He shifted his automatic into a shoulder holster. A tinkle sounded on his telephone as he tucked a linen handkerchief into his left cuff, in military fashion.

It was Tierney reporting. The sergeant had found plain clothes at the station, borrowed somebody else's hat. An efficient officer, Tierney. He would go higher.

Thirty-Nine was jumpy when Manning went down to him. He had finished the bottle of whisky, but it seemed to have had little effect, except to help bring out the sweat that glistened on his forehead.

"Wondering why I didn't telephone?" Manning asked him, pleasantly.

The Griffin's vassal shot him a look that mingled respect and fear in a cunning leer. He had gone through a very bad half hour.

"I didn't give you away, Hammond," said Manning. "Now, keep on behaving yourself."

He took the other in a grip above the elbow that could change instantly into a paralyzing vise. But Thirty-Nine was docile as a dachshund.

The cab had all the aspect of a private taxi, complete with inspection pasters, and framed license. The photograph resembled Hammond sufficiently, though the name was false, as were the number plates, the registration and the numerals on the engine.

It was a smart idea. A taxicab attracted small attention, day or night, so long as the driver obeyed traffic rules.

Manning fancied there was plenty of power under the hood, but Thirty-Nine drove at a steady gait, respecting automatic signals.

Somewhere behind, the faithful Tierney trailed. Manning made no attempt to be sure of it. Either the sergeant was there, or he was not.

They found the fog after a short drive. There was considerable traffic, with produce trucks, full and empty, running in both directions on the Queensboro Bridge, thin but steady stream of private cars, and a good sprinkling of taxis.

The mist vapored up from the East River. Melancholy hoots came from vessels trying to steal their way to a pier. Regular night water-traffic was over, except for a few barges, towed to take advantage of the tide.

The lights of the prison of Welfare Island were barely visible.

If the commissioner's men picked up the car under these conditions they were miracle men. Manning was just as well pleased. All cops were not Tierneys. He did not want to be made conspicuous.

Tierney's tailing him was like the tail to a kite. It helped to steady it. It was a good precaution. Manning would have used it even if the commissioner had not thought of it.

The cab was comfortable. With the fog, and no light, save on the dashboard, Manning was invisible as if he had drawn curtains. He did not smoke, though there was an ash-receiver and a cigar lighter; but he relaxed against the well-padded cushions; counting blocks after they got through the congestion at the Fifty-ninth Street end of the bridge.

They turned south, down town, zigzagging gradually west.

## III

## THE HIDDEN LAIR

THERE ARE certain sections of New York, notably those through the Twenties to the middle Thirties, that are partly commercialized but still preserve brownstone fronts that once were private mansions. They hold much of forgotten history.

Here are homes that have been closed for a century, where the dust lies thick on pre-Victorian furnishings. Clouded titles and the disputes of heirs keep them mysteries. They defy modern progress.

They are sandwiched between apartment houses and business buildings. Some have yards, deserted stables, spaces that once were gardens. They are at once the hope and the despair of enterprising realtors; bringing in nothing, paying taxes; worth thousands of dollars by the front inch.

It was easy for Manning to place himself as the taxi rolled on its way, occasionally passing, or being passed, by another vehicle. This was the city of his birth and preference. They were in the middle Twenties when they made the final turn to the west. Two blocks ahead, the new subway would run—when the city could afford to open it.

To the right was the shell of an incompleted apartment house, awaiting better times and lower taxes. On the left there was a high fence on the corner. The promoters had planned to build a movie theater, but they had got no farther than the clearing of the ground. To do that they had razed the ancient church of St. Jude's-in-the-Fields.

There had been farms all about the sacred edifice when it was erected, and was the sanctuary of the fashionable. But the edifice, and the dead and buried bodies of a host of parishioners had slowly moldered.

The bones had long since been transferred from the original cemetery. Now the church was gone. Only its stone pavings lay undisturbed, with the mortuary beneath them.

That was a maze of passages and crypts, where corpses had been held against interment. The papers had carried features about it when the theater was projected. It was mentioned as an eerie spot, with mysterious exits.

Next to the fenced-off corner, on the street that ran east and west, stood two houses that had been used by the clergy. They were gloomy and forbidding, a driveway between them, that led to a common courtyard beneath a dismal archway of stone, closed partly with heavy gates, and partly with a grille of iron.

It had an air all its own, that archway, somber and sinister. Windy eddies swept dead leaves, old papers, in and out of it. Children did not play there. Loiterers dodged it, even in bad weather.

Now the pseudo-taxi slowed down, moving in towards the curb.

Here, Manning told himself, might well be the Griffin's lurking place. It seemed to suit him, with the old cellars, the crypt, even the as-yet-unopened subway, with its unlit corridors of artificial stone, its exits merely boarded up.

The sliding glass panel between driver and passenger was pushed aside. Thirty-Nine looked over his shoulder at Manning.

"Is this the place?" the latter asked.

"Just a minute, mister. I've got to—"

Manning had not watched the eyes of tricky savages for nothing. For all the vague light, filtering from an arc through the wispy fog, he saw the shifting orbs of Thirty-Nine; and he reached for his automatic.

The cab halted at the curb with a jar of suddenly applied

brakes that jolted Manning. The glass panel closed with a vicious snap. The window on his right, which he had kept partly open, slid in its grooves. The light on the dashboard went out.

Thirty-Nine leaped from the car, leaving his engine running; hurled himself across the sidewalk ramp into the black gorge of the driveway beneath the arch.

The doors of the cab were locked. So were the windows, the sliding panel. Manning could not budge them. A shutter had blanked the window in the back of the car, working outside the glass. He could not see whether Tierney's car was in sight. The glass was all unbreakable. It was doubtful if he could have crawled out between frames, even if he could have smashed it, but he might have got a shot at Thirty-Nine, and let in some air.

IT WAS too late now. Thirty-Nine had been swallowed up by the big gates. The car was a trap of steel and crystal. Even the roof was steel. Manning hammered at all of it with the muzzle of his gun. Then with the butt. The glass shivered, seemed to become frosted—but he could not break through.

He fired at a window. The only result was to star the bulletproof pane and fill the space where he sat with choking powder fumes.

Next there would come carbon monoxide gas—the engine was still running. That would be a nasty death, but Manning expected it. It looked like the end. He would strangle like a woodchuck in its hole as the trapper pumps in the deadly fumes.

The car began to move, of its own volition, as if a ghost were at the wheel—or Death.

It backed, swung to the driveway, moved inexorably toward the archway. There came a voice, resonant, deep, infinitely mocking. It came through the radio transmitter of the car. It was plain, despite the closed panel. The voice of the Griffin!

"Welcome, Manning! Quite a leaf out of your own book— the laminated glass! You should have brought along my agent's acid-blower. But to cut your way out would have taken too long.

You will remember, I think, that I have driven a car by remote radio-control before. I do not often repeat my methods, but, in this case, the idea seemed appropriate—and useful."

Into the mental vision of Manning there flashed, like lightning at midnight, the memory of a self-driven car crashing into that of a famous physician who had incurred the Griffin's malice. That had been a hideous death, but a sudden one, comparatively merciful. Manning wondered if his would prove as easy—and doubted it.

The voice ended with a chuckle as the car swung into the driveway beneath the arch, and the grim gates opened. Now the car was in a courtyard, black as a cave. The gates closed in well-oiled silence. Manning could barely make out the loom of the old stables, of high brick walls.

His only hope was that Tierney had marked the car swing in. Tierney might have been able to see the crimson tail-light through the fog. If it had been lit.... If Tierney had not been lost on the road. It was a slim hope.

Manning was in the grip of the Griffin.

The car halted.

"I am going to open the doors, Manning. If you will then step out, with both arms well extended, there will be no immediate trouble. Do that within the next sixty seconds, or else the monoxide fumes will be diverted from the baffler that now protects you.

"They will sift in slowly. It will be a slow stupefaction, a long struggle for oxygen, while your lungs burn like fire. The sort of thing they do to guinea pigs in the laboratories. Guinea pigs under glass, as you are. And I shall watch your death throes with keen interest, Manning, with exceptional interest, I assure you."

The Griffin's derisive chuckle came again, as a spotlight from either side the car stabbed through the darkness, dazzling Manning, revealing him pitilessly—every move, every shift of expression.

There was a click as the windows and doors of the pseudo-taxi unlocked.

"While there is life, Manning, there is always hope."

The sentence, as the Griffin spoke it, was nothing but a sardonic sham, yet it appealed to Manning's aggressiveness.

Here, in the heart of the greatest, the most modern metropolis on earth, he was as helpless, as removed, as if he were in some medieval *oubliette,* deep underground, forgotten. But so long as he was able to prolong life, even though it only became something for the Griffin to torture, he meant to stay alive. The Griffin would torture him mentally, psychologically, at first; to break down his courage. Sooner or later, the fiend's latent insanity would rouse him to sheer sadism.

Manning holstered his useless gun and stepped from the car, elevating both arms. Instantly two more spears of light lanced the gloom and centered on him. He could see nothing, no matter where he turned. The direct rays were blinding. He could see when black robed and hooded figures passed in front the spots, took his gun, and frisked him expertly, patting him from shoulders to ankles in search of other weapons.

Then he was allowed to lower his arms. A hood of felted cloth was pulled down over his head. He was marched across the flagged courtyard, up carpeted stairs, through spaces that smelled dank and musty. They held him by the elbows. Manning thrust his hands into his trousers pockets, and went willingly enough. There was nothing else to do.

I V

## THE HOROSCOPE OF HELL

THEN HE was vaguely conscious of a rare perfume, the fumes of amber. Strange, exotic, barbaric music sounded softly. His hood was snatched off. The concealed lighting illuminated the room with a curious wave-green tint.

The Griffin sat in a carved, high-backed chair of ebony, inlaid with pearl and ivory stars. He wore a long robe of sable brocade into which cabalistic signs were woven in dull gold thread. He wore a skullcap of black velvet. His face was fantastically hideous.

The beaked nose, high cheekbones, the jutting chin, showed through a mask of gleaming yellow fabric that looked like the shedding skin of a snake, or the diseased tissues of a leper. It was thin, plastic, slightly transparent. It wrinkled with every change of expression, and distorted it. It puffed out from his lips when he chuckled or laughed through the mouth-slit. Through it his eyes gleamed wickedly. Dark eyes, with strange murky glints in them, like the lights in a black opal; fiery flecks of orange and red and blue; hideous and hellish.

The eyes of a madman, a murderer, a monster!

There was a table in front of him. Its top was black marble, its legs were crouching Griffins, with their eagle wings outspread, their lion claws clasping the rich oriental rug.

There was a gong, or brazen disk, suspended between two rods of brass. Under a paperweight of silver-gilt, in the shape of a crouching Griffin with ruby eyes, were sheets of parchment. In front of the Griffin, on the table, there was a single sheet of heavy paper inscribed with a long list of names.

Some of these had been crossed off with a crimson pencil.

It was the death-list of the fiend. Manning wondered if his name appeared there. Those scored through in red had been killed. The Griffin would say, "Executed."

There was another seat opposite the monster. Manning took it as the Griffin gestured. The hooded men disappeared.

The high and spacious chamber still held much of its original furnishings. The table, of course, was the Griffin's own. Also a great sky-globe, on a stand that brought the celestial sphere to the height of a tall man's head. It represented the heavens as seen both north and south of the equator.

About it ran a great circle that was the ecliptic, the apparent pathway of the sun amid the stars. And this line was the center of a belt—the zodiac, divided into its twelve houses, depicted with its twelve signs. The globe was, in all, divided into twelve sections. Halfway up the stand, a slanting platform made a desk on which was a pad of paper, printed with the design of a planisphere.

These were the blanks used by an astrologer for casting horoscopes. The top one had a sign set upon it. It looked as if the Griffin had been at work, trying to decide which of his victims was next ordained by the stars to die—at the hands of the Griffin, the "Avenger of the Universe."

There was one thing missing that had once been familiar as the Griffin's shadow. This was Al, the legless freak the Griffin had employed as buffoon and bodyguard. Al was deaf and mute. He had had about the intelligence of a chimpanzee, but the Griffin had found him useful.

Manning had eliminated Al. It was one reason for the Griffin's desire to do away with Manning, aside from the fact that Manning was sworn to the Griffin's capture and annihilation.

The Griffin set the jade mouthpiece of a hubble-bubble pipe through the mouth-slit of his mask. The rosewater in the container bubbled as he sucked the smoke, emitted it. Coming from that ghastly countenance, it seemed like hell-vapor out-breathed by a devil.

"This is but a temporary place, Manning; I must apologize for receiving you so poorly. But I will make the reception as warm as I can. I have been very busy lately; too busy to get properly settled, thanks to you."

His derision turned to hatred in the last three words, bitter and venomous as the bite of a mamba.

Manning regarded him serenely. He felt helpless. Hope was a rainbow dying in the dark, but his spirit held strong within.

"I feared," said the Griffin, "that Thirty-Nine might be baffled by some safety device of yours, installed too recently for me to know about. So I planned a second offense, that looked like a defense, on the principle of *judo*. And you fell for it, like the dupe, the simpleton, the *gobemouche* that you are. Once you amused me. Now you weary me. Any time I cared to concentrate I could have destroyed you. I have let you run, like a cur on a string. Now—it ends. Despite all your vaunted ability as an investigator, all your police, all your press, all your precautions. You are going to die, within the hour, Manning—and not at all pleasantly."

He hissed the last words with concentrated hate, the mask fluttering before his lips.

MANNING LOOKED at him steadily. He had faint doubt that this was his death warrant. The room seemed close. The amber fumes, the hasheesh, with which the Griffin tinctured his Turkish tobacco, were a little overpowering.

He took the handkerchief from his left cuff and patted his forehead. He remembered the sweat on the brow of Thirty-Nine, and was not ashamed to find it on his own.

But his hand was steady, his voice was calm, as he tucked the handkerchief into his breast pocket, looked at his wrist watch. The Griffin surveyed him mockingly. He had enjoyed that show of sweat. It was the first sign that he had affected his prisoner.

"It is a bit warm in here," Manning said. "You mentioned 'within the hour.' Am I to understand that my death is one of those appointed by the stars, that the Lord of my House had been careless, or cannot defend his domain against the aspects of evil on this night?"

It was his turn to jeer subtly at the Griffin's supreme belief in the omnipotence of the stars as controllers of fate.

"This is *my* vengeance, Manning. I have appointed the time myself."

"I see. By the way, I wonder if you noticed the recent announcement by astronomers that the obliquity of the ecliptic slowly changes? And that this upsets the astrologer's ideas as to what sign of the zodiac rose above the horizon at the particular moment of anybody's birth. Astronomy, as against astrology. I do not venture to declare which is the more exact science."

Manning had method in his talk. There was faint hope of successful interference through Tierney's tailing; very faint. But if he got the Griffin tangled in the erratic beliefs, he might cajole him long enough to play the hidden card he carried.

Already he had made movements he had feared he wouldn't be permitted. They had disarmed him, but he was sure he was being watched closely; that the first sign from the Griffin would start the final move.

He could see the mask pucker on the monster's forehead. It would not do to excite him too much.

"Astronomers! Einstein, and the rest! All charlatans! The stars have predicted every great event. They dominate all lives. It is proven."

"Nevertheless," Manning argued, "is it not true that there is now a discrepancy in the zodiac amounting to the breadth of a whole sign? That—"

The twitching mask smoothed out. The Griffin sat back, pulled on his hubble-bubble, and chuckled.

"You are trying to pull my leg, Manning; to make me angry, so that I will have you slain swiftly, and without much pain. But I refuse to be drawn out. That was a good move; the move of a brave man who does not fear death. But you, my Manning, will know fear, and agony, before you die. Your death has naught to do with your horoscope. It is the will of the Griffin. I, who am myself, alone. Unlike all others. The Destroyer! The 'Appointed One' of Abaddon and Apollyon."

Tiny flecks of froth broke through the mouth-slit, clung to the jade mouthpiece.

"I do not doubt your omnipotence," said Manning. He took the handkerchief from his breast pocket, dabbed his forehead, replaced the linen in his left cuff once more. "After I, of minor importance in your scheme of things, am blotted out; who comes next?"

"Ah-ha!" The chuckle was almost friendly. "So that you may win yourself recognition in the Land of Shades, by predicting an early entry? No, Manning. That I will not do. I have not myself entirely ratified the selection. I shall finish that horoscope after I am through with you—*rid of you, Manning!*"

The outbursts of maniacal fury that broke his speech were proof of his lessening control.

"But I will read you the list of those who will be chosen, each in their appointed hour."

It was to satisfy his own colossal vanity that the Griffin read his roll; of those who had died, and those who were about to die if his career of crime could not be checked. He gloated over the knowledge that the one man who might have accomplished that, listened, powerless.

Manning heard that roster of brilliant names, condemned by a madman to have their careers cut short, with far more emotion than the Griffin's pronouncement of his own death had stirred. For these men and women were geniuses. To slaughter them was to maim all humanity.

Once more he dabbed his forehead. Now he held the handkerchief crumpled in his right hand. The Griffin set down the list of those he had marked for death.

"AS FOR you, Manning," he said, "I have devised several means of shuffling you off this mortal coil. You have evaded some of them. This one you will not evade. These buildings are a part of old New York. In those old days, men went to see terriers tossed into a rat-pit. The terriers usually won, though terribly bitten, because they were equipped by Nature with punishing jaws, with the necessary teeth.

"You have good teeth, Manning, but they are not those of a bull-terrier. One annoyance of this place is that it is infested with rats. I have caught many of them, or had them caught. I have placed them in a special cellar, kept them hungry, but not so starved that they have become too weak. When they started to eat each other, I considered them sufficiently ravenous. I have kept them that way, for you.

"I am going to drop you into that rat-pit, Manning, as you are, unbound. And I shall enjoy the spectacle far more than Nero ever relished the casting of a Christian maiden to the lions. I hope you put up a good fight, Manning. There will be a spotlight—"

He half rose, in his mad frenzy. The jade mouthpiece fell from his lips. The flecks of foam clotted on the mouth-slit.

"A rat, devoured by rats—"

Manning moved the crumpled handkerchief, as if to stuff it automatically into the cuff of his left sleeve. His fingers worked for a moment.

"Not to-night!" Manning challenged.

The Griffin subsided into his throne-chair. He was not too mad to notice what Manning held in his right hand, brought from the elastic holdout on his left arm. The searchers had missed it, he held his arms aloft in the courtyard.

It was the pistol Thirty-Nine had carried. And it was pointed, with a hand that showed not the slightest tremor, at the Griffin.

"Sit down, and sit quietly," said Manning. "The aim, I think, is not very important. You know best what the poison will do to you. I think the rats will wait. I tested the trigger, and eased the spring. It will take but the slightest pressure to release the charge."

The mask stiffened. The eyes of the monster glared through.

"You are going to take me out of here," said Manning. "You will have to be very careful, for I shall be liable to mistake your intentions, being set on my own. To deliver you to justice, which, in the person of the police, will welcome you far more readily dead, or dying, than alive. All the psychiatrists in America will not suffice to send you to Dannemora again. It has been a long time since there was a lynching in New York, but—"

He was sure the Griffin had made no move, but suddenly the bronze disk clanged out a clamor of alarm.

"Sit still," said Manning. "I think the police you so recently derided are closing in. I had my own *judo*, my own second line of offense."

The yellow mask quivered a little.

"Get up, turn your back to me, make no false move. We shall go out arm-in-arm," Manning ordered.

The disk quivered with its message of imminent danger.

Slowly the Griffin rose, and turned his back. He uttered a high-pitched cry. And suddenly the wave-green light went out. The room was plunged into absolute blackness.

Manning heard the slither of robes, sensed the inrush of the Griffin's myrmidons. He pressed the trigger, but there was no spurt of flame, no sound. The compressed gas discharged the poisoned missile, but he could not tell if he had scored a hit.

He had to pull back a cylinder to recharge, a clumsy arrangement in the dark. He would have given much to swap this murderer's weapon for his own good gun.

The brazen gong ceased its discord. The Griffin had fled, careful not to expose himself against any light, fearful of the poison-gun he had himself devised.

His high-pitched call had not only summoned his men, but by a sympathetic vibration, had put out the lights. It had been an emergency mechanism.

It seemed as if Tierney must have made contact. The commissioner must have closed in. But that was not getting in.

There was a faint draft of air, suddenly shut off. The room was filled with unseen shapes.

The Griffin had left his creatures behind to kill Manning. He was in a rat-pit after all.

How many underlings Manning might destroy with the poison-gun would not count with the Griffin. He was ready to sacrifice them. If they guessed that, they would not show any mercy to Manning.

A voice sounded in the room, seeming to come from the ceiling.

"Kill!" it commanded. "Kill! He has betrayed you all."

His back against the long table, Manning awaited the on-slaught. He could hear their breathing, feel their motion. Then, with a rush, they were on him, swarming from all sides. They panted and grunted, uncouth, hideous and deadly, grappling with him, striking, clawing, seeking to get him down, to tear him apart.

V

## THE STRANGLING HORDE

MANNING FOUGHT for his life. Most of the Griffin slaves were weak and emaciated, but they seemed a legion. They knew him by the feel of his clothing, which they snagged and ripped to tatters.

Twice they got him to his knees, and twice he staggered up again, blood streaming down his face where their long nails had torn the flesh. Time and again he shook them off as they clung to his arms and legs. He struck out, and hit flesh and bone. Once he cracked two skulls together. The celestial sphere toppled, the table was upset.

Once, when someone he smashed fairly tripped over a connection, there was a brief flare of blue lightning. It showed him a score of gibbering faces, hollow of cheek, eyes blazing. They used their teeth and fought bestially. Only the darkness and their own numbers, which made them block each other, added to his own prime condition and fighting ability, kept Manning on his feet. Once down, they would trample him to death, mutilate him beyond recognition.

The greatest horror was the fact that they did not speak. They only uttered feral noises. He felt their hot breath on his cheeks. They stripped the pistol-gun from his grasp. He was just as glad to use his free fist. The gun was of little use to them in the darkness. It fell to the floor, trampled and kicked.

Manning began to weaken under the buffeting, the blows

and kicks. He had no definite goal to fight for. All sense of direction was lost. For all he knew, the Griffin had deliberately shut them in there to finish him; locked them in, and left them to whatever fate would ultimately come to them.

His throat was scraped and bruised. A dozen times he tore loose strangling holds.

Then one man closed with him again. He was of different quality from the rest, better fed, perhaps, or naturally more muscular. He seemed to have held off cunningly, reserving himself until Manning was worn down. His hands grappled Manning's windpipe, shutting off air and blood. Manning thrust his own thumb at the base of the man's neck, thrust with all his force.

This was *judo,* the deadly Japanese defense for a frontal attack. The man choked, an agonized rattle came from his throat. Then he collapsed, the tiny hyoid bone crushed. He went limp, dying in Manning's arms.

Manning was tired, but so were the others. Their courage had long since been leached out of them by the Griffin.

Manning charged them, and they fell back. He barked his shins on the edge of the overturned table, but he strode over it, carrying the man he had killed.

To the rest the table was a formidable barrier in the dark. They gave him a moment's respite while he crouched, stripping the robe and hood from the dead man, putting them on himself. A disguise might be useless, but if he ever got out of here alive—

The voice came again from the ceiling.

"Come, the way is clear! Leave him if you are sure he is dead. If not, finish him! But hurry!"

A subdued light began partially to illuminate the big room. The Griffin had calculated the horror of that unseen attack, the advantage that any light would have given to Manning, with his gas gun.

The Griffin had gone to see what the alarm might mean, to

set his defense against violent attack and entry; to prepare for his own escape. He had found flight necessary.

One of the doors was opening. There was a faint glimmer of light beyond it.

Now Manning saw that all these forgotten, nameless men, had numbers stenciled in white on the back of their black robes. Most of them showed wounds that he had inflicted or where he had damaged them. They stared about, bewildered, in a huddle, looking at the dismantled room, seeking the stranger they were bidden to destroy.

He had disappeared. Manning had his hood well pulled about his scratched face. Some of them started uncertainly for the door.

Manning led them. He was first through into the passage. A robed figure came hurrying towards him. Motioned him back. The wide sleeve only partly concealed an automatic pistol.

"Get back. I am to make sure of him," said the man harshly. His features were only a blur in his cowl, but Manning knew the voice, knew the man.

He stood aside as if to let the other pass, then flung himself upon him, left arm crooked about the neck, a knee set in the spine, right hand grasping the wrist above the gun.

Manning set out all his force, all the reserve strength that came surging to his aid. He felt the vertebrae snap in the small of the other's back. He heard him groan, and let him fall forward; to his knees, then full upon his face, while Manning tore loose the gun.

His own gun! With which the man had meant to give him the *coup de grâce*.

The white figures on the back of the gunman showed plainly enough. This was—or had been—Number Thirty-Nine.

BLACK FORMS blocked the doorway, irresolute. They were unarmed. Thirty-Nine was a murderer. The other man had been killed in a fight where the odds were with him.

Manning did not want to kill again—except the Griffin.

He fired over their heads. The heavy gun roared in the passageway. Plaster came falling down. The reek of powder was in the faces of the slaves as Manning turned and raced down the corridor.

That single shot, if the Griffin heard it, would be taken as the one that finished Manning. The Griffin would surely linger to know that his enemy was dead.

Manning prayed for that. He was willing to trade his own life in if he could know that the mad monster would commit no more murder.

Gun in hand, he hurried on. The passage ended in a door, unlocked. Beyond there was a flight of worn stone steps that led down to a hall of stone. It was dimly lighted with a single electric bulb. From it there led another passage, dotted with faintly glowing bulbs. On each side there were small chambers, like cells.

Manning knew where he was. This was the mortuary, the crypt below the ancient foundations of St. Jude's-in-the-Fields. He stopped for a moment. He fancied he heard a vague murmuring ahead.

Looking back, he thought he saw black figures, like shadows, wavering and uncertain.

They must know who he was now, and they were afraid of him. They had attacked him in a pack, hysterical, rather than hostile. But they were cowed now.

The corridor led into what must have been a chapel for the dead. The chapel was paneled to the groined ceiling, in conventional, ecclesiastical design. There was a spiral stair that led up, but it was solidly blocked off with masonry. That had led to the church. What of the other exits? He was sure the Griffin had come this way.

The black-robed slaves had trailed him to the entrance to the chapel. They stood there timidly, like so many phantoms.

They knew he had killed two of them, and had the means of shooting more.

"Any of you know how to get out of here?" demanded Manning. "If you do, I'll not interfere with your own getaway."

They barely moved. They might have been shrouded corpses, stacked against the wall.

"We do not know," said one of them in a hollow voice. "It would do us little good to go free, while the Griffin is alive."

"He won't be for long, if I can get at him," rasped Manning, exasperated at these remnants of manhood. "Haven't any of you got any nerve left?"

It was, he knew, an idle question. The bulbs were growing more and more dim. Manning fancied them fed by a storage battery of limited capacity; enough for an escape, insufficient to help a pursuit.

There was one thing he had brought away, and that was the knowledge of the Griffin's next intended victim. In his egoism, the Griffin had called off the list. And Manning had noted the sign upon the planisphere. The shallow curve above a circle that represented Taurus, the Bull.

If on that list there was one born between April 19 and May 20, that man or woman must be protected immediately, even if he or she had to be shipped secretly to the Gobi Desert.

Provided Manning did not get the Griffin.

In the end the police would break in, rescue him, capture the hooded slaves—unless the Griffin had prepared, which was likely enough, some final trap to cover his retreat, a contact-mine of some sort that would wreck the houses, the cellars, and all within them.

The bulbs gave a final dull flicker, went out.

VI

## THE SMEAR OF BLOOD

**M**ANNING WAS not afraid of being attacked again by the nameless ones. His own gun would be a real weapon, even in the dark; and the spiritless creatures had been already defeated. They thought themselves doomed. He snapped on his cigar lighter and began to search the paneling; sure there was somewhere a concealed outlet. The Griffin was on the other side. With every second the chance of getting him grew fainter.

He passed his lighter up and down the edges of the panels, bordered with Gothic carving. It seemed useless, but suddenly the flame wavered, blown by a draft that drifted in through an imperceptible opening at the side of the panel.

Manning tried every projection in the carving; rosette after rosette, with no effect. The paneling was heavy oak. He doubted if he could splinter his way through with his gun. Not without ruining the weapon.

He tried the other side of the corridor. There was a creak, and wood gave at last to his pressure on the center of a boss. The draft blew strongly, with a gust of cold air as the panel slid back. His lighter was blown out.

Light was of little use in the passage ahead of him.

He held out his hands and found stone masonry as he felt his way down a short flight of stairs. He touched the frame of a metal door, and groped out into a vast space.

Far away, down a mighty corridor the roof of which was upheld by massive, square pillars, he saw lights moving, electric torches and lanterns that now revealed, now hid a group of robed figures who occasionally showed the numerals on their backs.

Herding these slaves were a few men in ordinary clothing, the lieutenants of the Griffin. And the Griffin himself stood by, with folded arms, shown in a flash of light, then lost again in the darkness, in the enormous and distorted shadows that shifted and merged into gloom.

This was the unopened subway. There was some way out of it that could not be one of the boarded-up street exits.

Manning did not have to look at his watch. He knew that dawn had long since come, that New York was wide awake. Unless the fog was thick as that of London, even the Griffin would not dare to emerge in that fashion.

Whatever the exit, it was a narrow one. The group lessened one by one as Manning strove to reach them.

It was no easy job. There were only the far-off bobbing lights to be occasionally glimpsed. For the most part he blundered along, striking against the great pillars, hurrying all he could.

Now and again he saw the lights. They were moving no more. They were directed upon one spot where the group was dwindling, all too fast.

They seemed mounting some kind of steep, narrow and difficult ladder. And the Griffin was plain in one of the beams. It showed his black robe, his yellow, leprous mask.

Manning ran toward them, shouting, summoning them to surrender.

He spared one shot to emphasize his authority, reveal an actual threat. The report was multiplied a hundred times, until it sounded like a burst of machine-gun fire.

A flashlight was swung toward him. Its white light was strong and he shielded his eyes against it as best he could.

For a moment they were startled into inaction. They saw him as one of themselves, as the hooded slave sent back to finish Manning. They thought he had gone mad, run amuck.

But the Griffin knew.

He thrust his men aside.

It was the chance Manning had prayed for, but the glare of the light in his eyes spoiled a perfect aim.

He flung a shot at the Griffin at the same moment that the

Griffin hurled a bomb that burst into a streak of livid flame as it struck the floor.

There was a roar like a descending cataract, like an express freight roaring through a tunnel. The squat, sturdy pillars seemed to reel and dance, the ground heaved and split. Fragments of man-made rock came tumbling.

Manning was struck by one of them, blinded, and choked with gas. He fell stunned to the floor, his gun still in his hand.

The last thought his brain had registered was the belief that he had hit the Griffin. He had seen him stagger in the hellish blaze that had blotted out everything.

THERE WERE men about Manning. Some wore white. Light was stealing through his burning and still useless eyes. A voice spoke to him.

"It's the commissioner, Manning. We had the Griffin pretty well cooped up, but there was one thing we all overlooked. The old Croton Aqueduct. It hasn't been used for years—is kept only for an emergency. Parallels the subway for quite a ways. Marked on the blueprints, of course, but we didn't get at them. We blocked the street entrances, and left the houses, where Tierney thought he saw you turn in, guarded.

"There are manholes on top the aqueduct. And curving rung-ladders that lead to them. The Griffin and his crew got away through one of them, all except some in hoods we came upon, bolting like rabbits. We got them."

"I thought I got the Griffin," said Manning weakly.

"He almost got you," the commissioner said. "The surgeon says you're due for the hospital. But you hit *someone*. I hope it was the Griffin, and that you did more than wing him."

"Amen to that!" said Manning.

*Behind the Masks of Seven at the Charity Ball*
*Was the One Arch-Fiend Whose Cunning Had*
*Planned a Diabolic Trap for Gordon Manning*

I

## THE DICE OF DEATH

C HUCKLES, MALIGNANT and fiendish as the masked face of the monster issuing them, echoed in the hidden chamber of the Griffin. He was surrounded by the curious paraphernalia of astrology. A completed horoscope lay upon the great desk before him, and the name at its head was that of the Griffin's arch-enemy, Manning. The Griffin was satisfied now that his plans for Manning's elimination would be successful, though they were not as yet complete.

Gordon Manning, the man especially sworn to run the Griffin down, to destroy his power for evil, was as good as murdered. Once Manning had delivered the madman to the law. Medieval medical-jurisprudence had refused to send the Griffin to the chair. Instead, it had decreed Dannemora, but that institution for the criminal insane did not hold the crafty monster long.

Many times the Griffin had planned to murder Manning. His escape, the Griffin was sure, happened only because it was so decreed by the stars. But now, now—seeking as ever, by chart and astrolabe, to discover how the heavens felt towards Manning in the enterprise at present planned, the Griffin had discovered that the influences were ineffably malignant. Manning's star stood revealed in the House of Death.

Nor was that all. The Griffin referred to his own forecast, always logged to date. Destruction threatened him, as it did Manning, and as it did a victim already chosen; who was of slight importance save as the bait for Manning.

This was a situation to delight the inflamed brain of the Griffin.

He had no doubt that the menace that threatened Manning was himself. That his own danger would lie in the issue that, this time, by all the celestial signs and tokens, would be final. He had no doubt of the outcome.

This would be a trial to test his utmost powers. And he would win.

He stood erect in his long garment of sable silk brocade, woven with the signs and symbols of the zodiac belt. He wore a black skullcap, and he looked, with his tall, gaunt height, the high cheekbones and beaky nose, like the archpriest of some unhallowed cult.

Over his face he wore a mask of gold-colored tissue, thin like goldbeater's skin. His dark eyes glittered with incipient madness through the slits in the mask, but it was the madness of evil genius. The effect was weirdly horrible, as if the natural skin were shedding, like that of a snake.

Now he rubbed his thin hands together.

"Ha, Gordon Manning," he said in a harsh, imperative voice. "This will be good. The fates have brought us together in a glorious gamble, casting the dice of death together!"

JAMES CABOT FARNUM was a rich man by inheritance, and he had brains enough to keep his money by taking the advice of expert financiers who were his personal advisers. He was forty-two and unmarried; a big, healthy good-natured man who was by nature a philanthropist. He made a hobby of it, with a single purpose.

He was, perhaps, the best-loved man in America, a sort of

flesh-and-blood Santa Claus to deserving children. But he gave more than toys. He sent hundreds of youngsters into the country, and followed that up by seeing they were well-clothed, fed, educated and given their chance in life. He endowed clinics and built a hospital for them. He went into it personally and without ballyhoo. He was the hardest of men to interview and he got the finest write-ups, from reporters and editors who knew he was genuine.

James Cabot Farnum was in the "Social Register," and he used that fact to help his protégées. He promoted the Junior Charity Ball, an annual affair of elaborate fancy costumes, with fancy-priced tickets.

This year Farnum, as usual, was heart and soul in the preparations. It was at the end of a long day that he sat alone in his library smoking a pipe and reflecting pleasantly that the ball would be a huge success.

His telephone rang and he took the instrument from its cradle before he recollected that it should not have rung. His butler disconnected it every night at eleven. He was a meticulous servant. Farnum was surprised at the slip, still more surprised at the unknown voice that spoke in booming, resonant tones.

It was a voice with a sneer in it, distinctly unpleasant. A voice that held a hidden threat and a supreme confidence. Farnum was not a coward, but he felt the menace and resented it.

"Farnum," said the voice of the unknown, "this is your last week on earth. You will die on the night of the ball you so pride yourself upon, with your ridiculous schemes to avert the decrees of fate by attempting to guide the destinies of children. You are presumptuous. You have been condemned. No power on earth can save you."

Despite himself, the compelling nature of that arrogant voice had kept Farnum a listener. Now he got control of himself.

"I do not talk with cranks," he said quietly, and replaced the instrument.

*It was the Griffin himself.*

To his amazement a jeering laugh came through the receiver. It was a mocking, ghoulish, triumphant laugh that checked the flow of blood in his veins.

"I am not a crank, Farnum. I am the Griffin."

The instrument was disconnected. Farnum saw that it rested evenly in the cradle. But the laughter came again, the obscene merriment of a fiend, or a madman, or both. Then all was silence.

The reaction left him weak, in the grip of a horror his will could not instantly combat. He looked about him. The room was on the third floor, inaccessible. He was well-guarded with inner doors of wrought iron, with sensitive burglar alarms, faithful servants. Yet, with that jeering laughter still ringing in his ears, he felt that his doom had indeed been pronounced.

He knew, of course, of the Griffin, of the terrible trail of crime the madman had left. But he had never imagined himself as one of the victims, even though they were always chosen because of their usefulness to humanity.

Farnum pulled himself together. There was an automatic in a handy drawer, but he knew it was only a toy at a time like this. He was to die—so said the Griffin—on the night of the ball. That was three nights from to-night.

He touched a button. It was idiotic to think of a general alarm, but he opened the drawer where the pistol lay and stood by it, not quite sure who or what might answer his summons.

It was his butler, serenely efficient and impressive, even in dressing gown and pajamas.

"Did you ring for me, sir?"

"Yes, Saunders. Please have my extension connected with the central exchange. I find I have some telephoning to do."

Saunders bowed and departed. So natural was Farnum's voice that Saunders did not listen in.

"I should like to be put through to the commissioner of police," Farnum told the operator. "This matter is vital. Or else to the next in authority who is available immediately."

There was a slight pause. Then: "Mr. Farnum, this is Inspector Tennan speaking. I am going to connect you with Major Manning. He has already been in touch with the commissioner, concerning you."

## I I

## THE FIEND AT THE DANCE

THE JUNIOR Charity Ball was packed with a brilliant assembly of men and women, clad as their fancy prompted them.

It was a spacious place, lofty, with two balconies, and a dome of glass in the center of the high roof, used for ventilation. The higher balcony was vacant, for it was too far off for spectators to keep in touch with the carnival, when not actively sharing in it. It was cluttered with various properties used for decoration.

The lower balcony was partitioned off into boxes, curtained and festooned. These had been auctioned off and all had been taken, though all were not as yet occupied.

None but those assembled there to protect James Cabot Farnum against the Griffin knew anything of the grisly threat that haunted the occasion, like a deadly miasma that might be already in the air.

Farnum had led the grand march, as he always did, unmasked, in his costume of Messer Marco Polo, which had already been advertised in the public prints, photographed and pictured. But he liked to have all his friends, and those who might be his friends and aides to his cause, see him face to face, to smile at them, as he did to-night, despite the fact that he was well assured his life was in danger.

It was a brave thing to do, though Gordon Manning thought it close to being foolhardy. He had talked several times with Farnum, told him how the Griffin had talked with him, through the telephones he mysteriously controlled, before he had spoken to Farnum. He did not mention that the Griffin had boastingly, but solemnly, assured him that his own death was also certain.

Manning had heard that before, and he knew that the Griffin was always eager to kill him.

He had fifty picked men in the place, posted long before the ball had started. Some were waiters, cloakroom attendants, bartenders and kitchen helpers. Others were to be dancers. The commissioner himself was there, with a deputy, and two inspectors. The chief medical examiner had come. Manning knew how all of these were costumed.

Manning knew that the blow, or blows, would be delivered with devilish ingenuity. The Griffin struck with strange methods and weapons. The best Manning had been able to do with Farnum was to persuade him to change his costume after the march, and to wear a mask. Both he and Manning were now dressed alike, as mandarins. There were others on the floor, inevitably, and the loose robes helped to conceal identity.

None had been admitted, none would be admitted, wearing masks. The men from Centre Street, on the doors, would make sure that none of the exposed faces were those of men who were wanted, or who had ever been wanted.

While tickets had been at a premium, those who bought early enough had no trouble in securing them. This was for charity; and all who could afford the price were welcome. The hall had been searched thoroughly, including the roof. Manning had made that a personal matter, leading the squad. Box-holders had special tickets, and these too were checked at the stairways leading to the balconies.

TWO SPLENDID orchestras, and a famous military band, alternated. Manning, paired off with Farnum, always close to his side, waited, listening for some dread sound to break in upon the carnival, to know that Death, masked, or in the open, had launched his deadly dart.

It was more than possible, even highly plausible, that he himself might be the first victim, leaving the way open for the murder of Farnum.

"You and I, Manning," the Griffin had told him, "are gambling in the last game we shall ever play together. See that you throw a high main, Manning, for we play with the dice of destiny."

Whatever dice the Griffin played with would be cogged.

Yet Manning did not believe that the Griffin would try to kill him in a crowd. He might Farnum; but for Manning, his old enemy, he would want something more spectacular; or far more secret, for his own private satisfaction. The Griffin never meant Manning to have an easy or a sudden death. Manning was sure of that.

The night wore on, swiftly moving after midnight, and the tension increased for all the bodyguards with every passing minute. The stroke might come when the prizes were being decided upon, or given out. It might....

Manning felt suddenly as if an icy finger had traced the course of his spine. He was used to terror and to horror; but this gripped him, held him in a spell. It was beyond all reason.

A dance had just ended. Many of the couples remained on the floor, applauding for an encore. But there were open spaces, and through these there stalked a grim and awful figure, clad in black, skullcapped, the face masked with leprous tissue that enhanced rather than hid the bony beak of a nose, the protruding cheek-bones.

It moved silently, stalking, like Pestilence in person. It seemed to move with malign purpose, intent upon some horrible mission, unafraid; conscious of, and exulting in, the glances that were cast upon it, as the dancers drew away from it, whispering its name.

Manning had seen this presence before, and there were scores who had heard or read of it. Their recognition spread like wildfire.

Beyond all belief—*but it was The Griffin himself!*

### I I I

### THE GAS OF MOURNING

THERE WAS a movement of men gathering, closing in, groping for weapons. The figure on the now almost empty floor, where fearful men and women shrank from it, was in deadly peril. But it seemed more amused than astonished at its reception.

A man dressed as a clown stepped to Manning's side. A cavalier followed. The commissioner, robed as a cardinal, touched Manning's shoulder.

"There must be no shooting. If they miss—"

"Wait!" Manning's voice rang out. There was a measure of relief in it—and then he saw the real danger, the satanic ingenuity of the Griffin's move.

A few women had screamed, more had fainted. The fear might turn to panic at any moment. Then somebody laughed, the jangling laughter of overstrained nerves at a joke, an ill-advised jest, in the worst of taste, but still a joke.

For there was another Griffin now, on the edge of the huddling maskers. The second, and then a third, and still a fourth, all replicas, in cap and robe and mask. But these seemed uncertain, perplexed at the sensation caused by their leader. If he were their leader?

Two more Griffins were uncovered as people drew away from them, exposed them.

Which was the real Griffin?

Manning gave swift, short orders to his men.

He gave a signal, and a trumpeter, forewarned, an extra in the orchestra, blared out a shrill, compelling blast.

There were men on post at the exits who had been ordered not to leave their places, whatever happened.

The six Griffins found detectives, in stern mood, at both elbows. They marched them to the dressing room.

After the trumpet call there was a tremendous silence.

Farnum showed no sign of alarm. Manning's fist closed on his gun. This showing of six Griffins was not an accident. It was a cloak for action.

Through the silence there came a chuckle that rose to a mocking laugh. Manning glanced upward, swept his glance around the boxes on the lower balcony. Some were still unoccupied, the curtains partly, or wholly, drawn. It seemed to him that the drapes of one of them were slightly shaking.

Suddenly there sounded a tremendous bellow, as if from some hideous and enormous beast. Something came hurtling down to the main floor, a smoking missile that exploded, but cast no death-dealing missiles. Only a brownish-yellow fume that spread and mushroomed, bringing choking coughs and blinding, smarting tears.

Beside Manning, Farnum suddenly slumped, gasping out something that resolved itself into a scarlet froth, then a spurt of blood.

Manning caught him in his arms. He had heard no shot, but the bellowing sound might have covered that. And the missile he saw projecting from Farnum's body, a slender bolt of metal by the collar bone, where already a stain of red was fast spreading on the elaborate embroidery of the mandarin robe, might have been sped by air, or by powerful spring, even by a bowstring. It was not unlike the sort of bolt the medieval crossbow men used in battle and the hunt.

He could not guess how deeply it had penetrated, only that the shock to Farnum was severe. That was a job for the medical examiner and any other surgeons who might be on hand. What was done was done. But the assassin was at liberty, making his getaway. An agent of the Griffin, as those six mock Griffins had been his agents.

Manning's eyes were running, and burning. He turned and thrust Farnum into the arms of the commissioner. Holding his breath, he darted across the empty floor, through the rising mist of gas. Officers were fighting through the offensive fog to the stairs. Manning reached a pillar below the box where the curtains had waved, or seemed to, and swarmed up it.

The fumes mounted swiftly, in wisps that seemed like tentacles, reaching to halt him, to bring him down. All over the hall a pandemonium of strangling sounds, of inarticulate cries, rose from the crowd.

Manning clutched at decorations as he grew dizzy, and some of them gave way. But he got his head and shoulders above the gaseous tide, got a full breath of clean air. He flung a knee over the edge of the box, wiped his streaming eyes with the back of his hand.

The box was empty! Below, he could hear police giving assurance, announcing themselves, calling for order. He heard something else, that might have been meant especially for his ear, that would not be heard below: a malignant, satisfied chuckle.

That meant the close presence of the Griffin himself, keen

to know that the first kill had been made. Manning was pro-grammed to be the next, but it did not deter him.

A narrow aisle backed the boxes. Men and women gathered in it, alarmed, hesitating to move downstairs because of the gas. The Griffin would not have forced his way through these, nor would his agent. They had fled, upward, to the next gallery, to the roof?

STAIRS LEADING to the top balcony were immedi-ately outside the box. Manning mounted swiftly, gun in hand, eager to be at grips with the assassin and his master, the Griffin. It was a time for speed rather than caution. Others were fol-lowing him. They would be blocked by the frightened people in the aisle behind the boxes, but they would speedily get through.

The main lighting of the floor had been subdued with colored shades or substituted by spotlights. It was dim in the top balcony, which seemed empty of men, but was cluttered with strange shapes and deeps of shadow, from which might come at any moment the dart of death.

Manning had heard that chuckle too often not to be sure that it was genuine, had come from the actual throat of the monster. The Griffin was at that moment close at hand, actu-ally within the hall.

Fresh air came through screened ventilators, from the roof. Manning filled his lungs with it, driving out the last of the gas. For a moment he stood looking and listening.

There was a steep iron ladder that led to a scuttle hatch. More air flowed from there. The door to the hatch was open—and it had been closed, and bolted from within, when Manning had led his search earlier in the evening.

The ladder ended on a narrow platform. The door was ajar, as if it had been hastily closed but had failed to latch.

It was like the entry to an unsprung trap. Manning passed through.

He was on the roof, beneath the stars, a breeze blowing from the river with a tang of the sea to it. All about were the towers of Manhattan, lifting to the sky that had the first hint of dawn in it. Low mists were rising, with the inevitable change of temperature toward daybreak.

All about him the ventilators, cowled tubes, like those of a steamer, heading into the wind; looked like a company of hooded monks. They were excellent places for a grisly game of hide-and-seek. It was easy for him to imagine he saw furtive figures slinking swiftly out of sight.

To the left, he looked over the parapet into a narrow service-alley, with a fire escape zigzagging down the wall. The same to the rear. Manning knew those escapes were being watched. In front, the street.

To the right, a fifteen-foot drop, the roof of the next building, seemingly deserted. It had a small scuttle-housing, like a shark's fin, and in the center there was a structure of wood, windowless, painted gray, flat of top; that looked as if it might cover an unsightly water tank.

As he stood there, momentarily baffled, on the alert, tingling with the prescience of imminent danger, he heard a light *swish* in the air, and half-turned. Something settled lightly over him and fell, swathing him in light meshes of netting that were instantly drawn tight, as another and then another web entangled him and bound him.

He was helpless, pursed like a salmon in a seine, his arms useless. He could fire his gun only to shoot himself. The next moment something struck him at the back of his skull. It was the perfect disabling blow. It left him sick, weak and dizzy, with the certain knowledge that he could not fight off unconsciousness. He felt himself being lowered to the next roof with a precision and speed that suggested a team of well-trained acrobats. He vaguely saw a door sliding aside in the wall of a wooden shed. Then came oblivion.

I V

GETAWAY

THE FOUR detectives who had followed Manning by
the stairs broke out to the roof and heard nothing, saw
nothing. The roof was empty, and so was the one below it.
Beyond that the blank wall of a skyscraper forbade all idea of
flight or pursuit.

Manning had vanished.

They were picked men on the homicide squad, chosen by
the commissioner as Manning's personal aides and his bodyguard. Sergeant Gorman, first-class detectives Fallon and Doyle,
second-class detective Quinlan. All of them had fought it out
with desperate crooks more than once. They had the instinct
of their profession. They were crack officers, and, for all the
emptiness and silence—because of it—they knew themselves
in deadly danger; even as had Manning.

They wanted to ferret it out, to face it. Their guns were in
their hands.

"He sure came up here," said Gorman in a low voice, looking
all about him. "That scuttle was shut first time we came up, with
him. Take a quick looksee, lads. Quinlan, you an' Doyle scout
this roof. Look out for them ventilators and the dome. The
alleys an' the fire escapes are tagged."

Quinlan and Doyle went scouting carefully and Gorman
turned with Fallon to the parapet, and stared down at the roof
below.

Quinlan grabbed Doyle by the arm.

"Look at the shed! She's openin' up!"

The sides of the gray wooden structure that looked as if it
might camouflage a water tank were smoothly and quietly
collapsing, falling outward. The roof was folding down on one
of the walls, precise as machinery, well-hinged and oiled.

They saw a plane revealing itself. A strange ship, an autogyro far larger than any of them had seen, or imagined. It had a double set of sustaining and elevating blades that had been folded, but were opening up, like four-petaled flowers. The purr of twin-motors steadily increased.

"They got him in the ship!" said Gorman. "Come on!"

He set fingers between his teeth and whistled to Doyle and Quinlan. They came running across the roof. All four swarmed over the parapet, clung for a second, and then dropped.

Before they could get set to charge the plane, now fully in the clear, hell-fire broke out. Sub-machine guns riddled them from the gondola of the plane, tore them apart as they stood. Hot lead shocked and spun them about, leaving them bloody bundles that twitched, and then lay still.

Now the walls of the shed were down, level with the roof. The compact, powerful engines gave out their power. The overhead blades whirred and tugged. The twin-gyro lifted almost vertically, rose humming into the sky like an enormous top; up to where the last stars were paling and the river mist was spreading to a low ceiling.

ON THE ballroom floor, the commissioner took charge. Doors and windows were opened, to clear away the fumes of tear gas. None was allowed to leave. Farnum was carried into a dressing room, where the medical examiner swiftly started to give immediate aid, to find out the gravity of the wound. The great majority of the masqueraders did not yet know of the tragedy, though they were frightened and bewildered.

Of the doctors who offered their help, the medical examiner accepted the two that he recognized. The surgeons looked grave. Blood was jetting fast, dark blood now. It looked like a vein, an important one. Attempt to remove the missile might be immediately fatal, causing a hemorrhage that could not be checked in time with such means as they had at hand. Removal to a hospital was equally hazardous.

There was the added uncertainty that the dart, or bolt, might be poisoned, or barbed against easy withdrawal. The Griffin was capable of both.

"About one chance in a thousand," the M.E. told the commissioner, as the latter entered the dressing room, his face grim. "We'll do what we can. If we can get a powerful enough styptic, and stimulant, in time. I'll need a messenger."

"One waiting," snapped the commissioner. "Motorcycle. Can't you phone to save some time?"

"I tried it," said the M.E. curtly. "The Griffin is thorough. The phones are dead."

The commissioner's face set like stone. He had seen Manning swarm up the pillar, his own men making for the stairs. He turned to the inspector by his side, rapped out an order.

"See what happened to the squad that went up after Major Manning. They would go through to the roof."

The other left, and the commissioner followed to see himself to the M.E.'s special messenger. His heart was heavy with foreboding. If Gordon Manning was done in, he doubted if any human agency could foil the Griffin. The mad monster would proceed in his course of horror, encouraged, and unchecked.

Manning had spoken of his own danger, admitting he believed the peril greater than ever before. He had said he had taken precautions, yet the commissioner had seen him racing across the floor alone, swarming up the pillar like the hero of some forlorn hope, which indeed it might well be; determined upon sacrifice, reckless as any subaltern.

It was not somehow, like Manning, the commissioner told himself. He took risks when they were inevitable, as a man will take a death-defying leap. But surely he had gone straight into a trap.

The commissioner went to where the six mock Griffins were huddled, cowed and not all undamaged after their third degree. They had been examined separately, but their tales had been the same, and they had remained unshaken.

They were actors, out of work, out of money. They had seen an advertisement calling for professionals, offering twenty dollars for a few hours' work to men who were of the right size and otherwise qualified.

The address given was off Broadway, in the middle Fifties. The place seemed like that of any other curbstone agent. There was no name on the door. They did not know the name of the man who hired them. He was businesslike, short, squat, and swarthy.

He gave directions after he had weeded them out. There were tickets for the Junior Charity Ball, costumes to wear, all alike, with masks. It was a bet, a joke on somebody. They had no lines to deliver. All they had to do was to walk about mysteriously. He did not tell them what the costumes were. They were to wear them beneath black dominoes and take those off in the dressing room, put on their masks.

It looked like a soft thing and they jumped at it. They all swore that they had attached no significance to the costumes.

"I think you're lying," said the commissioner. "I'm holding you for further questioning. We'll try to round up that fake agent," he said to the sergeant who had quizzed the unhappy six. "Try and find out who made the costumes. It's going to be tough. Let me see one of those masks."

They were cunningly made, treated with wax so that the noses and cheeks could be moulded and stiffened.

The inspector he had sent after the men who had followed Manning, returned. His face was pale, his features working. He closed his lips, licked them and opened them again, twice, without speaking, evidently wrought up.

He was a man grown old on the force, earning his promotion. He had seen terrible things in his time.

"Damn it, Herron, don't stand there goggling and jibbering," said the commissioner, as premonition swept over him. "What's happened, man. Out with it!"

"Gorman, sir. Ryan, an'—"

"I know their names. What happened?"

"I think you'd better see for yourself, sir."

The commissioner was nearer fifty than forty, but he sprinted up the long stairway like an athlete, leading the inspector and a squad, summoned as they ran. He was not essentially a religious man, but he breathed a prayer as he looked at the shambles.

Quinlan groaned. His gallant vitality still clutched the last spark of life. The commissioner knelt beside the dying officer, as he muttered broken words through crimson froth.

"The—plane—they took—Mann—!"

The sun was palely gilding the tall spires. High up in the sky the commissioner saw a speck that seemed drifting, rising, a note that lost itself above the ceiling of fog.

It would take far too long a time before they could get pursuit planes into the air, to follow a wild goose trail. A curse took the place of prayer with the commissioner, a plea for the destruction of the fiend who had flown off with Manning.

He dared not hope for Manning.

"For God's sake, Herron," he said, as he turned away to do what might be done, however hopeless, "get something to cover up those bodies."

V

THE GRIFFIN'S AERIE

HIGH OVER the city, above the strata of mist that veiled it, the autogyro changed course, flew south and east. The double engines drove it at almost a hundred miles an hour. It seemed to skim through the air, like a mammoth dragon-fly.

In the enclosed gondola, Manning looked up, his head throbbing. As consciousness returned, he saw the gloating, ghoulish face of the Griffin above his own, unmasked—sure sign that the monster counted himself paramount. His eyes glittered, distended, all pupils; his thin nostrils flared.

He chuckled as he saw Manning's eyes open, and intelligent. The chuckle grew into a hideous laugh. Flecks of foam gathered on the madman's cruel lips.

"I could drop you into the sea, Gordon Manning," he said. "I could let you crash upon the sidewalks or the buildings of the City of Fools. I have thought of a score of ways to demolish you. And I am not yet decided. You must be made an eminent example."

Manning blinked, closed his eyes. The Griffin went on.

"The world shall learn not to dispute the decrees that are written in the stars."

Enraged at Manning's attitude, he forced the latter's eyelids apart with his lean fingers, thrusting the taloned tips into the corners of the eyes.

"You are in the grip of the Griffin, Manning, and this time I shall not let you go. You will amuse me, for the last time, when you writhe in your last agonies, and beg for mercy. So look at me, you miserable mortal, look at me! I am the Griffin, emblem of eternal vigilance!

"I caught you like a fish. My slave seined you as he used to seine a tunny in his native Italy. And I shall gut you, and scale you; scale by scale; while you are still alive."

The nets were still about Manning. He was quite helpless.

"If you hope to get any enjoyment out of that performance," said Manning, "why don't you let me rest up, beforehand?"

The Griffin cackled. His long-inflamed brain was breaking down.

"You are a victim after my own heart, Manning. You are still brave and bold. You have not my wisdom, you are not of the Appointed, or we might have worked together. Death sits in your House of Destiny, and the power of the zodiac is absolute.

"So take your ease, for a little while. Reserve your powers. You will need them all. Our orbits cross, our fates clash like swords in the dark. But I am the conqueror. So rest. It will not be long."

Manning forced himself to relax. He knew he would need all his wits, all his energy, if he were to survive. And he did not greatly care to, unless he knew the Griffin had been annihilated.

The astromancer had planned well and long, knowing before he sent out his threat that Farnum would be at the ball, where that was always held, leasing the empty building next door, erecting the shed that hid the autogyro, settling there at night.

Manning was not without his own purposes. He had meant to pit his sanity against the madness of the Griffin, to use his knowledge of the Griffin's reactions; but now he was in the toils.

Farnum was dead, or dying.

The plane hummed and whirred, driving on above the mists, through clean air, where the stars spangled the firmament. Other planes would be mounting soon, searching with no more chance of discovery than men hunting a needle in a giant haystack.

The revolutions lessened, the driving propellers stopped. They were going down, descending through the fog that still held, though New York must be a hundred, perhaps two hundred, miles away. By the persistence of the mist Manning imagined they were close to the coast.

Suddenly they broke through the ceiling into bright sunlight.

"It will not be long now, Manning," the Griffin hissed into his ear. *"Not long."*

THEY LANDED in what seemed to be a natural clearing, amid tall trees. The nets and cords were expertly taken off Manning, his gun was taken from him, and two men went systematically over him in search of other weapons, finding none. The contents of his pockets were turned over to the Griffin, who pouched them somewhere in the clothes he wore beneath a voluminous black cloak. With a wide-rimmed, high-crowned black hat, he looked, Manning thought, like a medieval Spanish brigand. It was a poor costume for flying, but it suited the Griffin.

"You will not need these things again," he said to Manning. "Perhaps I shall find something to keep as a souvenir."

He was being suave, infinitely polite, and infinitely deadly. He was the cat, playing with the mouse that could not get away, that presently it would kill, after physical and mental torture.

There was no road in the clearing, where the wiry grass grew high, but a car came into it a few minutes after they had made landing. Manning was transferred to it, with his arms bound behind his back. It was a big and powerful machine. A silent man, whose face wore the hopelessness of a convict condemned for life, took place on one side of Manning in the rear, another of similar type, his features expressionless, his form undernourished, sat on the other.

The Griffin got in beside the driver, and the car moved away, just as the autogyro took off with a splendid ease, soaring high, up again toward the still low ceiling.

It was a bright day in summer, the birds sang and flew, the morning shadows were long, and the air was fresh.

Here and there were broken-down fences. The place looked like a rundown and abandoned farm. Now and then Manning caught a glimpse of sunny water that must be, he thought, either Delaware or Chesapeake Bay. He was sure they had flown south, that they were either in Maryland or Delaware. Probably the first, from the hills.

He thought of the words of the condemned nobleman in the Tower of London, awaiting execution:

> "One more glimpse of the sun, one more sight of the sea;
> One embrace from my dearest one, then death come speed-
> ily."

He was not morbid about it, or sorry for himself, but he knew his chances were slim. The things they had taken from him did not matter much, but he was not sure if something they had overlooked were still upon him. He could not find out, bound as he was. Without it, the sooner the Griffin could be persuaded or taunted into killing him, the better.

Manning had a "dearest one," but he had not seen, nor spoken, nor written to her, for over a year. The Griffin had once tried to strike at Manning through her; and Manning had severed all communications, might indeed have severed the bond between them; vowed himself to eliminate the Griffin. Then, and only then, might he see her with safety to herself.

But he could not help yearning towards her, with regret for what might have been; as he looked at the bright glimpses of sun glare on the water. Life was never so sweet, the world never so fair, as when one was looking the last upon them.

They came to an old road, unworked for years, sandy and overgrown. Trees grew in close ranks beside it. Then they passed outbuildings that looked like ancient slave quarters.

The road forked, and they passed a wall, driving swiftly. Trees and shrubbery looked like a jungle inside.

All this time they had seen no human being but themselves. The place was infinitely remote, though cities could not be far away. But desolation had struck here, long before the depression started. It was a perfect hiding place. Save for the car tracks, there was no trace of anyone coming this way, to a spot so destitute of charm or utility.

But a fine lair for the Griffin, who was an adept at choosing his aeries, and concealing them. The tire marks could easily be erased, and Manning did not doubt that they would be.

An avenue went winding; trees, shrubbery and foliage thick on either side, tangled with vines, many of the trees dead. There were traces of a garden. Then came the house, once a stately enough mansion, fallen into decay. Planks were out of place, paint was only a vestige. One great chimney had crumbled, the porch tilted, with the gallery above it. Pillars were missing, and shutters hung crazily.

Yet, despite its deserted, haunted appearance, Manning did not doubt that, within, the Griffin had established a measure of comfort for himself, if not of luxury. He'd have some of his slaves here, men of once brilliant profession or useful occupation, bound to him by his knowledge of guilty secrets that would send them to jails they dreaded, to public announcements of their crimes and the ruin of the families who might—gratefully perhaps—now think them dead.

These men worked the Griffin's perverted will, devised his means of murder. Nameless creatures, known by numbers. Once Manning had freed many of them, but he did not doubt that they had returned. Their bondage would end only with the Griffin's death.

THE CAR drove through gaping doors into the ruin of a coachhouse. The Griffin got out, entering the house from a side porch. The two men escorted Manning through a rear door, holding him by his bound arms. They were more like automatons than men. It was no use to think of appealing to them. They were quite ready to strangle him if he tried to escape.

The room into which he was shown was dark, from drawn curtains, furnished with odds and ends of furniture, including a table and a sideboard. The two men stayed on guard. To Manning's surprise a meal was brought in, a well-cooked breakfast, to which he did ample justice, though he knew the motive was not one of hospitality, but sprung from the same cause that made the redskins feed their prisoners before they bound them to the stake—so that they would last longer.

When he had finished, the two cadaverous and silent men took him into a hall that led through the old house, down a stairway to a basement smelling of mold and decay, coming at last to a place that must have been the wine cellar in days gone by. It was flagged, walled with stone, lighted by narrow windows, set horizontally, and barred.

A heavy table stood beneath two gasoline lanterns that shed a brilliant light.

The Griffin sat there, in his black robe and skullcap, but his mask was still off. Manning saw that with relief, as he looked about him. There was a stool opposite the Griffin, no doubt for him to sit in, while the monster made a final arraignment. Manning was sure he would not forego that.

The table was not wide. It held on its plain surface a carafe and glasses, folded cloths, and what seemed some sort of case, covered with a square of black silk.

Posts stayed the flooring above. There was something that looked like a frame for growing mushrooms. Earth, several inches thick, was confined in the frame; rich-looking soil, evidently recently prepared, watered.

It was hardly a grave, but it suggested it.

Shadowy figures stood about. Manning counted six of them, without his own two guards, who stepped away from him at a gesture from the Griffin. The six others were dressed in denim overalls, numbers stenciled in yellow on their breasts. Their faces were all haggard, hopeless, abject.

"Sit down, Manning," said the Griffin. "I should have preferred to finish this matter between us in more elaborate surroundings, but, after all, that is largely your fault. You have made the vicinity of New York an uncomfortable place for me of late. I grant you that. You circumscribed my freedom. So I found this place, where I can be fairly well contented for a time. Until the hue-and-cry that will follow your death, and the exhibition of your body to the public gaze dies down. Until the yapping of the hounds ceases."

The Griffin was under self-control, temporarily. But red lights came and went in his dark eyes like the gleams in black opals, orange and crimson glints of murder and madness.

"I shall try to comply with any last request of yours," he went on mockingly. "It is the universal custom. But first, let me explain what I have finally decided upon."

He plucked the silk square from the case and showed, nested in velvet, an array of gleaming knives. They might have been a surgeon's scalpels, save for their settings. Each was handled in ivory, stained red, intricately carven. The case was of teak, inlaid about the edges. In the center was one long, thin dagger with a fluted blade, several inches long. The haft was of gray jade, carved to represent a skeleton in a squatting position, the end of it the skull.

The Griffin took this from the case and thrust its tip into the wood.

"You have traveled in the Orient, Manning," he went on. "You will recognize the cutlery of the executioner. This belonged to a man who once was an emperor's favorite, a master of the Death of a Thousand Cuts. If that man were alive, and available, I think I should have decided on that for your end. A superb demonstration of surface anatomy. But, to do it properly, one should first give the ceremonial cuts of mercy, removing the ears, the lips, the nose, the eyes, destroying—synthetically, I grant you—the senses of the victim.

"But the correct procedure would mutilate your face, and I want that to be very surely recognized. The body will not so much matter. And I could only obtain a substitute executioner, who proved, upon trial, most clumsy. He would have killed you far too soon, Manning, far too soon."

Manning looked steadfastly at the Griffin, knowing he could have little effect upon those eyes that regretted the abandoned spectacle of a man dissected, nerve by nerve, every sensitive part of his body quivering in agony as his life leached out from the sliced flesh, with all the main arteries and veins skillfully avoided.

He looked at the *snickersee*, the long-bladed knife with which the executioner of the *Grand Li-Chi*, might, if it were the will or whim of the emperor or magistrate, give the *coup de grâce*.

It was close to the Griffin's reach.

"So," said the Griffin, "I chose another form of Oriental disposal, wherein one honors an enemy with a lingering death. I have been at some pains, knowing you would soon be in my toils, to obtain the right kind of bamboo sprouts, also to arrange a swift-growing soil of rich humus. I need not tell you the process, Manning. You will be stripped, bound very securely to that frame, face and belly down, after the sprout, already for the purpose, chosen from a score I have been treating, is planted there.

"Within twelve hours at most it will have grown through your softer parts, no doubt with considerable unpleasantness. The tip should show beside your spine, to the right or left. I am not sure how long after that you will continue to live. Perhaps you can inform me."

## VI

## LAST REQUEST

HE LEANED forward, his face close to that of Manning over the table, taunting and contemptuous. Manning did not waver. It was a death so fantastic, so excruciatingly agonizing, that only the Oriental mind could have conceived it, only a mad monster like the Griffin have adopted it.

"When you are dead, Manning, I shall take pains to have your corpse placed on public exhibition. It may be found below Washington Arch, or on the Rocking Stone in Central Park. That is a matter of detail. But all the world will know how and why you died."

The Griffin licked his cruel lips, where once more curds of froth gathered.

"I am Alpha and Omega, Manning," he half chanted. "I am Apollyon, let lose upon earth to whip back mortals to the knowledge and worship of the true gods, or to destroy them."

In another moment, Manning saw that the Griffin would lose all control, and could no longer restrain his appetite to see his supreme enemy set to the living torture of the bamboo sprout.

"There was the matter of the last request," he said, in a steady voice.

"Of course. Name it."

"If I write a few words, will you see them delivered?"

"They shall reach the hands of the proper party, that I promise you."

The Griffin grinned beneath the curve of his nose, looking slyly down it. Manning knew the Griffin thought he would write to the woman he loved, and the Griffin could get additional zest over reading the lines that would be Manning's own epitaph. They would never be delivered, save to the Griffin, considering himself the "proper party."

"You took a notebook and a fountain pen from me," said Manning. "I can use them."

The Griffin cackled. "A leaf from the notebook, yes, but not the pen, not your pen, Manning. You have tricks of your own. The most innocent looking fountain pens have turned out to be gas-guns, even miniature pistols. I will let you use my own pen. You have often read what it set down. What more fitting than to use it for your own last testament, or whatever it is you intend to write? The ink is purple, as you know. Quite fitting the occasion, the—to you—mournful occasion."

The Griffin was squeezing the last drop of enjoyment he could out of Manning's predicament. He beckoned, and the case of knives was removed. Manning watched the departure of the *snickersee,* the knife-of-mercy, with longing. Then the Griffin handed over his pen, charged with the vivid ink that Manning had always seen in the Griffin's communications, which were always intended as death warrants.

Now he was in the toils. His arms were freed, on the Griffin's order. They were very sure of him. They had him helpless and unarmed. Soon he would be naked, bound to the frame that held the dirt, with the tip of the bamboo sprout; its outer skin armored with vegetable silica, a living dagger; pressed against his navel.

He tried out the pen-point. It was wide, a generous nib, fitted for the Griffin's striking calligraphy. The Griffin watched him with his face like a mask of malignant derision, his eyes glittering, the tip of his tongue showing between his teeth and his lips like a serpent's single tongue. Manning told himself he was surprised not to find it forked.

A moment more and he would know for certain if he were going to die horribly or whether he would be able to use the one chance for liberty with which he had provided himself.

He tried the pen again on his thumbnail, as if to test its flexibility. The ink ran freely, left a small purple splotch. But that was not going to matter.

Manning laid down the pen, sighed slightly, while the tip of the Griffin's tongue protruded, further in pleased malice. He passed his hand over his forehead, his hair, round to the back of his neck, forward across his right ear; his eyes closed, like a man disheartened and perplexed.

The butt of his right palm contacted with something, and Manning's spirit leaped within him. He was careful to keep his eyes closed lest they give him away.

It was still in place, though he had feared the nets might have rasped it loose.

Manning's ears were well-shaped. They lay close against his skull, the lobes generous. Behind the lobe of his right ear was a small capsule, attached with a special wax, impervious to moisture. A tiny pellet of gelatine.

But far more deadly than any bullet. The gelatine was thin but tough; the contents were drops of frightful virulence. Here was venom that, once introduced into the blood, meant hideous and inevitable death. Only large doses of anti-venine immediately and copiously introduced could save the victim.

Manning caught the pellet in the crook of his little finger as a thimble-rigger nicks his pea. He clasped both his hands nervously. The Griffin chuckled to see that sign of despair.

"It is hard to know what to write," said Manning wearily, "I doubt if you would ever deliver it. You seem to win this bout, Griffin, yet your victory will be brief. Madness rises steadily within you...."

As he carefully chose his barbed phrases, he watched the Griffin. The Griffin's hands clutched and unclutched like the talons of a beast that wants to rend and tear. And Manning transferred the poison pellet from his right hand to his left.

He once more picked up the pen, as if to test it, for the third time.

"Soon," he said to the Griffin, "you will be a raving maniac, no better than a mad dog. You...."

The Griffin half rose, leaning across the table with his face opposite that of Manning, his lips drawn back in a snarl. The attendants stayed still. It was theirs to obey, not to initiate.

"Write," hissed the Griffin, "*write*, you fool! Or—"

MANNING JABBED the broad gold point of the pen into the capsule. With a movement fast as the strike of a snake, he drove the envenomed nib into the Griffin's cheek, twice.

Blood showed, mixed with purple ink. The Griffin gasped with rage and astonishment, and with that indrawn breath, his doom was sealed.

"Deadliest venom known, Griffin," said Manning, coolly but swiftly, so that the Griffin would hear him before the frightful poison took effect. "Venom of the *boomslang*, the South African tree snake. You are a dead man as you stand there."

Curds of foam were thick about the lips of the Griffin. His voice rasped horribly as he sought to utter words his brain would not confirm.

"You lie, Manning! You lie!"

His eyes showed completely circled by the whites, and then the whites were suddenly congested with red veins, that broke and met until the dark irises seemed floating in blood.

His nostrils flared wide, trying to catch a full breath. His hands clutched at his throat as if he would tear it open to gain oxygen. His vitality was amazing, beyond all belief. Just as the mad monk, Rasputin, fought off poison, so the Griffin resisted the *boomslang* venom.

The attendants watched, spellbound and motionless. They did not know exactly what had happened, save that this had been a duel between two Masters; the Griffin, and the man who was the law to which they themselves were subject.

Manning watched, marveling. He knew the ink could not have diluted the venom. Unlike the viperine snakes, where the toxine destroys the blood corpuscles, the *boomslang*, like the mamba and the cobras, paralyzes the nervous system.

The Griffin swayed upon his feet, bereft of speech now. His face twitched. With infinite effort he moved one hand, one taloned finger quivered in the endeavor to point it at Manning.

There was a hideous cackle in his throat that changed to a rattle. His glaring eyes accused Manning of using cogged dice against his own prepared cubes, in this last gamble in which the Griffin lost.

He seemed to attempt to speak. Then his jaws became rigid, the ghastly grin of death fixed upon them, before he toppled to the floor, his bloodset eyes still staring horribly, his face the hue of old putty.

The slaves still stood silent, servile and irresolute. Their timid eyes moved toward Manning.

"The Griffin is dead," Manning told them. "You are free. I am the law, but I am not seeking you. After I leave, serve yourselves as best you can. I shall leave you so that you can soon release yourselves. The law may trail you eventually, but I am not your hunter. I have rid you of a monster. I am giving you a break for liberty."

It might not be ethics, but it was humanity; and not far from justice, he told himself. They all had suffered terribly.

They made no demur as he herded them into a smaller chamber and rolled a heavy barrel against the door.

He put the Griffin's pen, capped carefully, into his pocket, for a souvenir. The commissioner might like it.

The madness had gone out of the Griffin's feral features as Manning bent over him. The eyes were dead eyes. It was a magnificent cranium, the upper skull a case that had held a genius some taint had curdled, turning every thought to the desire to destroy all that was good.

Manning realized that the men who had been in the car, like those who had flown the autogyro, might not be so amenable as the numbered slaves. He found the Griffin's mask in a pocket of the robe he took from the dead body, and now put on. In another pocket was his own gun. He donned the skullcap and went up the stairs to the central hall, imitating the stride of the man who had once worn this garb.

The chauffeur sat there, springing to attention.

Manning snarled at him in a rasping voice, and the man cringed as if struck with a whip.

"The car, fool, the car!"

The car stood at the door with its powerful engines purring like lions in the sun. The driver opened the door—and Manning clubbed him neatly and efficiently with the muzzle of his gun.

He took the driving seat and rolled the car away from the old house.

The Griffin was dead! There was no doubt of that. And all of his slaves and sub-fiends were impotent without the head devil.

Well away, Manning took off robe and mask and skullcap. They were more trophies. The mask he meant to retain for himself, to place it among his other relics of grim adventure.

He struck a highway and drove north, rapidly and expertly. Within half an hour he passed the sign: BALTIMORE—15 MILES.

THE VOICE of the commissioner came through clearly over long-distance.

"There will be no trouble with the Maryland authorities,

Manning. They are sending men to meet you and will cooperate with us. I am flying down. They ought to elect you president for this."

Manning laughed. "I might get a medal—thirty years or so from now. I'll be waiting for you, commissioner. I've got a nice souvenir for you. But—how about Farnum?"

His face lit up as he listened. "That is the best news I've heard in a long while," he said as he hung up.

Farnum had won with his thousandth chance. The surgeons credited him with an escape that was literally made by a hair's-breadth. That much to the left, and the steel dart would have torn the vein beyond repair.

As Manning turned away from the booth a bellboy looked at him, bright-eyed and inquisitive as a sparrow.

"Gee, Major Manning," he said, "ain't there somethin' I can do for you?"

Of course there were leaks somewhere. Operators are human. But it did not matter. The Griffin was dead.

"Sure you can, son," said Manning. "Lead me to the bar. I need a drink."

www.ingramcontent.com/pod-product-compliance
Lightning Source LLC
Chambersburg PA
CBHW061518020726
47502CB00006B/2124